THE MAKER'S DREAM

Swati,

Thanks so much for being a great
Artist's Way partner. Happy reading!

~ Arvind

The Maker's Dream

ARVIND NAGARAJAN

NEW DEGREE PRESS

THE MAKER'S DREAM

ISBN   978-1-63730-657-4   *Paperback*
         978-1-63730-740-3   *Kindle Ebook*
         978-1-63730-931-5   *Ebook*

For Regina, who never clips my wings

CONTENTS

AUTHOR'S NOTE

The idea for this book was born a few years ago when I stumbled onto the topic of artificial intelligence. Specifically, the pursuit of artificial general intelligence. My interest was sparked by reading *Superintelligence* by Nick Bostrom, which I highly recommend if you have even the slightest interest in the subject.

Afterward, I found myself spiraling down a rabbit hole. I spent time reading books, papers, watching YouTube videos, and listening to podcasts. The kind of education that only happens when you combine curiosity with twenty-first-century tools. The kind of education that ends with me watching a YouTube breakdown of two computer programs playing chess against each other.

On one side was AlphaZero, an AI computer program that had learned the rules of chess merely twenty-four hours ago. On the other side was Stockfish, an open-source chess engine that had recently won the world computer chess championship.

As expected, the match was no contest. The unexpected part was AlphaZero, with twenty-four hours of training against itself and no theoretical knowledge of the game of chess, came out on top in convincing fashion. I watched the recap videos in amazement— AlphaZero played chess like no other computer engine before it. It defied decades-old theories around the value of pieces and space in a game that most laypeople thought traditional chess engines had nearly solved.

Watching this recap, I knew artificial general intelligence was going to change everything. I knew I had to do something with the ideas swirling in my head. What could be more fun than trying to write my own story?

A funny thing happened when I started writing. My interests started to weave their way into the book. My love of magical realism came to life through three of the most fantastical technologies I could envision:

1. The iLink: a neural chip that executes your thoughts in the real world. A smartphone in your neck, controlled by your thoughts, connected not just to a wireless network but to all nonhuman networked devices. Ready to do your bidding, from making your morning coffee to helping you soar like a bird through the sky.

2. Endeeze: nano-drones that blend into the natural environment while having the ability to form groups depending on the nature of the assigned task. These are the primary recipients of iLink messages. They represent the world's most effective DAO or decentralized autonomous organization.

3. iHERO: a piece of software on the iLink that trains each individual to become the best version of themselves. Through a lucid dreaming protocol, each human is guided on their own personalized path to fulfillment. Whatever you were meant to be in the most positive of lights—an artist, a stargazer, a philosopher—is nothing but a dream away.

Beyond the technology, there's also my perpetual quest for self-improvement. One of my struggles in getting to the best version of myself is a feeling of selfishness and unearned privilege weighing me down. So I imagined a world where that weight was lifted—a societal structure where there was no need for my pursuit of fulfillment to come at the expense of anyone else.

These interests came together in a story about what it means to be human and what constitutes a fulfilling life. My protagonist, KB, is a young girl thrust into this technological utopia, struggling with questions that don't have easy answers. We all know what it's like to question things that others take for granted. In the end, it's not about finding the answer. It's about finding people to explore and connect with. I hope you enjoy reading, and most importantly, I hope it sparks a few questions of your own. Nothing sparks curiosity like the magic of a story.

—Arvind

PROLOGUE

We were careful in what we wished for. Then the Maker gave it to us.

— FROM THE WORLD OF THE MAKER

She had spent thousands of hours with him, but she stared intensely as if truly seeing him for the first time. She knew instinctively where to look. Not at the strong cheekbones and flowing auburn hair. No, she lingered on his narrow eyes, evidence of his lack of warmth. She moved to a view of his overarching silhouette, noting the wiry frame and the hunch in his back. The natural pose of someone for whom ambition looms large. She pushed her rounded glasses up her nose, a nervous tic during times of distress. Maybe subconsciously, she hoped the nudge would fix her vision so she'd see him once more as a cute, insanely smart potential partner. If that were the case, those hopes were quickly dashed. This had always been who he was.

The two of them sat in silence on the rooftop patio, waves crashing in the distance with a thunderous resonance. She finally broke the silence, speaking softly as if to restrain the strong undertow of her hidden feelings. "This was supposed to be our time to celebrate. I thought you wanted this. I thought we wanted this." A small part of her hoped there was still a way to reach him. That his arms would open up to embrace her and the dreams they had so recently shared.

But it wasn't meant to be. The slight upward crease in his lips was the giveaway. Whenever he was in a deeply self-congratulatory mood, she saw it in him. As if he couldn't help being pleased that the situation was playing out exactly as he had anticipated. Here, it was a clear sign his mind was not on her suffering. It was on how accurately he had predicted these events would unfold.

He spoke with a measured practice to his tone. "Of course, and I do want to celebrate. We've both been eagerly awaiting the moment I finally passed the Maker's Dream. Today ought to be a joyous occasion." As his pause lingered longer than any plan would have called for, she felt her heart skip a beat. A stubborn little bubble of hope emerged once more.

Until he popped it. "I'm sorry. It's clear I'm meant for a different path than the one we were planning on."

She turned away, looking out to the ocean. She wished the next wave would rise like the tsunamis of old and engulf him. Passing the Maker's Dream had never meant as much to her as it had to him. *Proof they could forever access the best version of themselves?* She had always known that idea was too good to be true. She turned to face him and responded with a biting edge to her voice that she immediately regretted, "What do you mean, 'a different path?'"

She hated the distance she felt from a man she had spent so much time with. A man she had loved. She hated the desperation and anger it infused in her voice.

"I've seen the best version of myself, and I know the path I must embark on," he replied.

"Bil-vani..." she muttered under her breath, shaking her head.

His eyebrows creased in confusion. "I'm sorry, what did you just say?"

All she could do was chuckle to herself, finding the humor in her own naivete. "Bilvani. We had her name picked out, remember?"

For an instant, she caught the pain in his face before it quickly retreated behind a stoic exterior. "The Goddess of Knowledge. Still a beautiful name. But a name isn't a child, and we always knew we'd be deciding whether to have a child together only after we both passed the Maker's Dream and became Dreamers. My dream was clear. I know what I must do. And that doesn't include raising a child with you." He paused and scratched his chin before speaking again in a milder tone, "And, this *is* Keitaro, not some ancient civilization. One parent works just as well as two or any other number, for that matter. They can all raise children equally well. So, I don't expect you to change your decision because I've changed mine."

She let the silence fill the air. She knew it was the safest path to preventing an inner explosion. Counting her breaths, she closed her eyes for a moment until her equanimity returned. Gently opening her eyes, she rose from her lounge chair and walked to the door. *He's making a mistake, but he's right.*

The patio door opened upon her approach. After ensuring that he was following her, she looked at the rainbow-colored spiral staircase heading down to the main level. *My happy future with Bilvani does not depend on him.*

The bright orange door that served as the entrance to the house opened in perfect rhythm with her approach. She looked back at him and his slow, familiar stroll down the staircase. No longer bound by the kinship of their long friendship, she looked at him with the distrust of an intrusive stranger. He paused halfway down the staircase, looking at the one animated GIF of him that adorned this descent.

She remembered that one. Him crouching over a chessboard. The camera set up at this wonderful angle that captured his face almost through the prism of the chess pieces. She had always been proud of the moment she had captured. The GIF cataloguing the slow change in his facial expression, from the duress of intense concentration to the joy of having found a solution. He loved telling her about the move that he had made after, but for her, it was the expression she loved. Or used to love. Now, she wished he would just pick up the frame and take it with him.

She cleared her throat, disturbing his quiet gaze. As he opened his mouth to speak, she glared at him and shook her head. Their eyes locked, and he blinked and nodded in quiet understanding, bowing his head as he walked past her out the door. She looked at the back of a man she had planned to raise a child with. She couldn't help one last parting thought.

"You really believe this is the best version of yourself?"

He turned with a look of surprise at her question before he could catch himself. She saw the tears forming in his eyes before his head whipped back. His gaze drifted downward as his hardened voice betrayed no evidence of his sadness. "It may not seem like it to you, but the Maker doesn't make mistakes."

1

SOMEONE WORTH SAVING

We often look to technology to save us from our problems.

We rarely look at the problems technology creates in its efforts to save us.

—*FROM THE WORLD OF THE MAKER*

"Hey, Kali, want me to grab anything while I'm out?" Lila couldn't help but marvel at the athletic frame of Kali crouching on her knees in their living room garden. *What happened to that little baby who used to play there?* Every visitor had been so keen to point out the resemblance between her daughter and her when Kali was little. *How time flies.*

Other than the unmistakable cheeks, the young girl no longer shared Lila's gentle features. "No, thanks. I'm too busy playing with my friends."

Lila let Kali's note of sarcasm go. The garden was a former sandbox now filled with soil, an area usually reserved for Lila's gardening endeavors. But now, Kali was hunched over, tending to a line of identically-spaced little saplings. Her hands moved with surgical precision, using a syringe to draw from a collection of vials and inject various substances into the soil. Each sapling's plastic casing told Lila all she needed to know. This was one of Kali's projects. A science experiment designed to satisfy nothing but her own curiosity.

"None of these plants are about to sprout antennas, are they?" Lila shook her head and smiled when she realized she was speaking only to herself. Kali's angry expression was indicative of a focus that made her oblivious to casual conversation. That used to worry Lila. *"She doesn't look like she's having fun,"* she would comment to her brother Chakra. He had always reminded her that looks can be deceiving. That Kali's sharper features and stern expressions made it easy to confuse concentration with anger.

Lila decided it wasn't worth bothering her anymore. They'd have plenty of time at dinner. "Alright, I'll be back in a bit. Love you."

Kali was too engrossed in her task to even look up, responding as if on autopilot. "Love you, too."

Lila stepped out, taking one last look at Kali before the orange door gently closed behind her. She took a deep breath. *Ahhh. Life's greatness can be captured in the smallest of moments.* For Lila, the first breath of ocean-tinged air was always one of them.

Lila started walking away from the beach toward the main road. She turned left upon reaching it, looking upon the thick cover of the forest that lay a few hundred meters ahead. Noticing the kiosks lining the side of the road, she smiled when she saw the red, gold, and green kiosk with the word *HAPPINESS* etched on the side. She couldn't see it without remembering her brother Chakra standing next to it, a mocking grin on his face. *"Anything you want, you can get here!"* he used to say.

Mostly true, but not in this case. Today, what she needed was elsewhere. In that forest, beyond the edge of this Keitaro settlement. That was where she had found the only environment hospitable for growing radishes. Or, to put it more accurately, the only unenhanced environment, for Lila was a traditional gardener for whom that mattered. She didn't use an iLink to make the entire gardening process effortlessly exact.

She walked by the last of the kiosks, her pace slowing as the smooth surface gave way to a wooded path filled with cones and brush. When she had first explored this stretch of woods, not stumbling over the uneven surface had been enough to keep her busy. Now, though, her muscle memory took over, guiding her to that familiar stretch of dirt, leaving her mind free to experience her surroundings.

She felt a pine cone crush under her foot, sending a strange feeling shooting up her leg through her spine. Somehow, the crunch of the cone didn't remind her of uninhibited nature but rather the deep technological power that lay within.

Barely one hundred meters into the forest, the trees gave way to an industrial setup that looked like it was fit to withstand nuclear attacks. Lila ignored the frenzy of drones moving from one bioreactor to another. The quiet buzz of activity supported all the needs and desires of those in Keitaro. Lila walked right through this technological work zone, making her way to the desolate area beyond that still resembled a natural forest. A place where her hidden garden lay.

As Lila gently loped across the forest floor, she felt a subtle but noticeable shift in temperature. It felt a little hotter. A little more humid. The machines themselves were all engaged in their normal activities, but it felt different. She wiped a bead of sweat off her brow and slowed her pace even further, wondering if it was her own hurry causing the change.

Any lingering stress disappeared as she saw her small soil patch in the distance. She hurried to see how the newest crop of radishes had turned out.

Suddenly, she felt tiny stings on the back of her neck. As she reached behind her, a cloth came over her mouth. She took a shaky step and then collapsed, her muscles utterly unresponsive. Her shoulder hit the ground, the impact almost deliberate in its slowness. She heard the unmistakable sound of a man's controlled sobs. Then everything went black.

With her next backstroke, Kali felt the gentlest of stings. She turned over, treading water while she looked at the blue jellyfish she had bumped into. Next to hundreds of others, the jellyfish together formed a wall designed to protect swimmers in Keitaro from external marine life. It was also designed to notify swimmers that they had reached the end of the designated swim zone. The setting red sun gave the jellyfish a purplish glow. *Lila must be home now, probably wondering where I am.*

She leaned forward and started an easy freestyle stroke back to the beach. Her long frame and larger feet made her a natural swimmer. She emerged from the water wearing nothing but a purple one-piece swimsuit. She picked up her red towel and wrapped herself up.

Kali started walking, smiling as she took in the beach scene. A beach volleyball game. Cabanas with people enjoying the sun. A few young adults frolicking in the water. She turned as she reached the familiar signpost. Her house was set behind two others, one pink with a large outdoor spiral staircase leading to the deck. The other a sprawling mansion that looked like it could have been a kingdom in the olden days.

By the time she looked at her own house, two unfamiliar faces outside the front door had caught her attention. *Why hadn't Lila dealt with them?* She could always spot these bureaucrats. The ones who assumed manual data collection was necessary simply because of the location of their home. It was always their look that gave them away to Kali—a mix of pity tinged with curiosity.

"Can I help you?" Kali asked with a faked sweetness that only Lila would have seen through.

The short man on the left responded, "Hi, young girl. Maybe you can. Do you live here?"

"Yes." Kali found the less she spoke, the quicker these interactions usually went. Less time wasted so they could get on with whatever pointless survey they were conducting.

"Of course, we believe you, but would you mind if we scanned your iLink just to confirm?" The taller woman on the right spoke with a barely perceptible note of desperation masked by an air of politeness.

Kali's brow furrowed. *They know I have an iLink? So these aren't people gathering information from the disconnected? What are they here for?*

She raised her hair over her shoulder as a floating device scanned the chip in the back of her neck. She felt naked as both strangers took on a dead stare while reviewing her personal information. "KB. Is that short for anything?" the man asked.

"Keitaro's Bride," KB joked, her sarcasm not seeming to register judging by the pained expressions on both of their faces. In truth, KB hated having her details freely available, even her name. She had made Lila replace her name with the acronym, joking at the time, "Only those who love me get to call me Kali."

"There's no easy way to tell you this. Lila's had an accident," the woman said as she placed a hand on KB's shoulder.

KB bristled at the unfamiliar touch, backing up a step. "What do you mean, accident?"

The man spoke plainly. "She's dead. A machine malfunction. Literally a one-in-a-trillion accident."

"We're so sorry," the woman quietly added.

KB felt her legs giving out, stumbling before catching herself. *Dead? How?* It didn't make any sense.

The next few minutes were a blur. The two of them guided her inside to the living room couch. They told her how the technicians had discovered Lila when they responded to the machine malfunction. One of them even described Lila's death with detached simplicity. "Found crushed under the weight of a builder drone."

KB spent most of the time staring straight through them, occasionally nodding.

All of a sudden, out of the corner of her eye, she saw it. Through the living room window. An owl perched on a branch outside the house. Or what looked like an owl. Even from a distance, KB could make out the glint of the individual pieces. Hundreds of nano-drones combining to form this moving sculpture, a playful homage to the Harry Potter series Lila had loved. KB's eyes bulged as she realized this robotic owl meant there was a message. A message from Lila.

She tensed up and sprung to action. "I'm going to go get some tissue. I'll be right back." Instinctively, she didn't tell them the real reason she jumped to head up the stairs. *Might as well see what it says first.* Galloping up two at a time before turning into Lila's bedroom, she quietly opened the window in the corner of the room. The nano-drone owl rose in recognition, entering with a gentle flight and landing on the end table next to Lila's queen-sized bed. She stroked the head of the owl. Unlike its counterpart found in nature, this owl felt rough as her fingers passed along the edge of each nano-drone interlaced with the next. But the motion was enough—the owl's mouth opened, and the piece of parchment fell out.

The use of physical parchment would make no sense to anyone except KB. Despite living together, KB and Lila loved writing letters to one another, from notes of gratitude to scavenger hunts. If they had a thought for each other when they were apart, they often chose to deliver it via these nano-drone owls. As KB slowly opened the tiny piece of parchment, she felt her heart beating faster and faster. She couldn't quiet the hopeful feeling that this would be a note from Lila explaining this sick joke and where to meet her.

Whenever one door closes, another one soon opens.

KB's face fell into her hands as the piece of parchment absorbed some of her tears. The reference to a childhood lullaby she used to sing was so Lila. Exactly how she'd want KB to find out. *Lila's really dead.*

She looked up, and the tears stopped as if snapping out of a trance. *Whenever one door closes, another one soon opens.* Lila had shown her. She went to a familiar spot on the far wall close to the floor. It looked inconspicuous, blending into the soft green paint and well below the animated GIFs hung up higher on the wall. But this spot was different. KB had never actually looked inside, but Lila had shown her it was there and told her how to access it in the event of an emergency. KB tapped two times then put her thumb against the wall for the fingerprint scanner to detect. The wall moved aside, revealing the contents within.

KB couldn't believe her eyes. An iLink was on and plugged into a contraption she'd never seen before. *Why did Lila have another working iLink? Isn't there supposed to be just one for each individual?* KB looked at the implantable brain-machine interface designed by the Maker. The size of a fingernail and in the shape of a pear, the iLink had a grayish translucent hue. Practically invisible to the naked eye, tiny filaments surrounded the device as if grasping for something to connect with.

How is it on? The iLink was only supposed to function within humans. In fact, each iLink, when implanted, was only operable within that individual.

KB turned over the device that seemed to be fused with the iLink itself. The case was multicolored, like a disco ball made of some sort of claylike substance. This wasn't just any iLink—the markings revealed this was Lila's.

The questions arrived in a flurry, way faster than she could process them. *Did Lila remove her iLink? Why is it hidden here? Why does she want me to get it?* KB started to feel lightheaded.

She had more questions, but she knew the answers wouldn't come now. KB closed her eyes and took a deep, calming breath. She put the iLink and its container in her back pocket and closed the safe she had opened. As she descended the stairs, she felt the tears starting to cake under her eyes. She turned around, quickly grabbed the box of tissue next to Lila's bed, and made her way back down.

"Are you okay?" The man's single raised eyebrow made KB fidget nervously, turning the tissue box over in a rhythmic fashion.

She looked back and forth at the two of them, sniffing in an exaggerated fashion. "Yeah... but I think I'd rather be alone right now. Do you need anything else?"

"No, I think we're all set," the woman replied. "Keep your iLink on. You'll receive some messages over the coming days about where you'll be staying and who will be your guardian for the next few weeks."

My guardian. Hearing those words nearly caused the dam holding her tears back to burst.

As the two of them stood up from the couch, the man looked at her quizzically. "Is there anything else we should know? Lila's iLink seems to have been destroyed during the accident, so we're flying a little blind here."

Even though the iLink in KB's back pocket was secured in a smooth ball-like container, it seemed to be digging into her skin under the weight of the man's gaze. *Should I just give it to them? She's dead now. No way to know what she would want me to do with it.*

"Look, now's not the time, but if it's okay, we'll stop by again in a day or two just to check on you. We can catch up then." The woman spoke with a warm smile, but at that moment, KB's decision was made.

"That won't be necessary. I'd prefer not to have visitors right now. I'll reach out if I think of anything. You can reach me on my iLink." KB declared with a firmness that belied her age.

Whatever the significance of Lila's final message, KB trusted it wasn't meant for strangers.

2

A HANDWRITTEN NOTE

To understand Keitaro, we must first understand the
world before it existed. Before the advent of artificial
general intelligence. Before everything changed.

At that time, the place was called Chennai. Even relative to the
rest of the world, Chennai was in a bad place. Climate change
had made it nearly uninhabitable. Disease brought through
warfare had ravaged the population. Digital attacks had left the
infrastructure crippled. There were fewer than 1,000 people left.

Until one day, in the area formerly known as Besant Nagar, on a
nondescript street best known for a temple dedicated to the Hindu
god Ganesha, a large package was discovered in the center of the
otherwise empty street. On it sat a handwritten note. Who would
have thought humanity's savior would be found inside?

—*FROM THE HISTORY OF KEITARO*

In the pure darkness, the musty air carried a deathly odor. The only
light came from the silvery shimmer of the object in the center of the
space. It was the size of a refrigerator with gentle, beveled edges. A
dispenser sat at the center and a small keyboard terminal above. No
one knew what lay inside that smooth exterior, but as a cage warns of

the potential power of the animal trapped inside, so too this machine radiated amidst a confining setup.

The fridgelike object sat encased in several enclosures. A chain-link fence. Kevlar-reinforced fiberglass. An anechoic chamber made using carbon nanotubes. The entire structure burrowed deep underground. Outside of all this security, there was only one way out. One way to escape this prison.

The gray door led to a room that gave no indication of the setting on the other side. In fact, it looked like a typical boardroom, stocked with various snacks and drinks along the walls. Fresh mountain air flowed in through a filtration system, providing a pleasant aroma that stood in stark contrast to the surrounding prison. The walls of the room were completely undecorated, except for one digital display with a thin cursive font.

In Loving Memory: Heitaro Abeh

Three people sat in the room, looking at the opposite wall, seemingly oblivious to the strange setting through the door behind them. They watched footage projected on a 3D screen of a builder drone approaching a middle-aged woman asleep on the ground. Instead of adapting its instructions to avoid her, the drone acted as if she weren't there, placing a piece of prefabricated timber down directly on her face.

Anthony averted his eyes from the gruesome scene of blood splattering everywhere. "No need to see it again." He waited for Dush to turn the screen off. "We aren't going to figure out what happened to that drone from this footage."

Anthony's white hair had receded far enough to reveal a prominent forehead, which, when combined with his strong jawline, gave him a distinguished air. Yet it was not his looks but his authoritative tone and measured pace that left the other two with their eyes locked on him, hanging on every word. "We'll have to do a full investigation of the accident and be sure to anticipate any potential fallout."

After a deferential pause, the woman to his left weighed in first. "With all due respect, Anthony, we shouldn't overreact. She was asleep in the strangest of places, technically outside Keitaro, and fell victim to the ultimate freak accident. In fact, this is the first accident in almost two years and 490 trillion interactions. I doubt there will be much fallout."

Anthony's penetrating blue eyes lingered on Tara as if trying to discern the motivation behind her comment. "If only more people had passed the Maker's Dream, you might be right. But a majority of the population aren't Dreamers. They won't think like the three of us. Are there any immediate risks?"

Dush responded eagerly as if anticipating this very question. "Her brother Chakra." He lowered his head quickly.

Anthony looked confused as he turned to face the diminutive man. "The Ultimate player? What's the issue? Is he questioning things?"

"He doesn't know yet. But he already showed up as a high-risk threat."

As a historian, Anthony was one of the few members of Keitaro who still felt comfortable flipping through sheathes of paper. He flipped through the report he had printed out in front of him and turned to the page with Chakra on it. "It's all relative. As Tara just said, we haven't really had many incidents of late. Keitaro is no longer a place under siege. This is only a threat in relative terms. Put an active locator out on him. Once he's located, engage a surveillance drone team to monitor his activities but no need for any other actions."

Anthony closed the report and pushed back from the table, readying himself to stand up. "Anything else?"

Dush shuffled his feet under the table. "Well, they couldn't recover her iLink."

"What do you mean?"

"Well, when the technicians showed up, they removed her iLink to download contents and pull up her last will and testament as per protocol. But I guess it had taken a beating from the timber, so the iLink couldn't be read."

The shining auburn strands of Anthony's left eyebrow arched. The remaining white hair on his head remained unruffled. His long, bony fingers unclenched so his thumb and index finger could press together. His hand moved in front of him as if to underline the words as he spoke. "Where is the iLink?"

Dush's head bent to avoid meeting Anthony's eyes. "We went to deliver the news to the child like you asked. The girl said it was her parent's wish to have it reused, so we had the technicians send it for recycling." He paused, his voice lowering to a near-whisper. "And it wasn't functioning anyway."

Anthony sighed. He wished Dush and Tara hadn't acted so hastily, but of course, they had followed suggested protocols. "How did..." He caught himself from saying her name. "...the girl seem?"

"She seemed tough," Tara replied. "Obviously, the news hit her hard, but I was impressed with her composure."

"I would agree, except for her extended bathroom visit," Dush couldn't help adding.

"What happened?"

Tara rolled her eyes. "Dush is ridiculous. She went upstairs to be alone for a few minutes, probably to let all the emotions out. She had pulled herself together by the time she returned."

"The way she ran up those stairs, she didn't look like a girl about to cry. I think the little girl had to use the potty!" Dush laughed as he spoke but stopped as soon as he realized the other two didn't see the humor.

Tara took the opportunity to steer the conversation back to the necessary actions. "There's one more thing. When I pulled up her report, I noticed something strange." Anthony waved an arm impatiently before she continued. "She's never played iHERO."

Anthony's eyes shifted back and forth. "Wait. Never?"

"Never. May mean she's at risk of disconnecting?"

Anthony scratched the hair behind his ear and grimaced in thought, tossing over the possibilities for the girl.

Dush squinted at Anthony as if he had fallen out of focus. "Uhh... it's not a big deal, though. We'll make sure she's moved to a family home. She'll have to play iHERO until the annual Update Festival. We'll keep an eye on it but...." Dush paused before nervously adding, "It doesn't seem that serious?"

"You may be right. But actually, in this case, I think I'll take her myself." Anthony paused to let the shock sink in, savoring the startled looks on the two faces looking at him. "As you said, she has less than a year. I don't want this little accident to spiral out of control in any way, so best to keep a close eye on things."

As Anthony started to stand up, Tara and Dush looked at each other in shared confusion. Anthony pretended not to notice as he buttoned his plaid blazer. He turned toward the elevator tube leading out of their underground confines. "What can I say? I've never had children of my own..."

3

SURVIVAL

The package sat in the center of the street for days. With the rising sea levels, the street was now largely deserted, too close to the shoreline for recurring traffic. We don't know which impoverished survivor first laid eyes on the package. We do know that eventually, the townspeople gathered around the note to consider a course of action.

Terrorist groups, even nascent ones, were too advanced for bombs at the time. These days, biological and chemical warfare were most common, even surpassing physical drone strikes. But any sort of attack wouldn't have been a likely worry for the people of Chennai, for they were barely relevant on a global scale. It was a town of forgotten survivors with little to lose.

As a result, curiosity trumped concern. The people opened the package, and for the first time in recorded history, humans laid eyes on the machine that would come to be called the Maker. On the front was a note. It read:

> *This is the first artificial general intelligence, preloaded with all the data on humans I could find. I want the people of Chennai to decide whether to turn it on. Below are instructions on how to 'box' it in and my best guess on how to ensure humanity survives the machine's emergence. Good luck. Keitaro Abeh.*

—*FROM THE HISTORY OF KEITARO*

Frankie's eyes darted upward toward a blinking notification in the top corner of his iLink. Designed not to be visible during a 'flow' state, Frankie wondered if it had appeared hours earlier or a moment ago. He chuckled, remembering the time Teddy had been temporarily disconnected and needed to be picked up. When Frankie didn't show up for hours, Teddy was, quite understandably, not pleased.

He lowered the microscope and, with a flick of the eye, a small silicone arm extended out. The arm took a glasslike object the size of a ladybug and returned it to its casing.

With his lab space clear, Frankie blinked and the notification moved to the center of his eye line, blurring the background of his normal visual field.

The iLink display had the wonderful capability of interrupting the signals from the eye to the brain to alter visual reconstruction. It was augmented reality to a stunningly accurate degree.

Chakra found. Location: Elliott Beach.

Frankie let out a sigh as he watched the live feed of Chakra throwing a frisbee come up.

"What's wrong, Frankie?"

The message collapsed, dissolving until his normal field of vision returned. He saw Teddy peeking in his home lab from the kitchen.

"This is why I need an office outside the house," Frankie said.

"Or at least put on the black shades for 'do not disturb' mode." Teddy shrugged and went back to his kitchen work. Thousands of the ladybuglike objects swarmed like schools of fish under his command. The nano-drones. Once people started referring to them as NDs, their name quickly morphed into the endearing term 'endeeze.'

Frankie stood up and marveled at Teddy's incredible efforts. On his left, Teddy had one group of nearly a hundred endeeze combine to form the shape of a chef's knife, with a blade sharp enough to demonstrate a mastery of onion slicing. To his right, Teddy had the chameleonlike endeeze take on the shape of his hand holding a pen, transcribing his reactions to the research podcast he was listening to through his iLink.

Frankie continued, hoping he could still get Teddy's attention. "Remember that friend of mine who was killed in the accident?"

In an instant, the two groups of endeeze paused their work, the knife lowering to the table and the hand coming to rest on the screen. Teddy turned to face Frankie, but his confused expression showed he had no idea what Frankie was referring to.

"How could you forget? It was literally right before I went into the lab. She was a year younger than me, remember?" Frankie asked.

"It is sounding familiar... How did it happen again?"

"Machine malfunction, can you believe it?" Frankie regretted the question instantly, knowing Teddy wouldn't be able to help himself from answering.

"I do believe it, but it is statistically improbable. What, it's been at least four years since the last incident? That must be billions, if not trillions, of machine-human interactions without a fatality."

Frankie shook his head. "Yes, Teddy. She won the lottery, I suppose."

Teddy must have recognized his insensitivity, as with a slight wink, he had his hand-shaped endeeze fly over and start massaging Frankie's shoulders.

Frankie couldn't help but laugh at the gesture. "You know, by next year, I'm hoping you'll be able to control a full clone-sized endeeze to handle things like this."

The nano-drones were the most powerful tool in Keitaro. And Frankie was the geek making them even more powerful. He was working on the latest connective tissue to allow the endeeze to work in groups of 10,000 or more in more dynamic arrangements. They were currently limited to a collective capacity of 7,500, and when they approached that, their movements were quite stiff and limited.

Teddy walked over to Frankie. "Will they be able to handle this, too?" He gently kissed Frankie's cheek, his pale white skin in stark contrast to Frankie's dark skin tone.

"If only your students could see you now."

"They do think I'm a little stiff."

"I think *robotic* is the word most frequently used to describe you."

"I'm not out to prove anything about my character to them. In any case, what about her?"

Frankie's mind returned to the original message that had disrupted his project. "As soon as I heard, I got notified of someone who needed to be personally notified of the accident. So, I put out a search, and they just located him."

Teddy's eyebrows creased, making his buzz cut more prominent. "You mean someone who's disconnected?"

Frankie didn't want to go down that rabbit hole at the moment. "Yeah, there are still some crazy ones out there. I'll see you later. Love you."

He mentally called for his coat on his iLink. He found the ocean breeze a little chilly for his taste. Thousands of nano-drones appeared, flying off the wall next to the front door. They pulsed from a pristine white to a checkered blue. The endeeze gently lifted the coat off the rack and floated toward Frankie as he started walking to the front door. Frankie concentrated, trying to execute a complex flip to have the coat seamlessly adorn him, but instead, he ended up with only one hand in it. He sheepishly pulled on the other arm of the coat as he walked out the door.

Out of the corner of his eye, Chakra saw the nano-drone approaching. He took a step and then jumped, executing a twist midair. His outstretched hand grabbed the frisbee. As he landed, his arm continued rotating and the frisbee collided with the nano-drone, a heavy thud marking the collision.

The nano-drone started to drop like a bee hit by a flyswatter but then steadied with alarming resilience. Combining with two other approaching endeeze, they together rose and ran a visual scan of Chakra, much to his annoyance.

"Hey, Chakra, this is Frankie. I have to talk to you about something important. I'll be there in seven minutes. Please stick around."

Chakra bristled at the accurate portrayal of Frankie's voice coming from the endeeze. He thought about leaving before thinking better of it. *These damn things would probably just follow me.*

He continued tossing the frisbee with his teammate until he saw Frankie's approach. A checkered blue jacket partially covered an oversized T-shirt, jeans, and a pair of black shoes that looked out of place, half-buried in the sand.

"Still using a plain frisbee, huh? You know we've moved on from those, right? Man, Chakra, you look... different," Frankie said as he approached.

It was true. The frisbee next to him was probably the only thing that looked familiar. He was darker than ever, a deep brown hue that bordered on black. His long black hair flowed to his shoulders and covered most of his forehead. A few stray red hairs shone vibrantly near the tips but seemed to lose their luster amidst the gray tinges near the roots.

"You can say it, Frankie. Older."

Frankie grinned. Chakra's hair connected to a grizzled beard, trying their best to distract from the sharp, handsome features of his face. But there was no distracting from his emerald-green eyes above a jawline that could cut stone.

"No, no, no. You still look amazing, Chakra. I love the beard. Honestly, I do. You just look... like a grizzled veteran. Someone who's seen something terrible and lived to tell the story."

Maybe I have. Chakra felt the weight of the bags under his eyes as he watched the waves crash, one after another, in slow succession. "Frankie, I need to get in touch with you whenever I'm looking for a compliment."

"You could always get in touch if you were connected."

"Don't get me going, Frankie," Chakra said, shaking his head. "You happened to have caught me in a good mood."

Frankie's smile disappeared. "Look, Chakra, I am going to have to ruin your mood regardless. There's no easy way to tell you this. It's about your sister. Lila's dead."

The words caused Chakra to stagger backward in the sand as if on the receiving end of a physical blow. Frankie reached out a comforting arm, but Chakra reflexively pulled back. His eyes narrowed as he looked at Frankie. "How did it happen?"

"Machine malfunction. Completely random nano-drone accident."

Chakra couldn't restrain the anger in his voice. "What the fuck? When have you heard of a 'fatal machine malfunction?'"

"Years ago. I know, Chakra, it makes no sense, but —"

Before Frankie could continue, Chakra cut him off. "How long has it been?" Chakra's voice dripped with urgency.

Frankie had a distant gaze as he peered at his iLink to confirm the timing. "Almost four hours ago. Why?"

Chakra's eyes darted around, looking for nano-drones in the vicinity. His voice lowered to a seething whisper. "This means Lila was close. She was close to figuring out how to defeat the Maker. Destroy the whole system. They must have killed her because they were afraid."

"Chakra, there's no 'they.' No one killed Lila. You can't honestly believe that." Frankie's patronizing tone did little to mollify Chakra.

Chakra's nostrils started flaring, and his fists clenched up. "Frankie, I'm not going to try and convince you. I know what a tech lover you are. But they won't stop with Lila. They won't stop until they're forced to."

His warm demeanor at the beginning of the conversation seemed like a distant memory now. He looked derisively at Frankie, recoiling at his very presence. *I wish I could wipe that look of pity off his face.*

Frankie reached out a hand to Chakra. "Look, I just came to tell you that the service is in three weeks at the beach near her house. I hope I'll see you there."

Chakra looked down at Frankie, both literally and figuratively. He turned and walked away in disgust.

Chakra could still feel some sand between his toes as he sat down in the underground tube. He usually had little reason for any transport other than walking, but this was an exception. It wasn't nanoflight, but he'd cover the twenty kilometers to Uthandi at the edge of Keitaro in exactly one minute.

Underground, while traveling in a tube at high speeds, the surrounding tunnel dynamically displayed the landscape from a different vantage point. It showed the passing ocean, beaches, and waves as if they were flying high above the ground instead of the actual view from deep underneath.

The tube system was a relic used mostly by tourists. Or disconnected residents like Chakra who lacked the power of an iLink. On this particular tube, there was one group of five visitors. A typical male-female pair with three young children. Though there was no physical resemblance, the mere presence of three children together was enough to take Chakra back to his own childhood. To the last time he had lost a sister to the Maker.

Most people accessed their memories through their iLink, visually reconstructing their memory in full, stunningly vivid detail. Without one, Chakra relied on his spotty memory. In this case, it was even more hazy since he was only six at the time.

But there they were. His sisters Lila and Seina on either side of him. Sitting on the tube on their way to the festival back before nanoflight had emerged.

They had eventually come to that perfectly pedicured lawn. Chakra remembered the crowd—maybe a thousand people—all gathered in jubilation. The festivities kicked off with some old guy speaking.

"Welcome to this year's Update Festival. Our 11th edition! Let's take a moment to appreciate that we're even here. We're very lucky. It wasn't predestined we were going to make it. Humanity was on a terrible path. Climate change. Scarce resources leading to warfare on many

fronts: biological, chemical, physical, and most importantly, digital. Consuming the planet to its eventual depletion. The end was near."

At a young age, Chakra loved the mythology. He loved hearing how they had come to live in paradise. He used to hang onto every word.

"But we always had one final trick up our sleeve. You see. Humans, of all their unique properties, this was perhaps the most interesting. We had the ability as a species to save ourselves from any problem of our own creation. We built the atomic bomb. Then we had a nonproliferation treaty. We caused the explosive growth of cancer through our actions. Then we cured it. We dug ourselves into holes, but we always figured out a way to escape. The escape always led us into a deeper hole, but hey, we live to die another day."

Chakra had read the stories of the battles to rid Earth of war and disease. At that young age, of course, he had believed them wholeheartedly.

"This time, it seemed like the hole was too deep. This little settlement, much like the rest of the world, was on the brink of collapse. It seemed like even humanity wasn't smart enough to figure out a way out of this hole... until we were. Or maybe 'we' isn't the right word. He. Keitaro Abeh. The man who created the Maker and released it here in the land formerly known as Chennai but forever now known as Keitaro."

At this moment, he remembered the look on his oldest sister Seina's face. She looked deeply interested as if she were somehow looking through the words to something beyond them.

"Now, look how far we've come here on Keitaro, A small but growing group. Through our open border policies, Keitaro settlements have been established in many places. The populations in the countries formerly

known as India, Pakistan, Bangladesh, and Nepal have created thou-
sands of their own settlements in this short time. Within a few decades,
based on immigration trends, we expect all of the former continents of
Asia and Europe to be part of Keitaro."

Chakra remembered Seina's furrowed brow amidst the sea of roaring approval.

"Of course, we shouldn't be prideful about size, but being proud is nat-
ural. Here we are in a place where people are on a path to fulfillment.
Where every need is met. Every desire attainable. We realized that
the key to not digging a deeper hole was to focus on internal devel-
opment, not external. If we just trained our minds on what matters,
we could live peacefully, harmoniously, and happily. Not just some of
us. All of us. And we didn't have to give up control to do it. That, my
friends, was the promise of Keitaro. That, my friends, was the promise
of the Maker."

At that young age, Chakra felt free from the burden of expectations. An iLink to provide him everything he ever wanted. Loaded
with the software known as iHERO, the mysterious lucid dreaming
protocol that guided each individual in moderating their desires.
With the Maker's gifts, Chakra had no doubt he would find his personal path to fulfillment. How could he not?

Now, he recognized it sounded too good to be true, but at the
time? Chakra didn't question it. Very few did.

"So, before we go on to celebrate this year's Update Festival, and believe
me, it's a great one, let's all take a moment to appreciate that we're
even here."

On cue, he started the chant and Chakra joined in, along with
nearly everyone in the crowd.

"To happiness! To joy!"

"To bliss! To fulfillment!"

The look on Seina's face was seared into his soul. Her lips sealed, looking around in silent disapproval.

He only found out why on the walk home. While he was twirling a lollipop in one hand, his other gripped Seina's. She had high cheekbones and thin, crescent-shaped eyebrows. Her forehead always shone in bright contrast to the jet-black hair streaking behind her.

Chakra looked up when she started speaking to Lila. "It all sounds too perfect, doesn't it?"

"What do you mean?" Lila always smiled with soft deference to her older sibling. Her dimples and lighter skin tone combined to give her smile a quiet warmth that always put Chakra at ease in her presence.

Seina seemed to have no idea Chakra was even paying attention. "I mean, humanity was on the brink of extinction. Falling apart. Until the Maker somehow saved us. Somehow saved us with no consequences. No negative externalities. Of course, everyone wants to believe it. Life is perfect here. Look at Chak sucking on that perfect lollipop. Somehow the perfect taste. Perfect nutrition. Sustainably processed and synthesized."

Lila and Seina both giggled as they looked at Chakra slyly taking another lick.

Seina's serious expression returned. "Don't you think... if all we've ever done is dig a deeper hole, that we might... well, be in a deeper hole right now?" It was her trademark expression. That I'm-not-buying-it face that he'd only ever seen in one person since. The person he was on his way to see.

The tube started to slow, snapping Chakra back to the present moment. Chakra looked out at the southern edge of the settlement that had now come into view. A forest that extended as far as the eye could see. But Chakra knew the tall trees conveyed a stillness that belied the activity on the forest floor. The surroundings were dedicated to providing a seamless, carefree existence inside the settlement. Endeeze at work, synthesizing and cooking food, operating factories, constructing new homes.

None of that was visible from the holo-field displayed on the tunnel, but Chakra had seen it with his own two eyes. Those with an iLink had to trust that the device wasn't manipulating their visual field without their permission. Unlike the blind followers of Keitaro, he knew his vision could be trusted.

As the tube stopped, he saw the familiar station surroundings. He stepped into one of the elevator tubes and popped out at the surface level a moment later. Compared to the eerie silence of the underground tube, the loud sounds of laughter and merriment were a shocking return to the present. It was nothing like the quieter Elliott Beach, where Chakra could hear the waves crashing against the sand.

On this beach in Uthandi, he ignored the happy faces and waves from people along the way until he reached his destination. It was not an excessively large home, but it was a vibrant one. Like a colorful sari, purple and green wrapped around in a pattern that seemed to personify the house.

Chakra still had that old Update Festival on his mind. Seeing the door to Lila's house, he started to relive the nightmare he had lived through that night. Or, to put it more bluntly, the Nightmare that had killed his oldest sister Seina. The Maker's Nightmare that had left her worse than dead—comatose. Chakra could still see the drool that had caked on the sides of her face. It was the cruelest form of torture he ever could have imagined.

Seeing his sister go through the Nightmare didn't just affect him. Chakra never forgot the steely expression of determination he saw in Lila's eyes at the time. Closer in age and sharing the bond that only sisters have, Lila and Seina had always been inseparable.

Tears started to form as he stared at the orange door right in front of him. Chakra wiped them away, resolving not to let them reappear when he saw her. If what he suspected was true, he was now at the door of the person the Maker would go after next. The girl with the same cheeks as Lila, but in most other ways, a marked resemblance to Seina. Lila's child KB. Chakra had to warn her. Before it was too late.

4

THE FATEFUL ILINK

The people of Chennai looked at the machine that would come to be called the Maker. Should they turn it on? Was it a trick? Keitaro's handwritten note foretold of a utopia unleashed by this AI machine. Armed with untold intelligence but constrained by an unflinching commitment to truth and obedience, the machine would provide all the answers they needed. Though with no proof to substantiate the claims, skepticism was widespread. Ultimately, desperation spoke the loudest. With little to lose and a potential paradise to gain, they decided to follow the instructions. They built the anechoic chamber and boxed in the Maker.

They turned it on and typed the command into the terminal as instructed:

```
Maximize every individual's path to happiness,
joy, fulfillment, and bliss without compromising
their humanity or their freedom.
```

Then, they waited. And waited. Nearly twenty-four hours passed before the Maker started to roar in anticipation. The Maker's 3D printer engaged and out popped one thing: a small implantable chip. The chip known as the iLink.

—*FROM THE HISTORY OF KEITARO*

KB lay under the covers, wondering how long she could go without her iLink notifying the authorities. The tears had stopped at this point, replaced by something worse. A feeling of loneliness left her lethargic, lying still in the bed with glassy eyes. Sleep would have been a welcome change, but closing her eyes brought terrorizing thoughts of her dead parent that she couldn't wrestle with yet. *What will life be like without her?*

The notification of a visitor interrupted her dead gaze. *Chakra.* Normally, the thought of his familiar gaunt face would be welcome, but now, she considered ignoring him. *He won't go away until I talk to him.* KB sat up in the bed.

When she signaled for the door to open, Chakra rushed in, grabbing her by the shoulders to look her up and down. KB provided no resistance, her weight falling onto him like a rag doll. She wished the tight embrace of her only remaining family member might make up for Lila's absence, but she felt nothing.

After what felt like several minutes but might have only been a few seconds, he whispered softly, "What happened, Kali?"

KB felt his jagged shoulder blades and the roughness of his beard against her hair. If only it could have been Lila's nook, the affectionate name she had given the spot on Lila's shoulders she used to snuggle in most mornings. The place where she'd so often nestled as if in a cocoon. Never again.

Finding her voice was harder than she expected. "I don't know, Unc. She said she had to run some errands. Then I got a notification saying there'd been an accident..."

Her voice strained to get out the words between breaths. She felt Chakra squeezing a little tighter.

He took her by the hand, leading her to the couch. "What exactly did they say?" Chakra said while taking a seat.

"Some sort of machine malfunction. The endeeze were moving a large piece of building equipment. The configuration was too large. Some sort of sensory problem. They weren't aware of her presence until it was too late."

Chakra looked up at the wall above her, which was covered in black and white GIFs. Animated shots of the children of Keitaro. Each seemed to capture the subject's joy at its very essence. The sparkle in the boy's eyes as he clapped among a crowd. The gaping mouth of the girl gazing out at the ocean, a large wave cresting in front of a radiant sunset.

"Tell me this..." Chakra paused. He shifted uncomfortably on the black futon. The teak frame, covered in engravings of elephants, snakes, tigers, and other wildlife, creaked under the moving weight. "Did Lila say or do anything recently that didn't make sense?"

The reminder of the mysterious message shook KB out of her grief-stricken state. "Crazy you should ask, Unc. There is one thing..."

As she told him about the note and the iLink, Chakra's eyes bulged, and he shifted forward on the futon. He eagerly grabbed the note and the contraption from her. He scanned the note before examining the contraption and the iLink, turning it over in his hands. "How did she do this?"

"I have no idea. When I opened it, the iLink was still on! Somehow, it was on even though it wasn't in her!" KB leaned back, confused at the excitement she heard in her own voice. The last few hours had felt like years, but talking about something other than Lila's death had briefly revitalized her.

Chakra's jaw dropped as he rubbed the multicolored ball. "Are you kidding me? These are nano-drones!" Underneath a light coat of paint were hundreds of endeeze no longer connected to the broader nano-drone network. These nano-drones had been fused together into this contraption that somehow operated an iLink.

KB started to frown, noticing a glint in Chakra's eyes. She reached out a hand to take back the contraption, but Chakra was faster pulling it away. "Kali, I'm going to need to keep this for a little bit. Figure out what Lila's been up to. This is too big a mystery to unpack right now."

"Hell no!" KB couldn't control the anguish in her voice. "She left that for me!"

Chakra handed her the parchment with Lila's message on it. "No, she left this note for you. This, on the other hand..."

She grabbed the note from him and clutched Lila's final words tight in the palm of her hand. He looked at Lila's iLink with a hunger in his eyes that was all too familiar to her. The type of look that led to him disappearing for months at a time. Where he'd be using that red psychoactive substance he always carried, off chasing some dead-end conspiracy theory.

"Let's see what the authorities say about this when I let them know you've taken it."

Chakra looked at her with wide, bloodshot eyes. "Don't even think about it," he hissed. "Wait, do they already know this exists?"

"They were here when the message came, so..." She considered lying to him.

With a look of panic, Chakra's eyes started darting around the room. "And they let you keep it?"

"No, they never even noticed. I opened the message upstairs." She figured lying might drive him even crazier. "What are you looking for?"

"Thank goodness, that's my girl. I'm looking for any of those nanodrones in here."

"We've never had endeeze in this house, Unc. Other than the ones in your hand holding that iLink, I guess."

He grimaced. "Kali, I can't be sure, but I don't think this was an accident. I think Lila was killed."

There it was. The dead-end conspiracy. KB shifted back, sinking deeper into the cushion. "Let me guess, Uncle? Was it the Maker?"

Chakra nodded. At this point, KB wanted to return to the loneliness of her bed and grieve undisturbed. "Get the hell out of here."

He recoiled at her harsh tone. "Kali. Look. I'm so sorry. Lila was an amazing gift to the whole world, but I can't even imagine what an amazing gift she was to you. She was your parent. I'm not going to lie to you, kiddo. Nothing will ever replace her."

"From the sound of it, you need to be giving that speech to yourself."

"I know everyone thinks I'm crazy. But not you, Kali. I've heard your questions. Heck, I know how Lila raised you..."

Her gaze dropped to the Persian carpet at her feet.

"The Maker did this. I don't know how, but I'm going to figure it out." He put Lila's iLink into his pocket. "The Maker is out to destroy us." He paused. "And I'm worried you might be the next target."

He's really doing this? All she could do was shake her head.

"I know what I'm about to say isn't fair, but I wouldn't make you if I didn't think this was best for you..." Chakra's voice trailed off.

KB raised an eyebrow, wondering what his unresolved anger had to do with her.

"I think it's best for the time being that you live in a safer place. A place where those without parents are protected with the most advanced security protocols—"

"I know you're not about to say a family home." She couldn't help interrupting as she caught on to his intentions.

Chakra's stern look made clear he wasn't ready to stop. "They'll accept you, no questions asked. I know this family home. It's not too bad. It'll never compare to living with Lila, but it'll do. When you meet people, talk about the accident but never share too much about Lila or your relationship with her with anyone you don't trust."

"No fucking way. I'd rather get killed by the Maker. Maybe I'll see Lila again in the afterlife."

"Unfortunately, you don't have a choice. I'm technically your guardian now." Chakra cleared his throat, his hand sliding into his pocket to feel the iLink. "And my current lifestyle isn't conducive to raising a child." A look of embarrassment briefly crossed his face. "Honestly, Kali, I think you're going to be happy there. Kids your own age to hang out with. It'll be good, I promise."

Her jaw tightened, and her fists started to clench. She opened her mouth to speak before catching herself. *What's the point? Change his mind, maybe even have him move in? Have him try and fill the gaping hole Lila's death left behind? Ha.* When she was younger, she had looked up to her uncle as the dashing, rebellious one. Now, as she watched him avoiding her gaze, she had little interest in rekindling their relationship.

Chakra stood up and held his arm out to her. She didn't budge.

"Pack up what you need, and I'll pick you up later tonight to drop you off. I have to do a couple of things before we head there."

As he shuffled slowly to the door, KB said nothing, hoping her silence would lead to a quicker departure.

He stopped and started scratching his beard nervously. "I promise I will get you out of there when I have more answers. Oh, and we can talk more about this tonight, but I wanted to mention that I know your Update Festival is coming up. You're probably thinking about disconnecting." Chakra paused and turned away, using his shirt to wipe his eyes before looking back at her from the doorway. "Whatever you do, please don't do it. The Nightmare isn't worth it."

5

A HOME FIT FOR HEROES

Any sufficiently advanced technology is indistinguishable from magic.
So it was with the iLink. The power to control the connected world
around you with your thoughts. At first, with limited networking
and drone technology, the use cases started small. Tasks like
flipping switches or carrying plates. But what was possible rapidly
accelerated with advances in technology. Soon, entire meals could
be made, or homes reconfigured based on thoughts alone.

Many worried about the unintended consequences. If everything you
desire is only a thought away, what's to stop you from wanting too much?

Yet, something strange happened in the face of such power.
People wanted less, not more. While iLinks fulfilled more of
our collective wants, our wants narrowed instead of expanding.

For there was one additional component to the iLink. It came loaded
with a piece of software, iHERO. A lucid dream, completely personalized,
individually optimized. "Become the hero of your own journey. Become
the best version of yourself." That's what our ancestors were told. No
one knew how it worked, but soon enough, no one cared. For it was so
widely loved and the effects so real that how it worked didn't matter.

—*FROM THE HISTORY OF KEITARO*

The car KB had ordered pulled up in front, and she turned to face her home. The one she had shared with Lila. The door swung closed with a thought, gliding soundlessly on perfect hinges. She gazed from the car's backseat with only the panoramic windows keeping her company. With a weak smile, she imagined Lila was taking a picture to commemorate the event.

A few hours ago, she had no intention of leaving. She had planned to confront Chakra. Call his bluff and request an arbiter to enforce his rights of guardianship. Chakra might have blown up at the idea of any sort of higher authority. But then, staring at the 3D wallpaper of the universe hung up on her ceiling, it dawned on her. Maybe a change of scenery would be nice. Being in a setting that didn't remind her of Lila in every way might be good for her. Even if not, climbing under the covers there couldn't be that different than home. After her Update Festival in a few weeks, she'd be free to move back in.

Her lips curled into the tiniest of smiles, imagining Chakra showing up to find her gone. He'd have to figure out if she'd actually made it there or had gone elsewhere.

The journey was quick and uneventful as the car glided through the mostly empty streets. She mindlessly glanced at the passing neighborhoods until the car pulled into a less residential, wooded area. The former Guindy National Park, an evergreen forest near the heart of Keitaro. With no houses in sight, the evergreens crowded the road, making it feel more desolate than it was.

The car came to a stop, and the door opened with a look from KB. Even in the dark, her first glance took her breath away. A massive open area, replete with playing fields and a mansion sitting in the center. It had a tall tower and surrounding smaller structures that seemed to spread out like veins. The late hour and surrounding darkness only emphasized its grandeur. A beautiful red parapet surrounded the building. As she approached, KB turned her attention to the Fungi family sign shaped like a mushroom above the door. She stepped onto the welcome mat, peering through the gate at the mansion looming over her.

Here she was, in a part of Keitaro she had never set foot in before. She sighed, resolving to try to leave the cloud of Lila's death behind, at least until she made it to her room.

She put her face near the scanner and announced, "Here to check in to Fungi as a new resident."

It completed a facial and retinal scan before she was asked to turn around. She turned, lifted the long brown hair from below her shoulders, and let the device scan her iLink.

"Welcome, KB. We hope you enjoy your time at Fungi. Please walk to the main hall to meet Quell, Fungi's Chief Resident."

The gate slid open, and KB walked through. The front doors of the mansion automatically opened as she reached the top platform. An older woman with high cheekbones and yoga pants that emphasized her athletic frame emerged. Her sharp features were offset by the warmth in her smile. "Welcome. I'm Quell. It's so lovely to see you. I'm so sorry for your loss. Do you go by KB or something else?"

"I go by KB." The short response carried a little more edge than KB intended.

"Oh, sure, I'll make sure the local operating system knows that." If Quell felt aggrieved by the tone, her dimpled smile betrayed no signs. "I know the last thing you must want is to be in the company of strangers at this late hour on such a terrible day. Let me show you to your room, and we can handle the introductions later. Follow me."

KB tried to give Quell a weak smile as she followed a half-step behind her. KB's eyes followed a girl flying through the hallway.

"Endeeze flying privileges are automatically granted for anyone ten and over as long as they remain in good standing in iHERO," Quell said, noticing KB's prolonged stare. "There's usually a three-day waiting period for new residents, but I'm happy to waive that as soon as you take part in your first session here."

Quell stopped at a mahogany door engraved with the words, *Seek wisdom within*. KB traced the smoothness of the engraving with her finger.

"Of course, this wing is still set up with the previous occupant's settings. Please do make it your own. We've connected your iLink for all basic safety and security functions, so we'll provide the necessary meals. Feel free to ask for anything else. Let me give you my direct line."

KB turned away from Quell, flicking her hair over her shoulder once more. Quell put her thumb on KB's iLink until the scan was complete. "Okay, my contact is in your database. KB? I'm sorry once again. I know it's not the same, but I promise we'll do everything we can to make this place feel like home." Quell rubbed KB's shoulder gently as she turned to walk away.

For the first time since Lila had died, KB felt a strong urge to avoid being alone. "Quell?"

"Yes?"

"Maybe being by myself isn't ideal right now. Do you have someone who might be able to show me around Fungi a little bit?" KB paused as she thought about what she was looking for. "Someone... who... you know... might.... carry the conversation?"

Quell smiled with understanding. "Of course. I know someone who should be up and about at this hour. I'll send up Kumi right away."

KB didn't even unpack her duffel bag. She was too engrossed in admiring her surroundings. This wasn't an amazing room. This was her own house, attached to the larger family home. The wing extended down for what felt like kilometers. She stopped counting after the first six rooms, and she couldn't understand why three bathrooms were necessary for one person. She picked out her favorite bedroom to throw her duffel bag in, where there was a king-sized bed with ergonomic pillows, all resting on a gorgeous wooden bed frame. A beautiful dark green and red canopy hung over the high posts of the bed.

The room next door was completely outfitted for entertainment. A bright green and blue gaming chair sat upright in the corner, replete with massaging capabilities and over twenty positions to choose from. No matter what position, the neck rest provided head protection, and the rest of the chair ensured full-body haptic capabilities.

Her entire room from Lila's place could fit into the entertainment room here. As she took out her toiletry bag, she heard knocking at the front door. She made her way back to the entrance. When she opened the door, she was surprised to find a boyish face on what looked like a grown man's body.

"Hi, KB? I'm Kumi. Quell asked if I could show you around." The bald head and chiseled frame seemed like a misplaced home for the gentle voice emerging from it. Everyone had perfectly white teeth, but somehow Kumi's looked more perfect in contrast with his dark walnut complexion.

KB stuffed her hands in her pockets, exhibiting a shyness that surprised herself. "Yeah, thanks a lot. Nice to meet you."

Kumi looked around at the setup behind her for a few moments, then asked, "Have you found wisdom?"

"Huh?" Her face couldn't hide her obvious confusion.

"Oh, I mean, the door. It says, 'seek wisdom within.' Just wondering if you found it? You know, a joke? Never mind."

She wondered what Quell had thought she meant when KB asked for someone who could carry the conversation. Strangely, she found Kumi's authenticity endearing. "I think you need to get out more, but I guess this place is so big you don't need to?"

He looked behind her, "Yeah, they are all massive, but they aren't all the same. I like the kind of library feel of this place. Anyway, let me show you around before it gets too late. Even night owls need sleep."

Kumi kept a brisk pace as he navigated the hallways. KB was nimble and athletic, but she had to exert some effort to keep up with his longer strides. They made their way back to the front door, taking a path that seemed to have too many left turns to be optimal.

Finally, as they approached the main hallway, he let out a sigh of relief.

"Were you lost? I feel like I didn't get the best guide here," KB said with a playful grin.

Kumi chuckled. "I knew we'd get here eventually. Now I'm good, though. I wanted to orient you from the front of the building because I kind of need to understand things spatially. So, if you're looking out the front door, out to the right, that's what we call the Wood Wide Web. Don't shoot the messenger with all the naming here. We're in the Fungi home. I mean, I've come to appreciate it, but it's an acquired taste for sure."

She smiled at his explanation. She had spent enough time in the woods with Lila and Chakra to know all about fungi. She considered telling Kumi about her experiment testing the mycelium network but thought better of it.

He continued, "Anyway, the Wood Wide Web is basically our outdoor playground. There are three actual playgrounds, a bunch of games, and hiking trails even farther back. Honestly, it's where most of us spend most of our days. You can explore it more later. I recommend doing so once your nano-drone flying privileges are enabled because there's a lot to explore at the higher levels of the Fungi dome in the wooded trails. Everything you can see—mental games, athletic games, group activity setups, performance arena—I'm sure you're pretty familiar with, right?"

"I mean... yeah, but this all looks like top-of-the-line equipment. I guess I wasn't expecting this at a..." KB's voice trailed off.

Kumi jumped in, showing no signs of embarrassment. "At a group home. Yeah, it surprises a lot of people. But think about it. We may not have our parents, but we have Quell and a few others who have passed the test here. That's really all you need, especially when you're given one of the biggest mansions in Keitaro! I mean, we each have our own wing in this place!"

KB couldn't help asking, "How many kids are in here?" If everyone had their own house inside, even a mansion like Fungi couldn't accommodate too many.

He gave her a sheepish smile. "Well, it's a little nuts. We call each little residence a Hyphae. It looks overwhelming, but there are only twenty-six. Each Hypha has a letter, and they go from left to right in their naming. You're in Hypha R. Not all of them are occupied. We have twenty-one of us now, including you."

All this space and only twenty-one people? Her jaw dropped. There were actual families with more people.

If he sensed her surprise, he didn't let on as he continued. "See how the Hyphae kind of team up in four bigger strands? Those are called spores. Your Hypha is in the Shroom spore. I'm over in D, which is in the Dew spore."

Even as a fungi lover, this was a bit much for KB. "They really went all-in when they decided on Fungi, huh?"

He laughed. "Yeah, it's a little crazy. But let's keep it moving before it gets too late. So we call this whole central tower Mycelium. I know it looks big when you walk in, but it's even bigger on the inside. There are nine floors in this central tower. You have the cafeteria on two, auditorium on three, library on four, spiritual on five, athletic on six, immersion on seven, connection on eight, and iHERO on nine. Follow me."

KB stood in shock at the glorious facilities. He stepped into a tube and waited for her to follow him. She looked around at the translucent tube, admiring the attention to detail in even the smallest displays. After a few moments, she glanced at Kumi. "Um... why aren't we moving?"

"Oops. Oh, yeah, say the floor you want to check out."

She wasn't used to this level of technological wizardry. In her home with Lila, they had kept things pretty low-tech, quite deliberately. "Oh. Spiritual."

The tube immediately whizzed up, sending KB's stomach into her throat for an instant before their near-instantaneous arrival.

"Nice pick. So there you can see sensory deprivation rooms, both for individuals and groups. There's the yoga studio. The choir room's the big one in the middle. It's cool. They have it set up acoustically, so it sounds amazing when you're in there and you can't hear a peep outside. Meditation rooms. I got to admit, showing you all this makes me feel like I probably should have spent more time on this floor. Spiritual isn't really my thing."

"It's not your thing yet. There's still time."

He grinned as he shrugged. "Maybe... What next?"

They entered the tube. This time, she picked right away. "Immersion."

Kumi laughed. "Now we're talking my language."

An eerie feeling swept over her as she emerged from the tube. They were on floor seven, with two more floors above, but the space felt cavernous. The large open area was covered in a rainbowlike glow. KB imagined how others might be awestruck, but it felt too contrived for her taste.

He oriented her to the surroundings. "So, there are four immersion rooms. Each one can accommodate from one to ten people. You select your experience, you scan your iLink, and you're off. They monitor your immersion time by age. We can do up to two hours a day."

She had been in immersion rooms before, but she still had naive curiosities about the phenomenon. "Do kids here prefer immersion to iHERO?"

Kumi stroked his chin while looking at one of the rooms. "I don't know; people like both. The immersion experiences are amazing. Full-body haptic suits make virtual reality an incredible way to see the world. And at least you're awake, so you know everything that happens. With iHERO, you feel amazing after, but not remembering much sucks. But still, each dream gives you this addictive happy feeling even if you can't figure out why. For me, I'd have to say iHERO. What about you? Which do you prefer?"

KB smirked as she replied, "Oh, I prefer something like the Wood Wide Web or Spiritual to either. But I guess I'd prefer immersion. I prefer the idea of an objective reality versus a subjective one."

He started walking back to the tube and shrugged. "Yeah, I guess. Come look out this window. It'll be easier to show you the rest."

She looked out the window facing the rear of the grounds. She was struck at the magnificent shape of the building below. As if a stream of water had spread out across a leaf, the building spread in what felt like an infinite number of narrow wings. KB usually kept her excitement to herself, but she felt a lack of judgment in Kumi's presence. "Wow. This place is pretty epic. I wish I was in a better place to appreciate all this."

His smile disappeared as he turned toward her. "Yeah, I know I didn't ask about you, but don't think it's because I'm not interested. I figure anyone new probably doesn't have the happiest reason to be here. We'll have plenty of time to get to know each other. Anyway, do you want to head back to your room? Happy to drop you off."

Before she could even respond, the tube opened, and Quell emerged.

"Kumi, thank you so much for showing KB around so late. KB, I hate to say it, but it looks as if that tour may have been quite useless. Even at this late hour, someone's here to pick you up."

6

THE NEXT STEP

We are part of an evolutionary journey. The Maker is the next step in that journey. From the quarks after the Big Bang; to amoeba; to humanity; to the Maker. The nihilist in me says to accept the Maker and acknowledge humanity was only ever meant to be a brief step on this long journey. The optimist in me wants to fight to maintain our humanity for as long as we can.

—FROM THE WORLD OF THE MAKER

Anthony rose from the chair in Quell's office and walked behind her desk. He couldn't help himself. It was so rare to see physical books these days that it offered a rare window into someone else's priorities. He hunched over and flipped through the books. *Transcend: The New Science of Self Actualization. Scott Barry Kaufman. Know What Makes You Happy (or they'll try to convince you they know). Dispatch Hannon. The Psychology of the Child. Jean Piaget.*

That one looked slightly out of place as if it had been returned rather hastily. Anthony pulled out the book and opened it to a folded page. The door opened, and he turned around.

He had studied her file, but it was still striking to see her in person. Her dark hair was reminiscent of Lila's. But unlike Lila's youthful features, KB's face seemed to convey a maturity far beyond her young body. He wouldn't say she had a pep in her step—after all, she had recently lost her parent—but there was still a purpose to her stride that impressed him.

Her eyes narrowed, and she looked over to Quell. "Wh—" she started before deciding on a different question. "I thought you said Chakra was here?"

Quell tilted her head. "Who's Chakra? This is Anthony." She gave a smiling nod in his direction. "I'll let him explain who he is. I'll leave you two alone, but if you need me, I'm just a thought away!" With a slight bow of her head, she scooted out of the room, and the door soundlessly closed behind her.

"You must be KB." He had seen her local OS and knew to go by the shortened nickname.

But KB was not impressed as she stood at the doorway stone-faced. "Yeah, but who are you?"

Anthony continued smiling as he placed the book back on the shelf. He knew winning over anyone raised by Lila would take time. "Of course. I'm Anthony. It's great to meet you. I'm sorry that the first time is under such unfortunate circumstances. Why don't we sit down?"

As he took one of the two seats facing Quell's desk, KB didn't move. "Why are you here?"

Now was the time for his first reveal. Anthony paused, and a look of sadness crept over his otherwise stately veneer. "Well, long before you were born, I actually was a classmate of Lila's." He paused to see if Lila's name sparked a reaction. It registered in the focus in her eyes, but there was no emotional outburst. "In fact, at some point, we used to be good friends. We fell out of touch over the years, but when I heard the news, I wanted to reach out to you. See if I could offer some assistance during this difficult time."

He could see the wheels turning in her head. He doubted Lila had ever mentioned him. He waited to see where she would take the conversation next.

"How did you even find me?"

Anthony responded in a demure tone, "iLink sends out a tracker for anyone who..." His voice trailed off as he searched for the precise words.

Before he could find them, KB jumped in, "... has lost their last parent."

Anthony nodded. He watched KB's eyebrow arch with a skepticism he was much more used to showing than receiving.

"And they let *anyone* see that?"

The corner of his lips turned into a slight smirk as he took pleasure in being faced with a dose of his own medicine. "Well, not anyone. Anyone who has passed the Maker's Dream in iHERO and makes a request."

KB continued to surprise him. Her face was blank. It was as if she didn't fully comprehend the magnitude of becoming a Dreamer. Anthony leaned his head one way and then the other, hearing his neck crack. Getting through to her was going to be harder than he had imagined.

Her eyes met his, and her feet shuffled as if impatient to leave the room. "Look, I appreciate you getting in touch. Thank you. But I'm not sure what you can do for me. I'm pretty much settled in here, and I'm a few months away from my Update Festival."

Before Anthony could respond, he saw her eyes grow large, making her look for a moment like Lila. "Wait, wait, wait. Are you the organizer of the Update Festival? I remember you giving the opening speech!"

Anthony laughed and leaned back in his chair. She still wasn't sitting, but she had moved closer and was finally showing signs of engagement.

"Not quite. I'm a member of the Maker Small Council. And I'm a bit of a history buff. That, combined with the faux gravitas that comes from this white hair, is enough for them to ask me to speak at the annual Update the last few years."

Again, Anthony let the silence fill the room. He never rushed conversations. Instead, he liked to use silence to strengthen his position.

See how much a partner was willing to be led. He saw her nod as she looked at him out of the corner of her eye. Maybe she was realizing now that he was one of the three people in all of Keitaro that the Maker had selected. He watched her face closely to see if he could discern any of her views. Passing the Maker's Dream may not have impressed her, but to be one of the three people representing the whole of Keitaro had to.

After interrogating KB's expressions, Anthony continued, "As to what I can do? I know you're already fourteen, and it's only a few months until your official Update, but I wanted to offer for you to come live with me until then. My place is no Fungi, but it's not bad."

KB's look of skeptical disregard forced Anthony to try again. "I can assure you I'm not one for false modesty. My place is very nice, don't get me wrong. But Fungi is world-class as family homes ought to be for their special residents. But a living space is about more than the amenities."

He watched as she rocked back and forth on her feet, her eyes darting around. He knew he still had work to do.

"This is a lot... Why do you even want to do that? For a childhood friend who you haven't seen in at least a decade? No offense, but Lila never even mentioned knowing you. Which is pretty strange for a member of the Small Council."

Anthony turned contemplative. Maybe bringing Lila up had been a mistake. "KB, I know it probably doesn't make much sense to you. I'm not sure how best to explain it. I've never been a parent..."

"I'm not about to be your child..."

He couldn't remember the last time he'd heard that disrespectful tone when someone addressed him. He let his teeth scratch the top of his tongue, the only expression of irritation he would allow himself. He only had himself to blame for how this was going. He would have to adjust his expectations and try to salvage a draw in the face of imminent defeat. Making no effort to hide the remorse on his face, he continued, "I'm sorry. I was going to say, 'So I don't have any expertise.'"

Her weak smile provided the assurance Anthony needed to continue. "In any case, that was a poor way to start my thought. Of course, I'll never be your parent. All I'm trying to say is... I really respected Lila back in the day. I'm at a stage in my life where I have some wisdom that may be useful. While I usually try to share that through my classes, I'm always a Chosen mentor for my students. I selfishly saw this as an opportunity to build a relationship in another setting while honoring a friend's legacy."

For the first time, he saw a crack in KB's tough exterior. As she turned away, Anthony caught a glimpse of the glassy tears forming in her eyes. He thought of continuing but decided to wait for her reply.

"That's very nice, Anthony. It really is. Lila would feel great knowing there were people who cared enough about her to want to look after me. Honestly, though, I'd prefer to be in a place without any ties to Lila at this point. And I'm pretty much set up here."

He let out a small sigh of relief. He maintained a warm smile as he got up from his chair. "Of course, I completely understand. Let's do this. I'll provide you my details and directions to my place. If you ever want a nice meal or need to get away, you can always come over, no questions asked. Consider it an open invitation."

"Alright, that sounds nice. Thanks."

An awkward pause ensued. Anthony rubbed his thumb and middle finger together, wondering why KB wasn't preparing to receive his details. He glanced at his fingers and back at her until she recognized her oversight. "Oh, can you tell me? I try not to use my iLink for directions. I consider myself a bit of a wanderer."

Of course. Only someone who had never played iHERO could live with such independence from her iLink. Only someone who had never played iHERO would even want to. This was going to be fun. "I should have guessed. Sure. Nano-flight or by car?"

"Not close enough to walk from this place in the middle of nowhere? Then definitely nano-flight."

As he wrapped up the directions, Quell popped her head in the doorway.

"Sorry for interrupting. KB, shall I have the endeeze bring your stuff down here?"

KB nodded at Anthony as she gathered herself. "Actually, Quell, if it's okay, I think I'm going to stay here. Anthony, look forward to a meal at some point."

Once she had left, Anthony turned to Quell. Now that the plan had changed, he needed her support. "Quell, thank you again. Can I bother you for a moment more?"

Anthony walked out the front door and turned back to face Fungi. It was an exceptional place. A sign of the incredible progress Keitaro had made. Even those with no parents—traditionally the forgotten orphans throughout history—lived blissful lives here.

The black car pulled up, and Anthony opened the back seat. Since the advent of nano-flight, driverless cars had acquired an antiquated feeling. But old habits die hard. And when nano-flight had arrived, he had been too old. He wasn't able to modulate and control his flight with the precision of those half his age, making his experience a jarring one. So, for the most part, he took his seat in modern electric cars like this one.

With a thought, the car pulled into motion, accelerating smoothly until trees became blurs of brown and green. Amidst the silent forest surrounding Fungi, only the rhythmic tapping of his bouncing leg could be heard as he reviewed the Small Council report.

He leaned back and put his iLink into full-screen mode. He scanned the headings and saw a few notes of progress on the nano-communication technology. He paused at Chakra's name.

Ahhh, the other loose end. Let's see what Lila's brother has been up to.

When he selected the report, his female colleague from the Small Council, Tara, appeared in his visual field. The iLink's ability to replace the visual field had become nearly flawless. Her holographic recording captured her glowing skin and energetic expression. "Anthony, the nano-drones have finally located Chakra. It took longer than we expected, and it only happened because... Well, see for yourself."

Tara's recorded face left the iLink, and his visual field turned into immersive mode. If he were in an immersion room, he would have felt like he had been dropped in the forest near the outskirts of Keitaro. Still, with only an iLink's inbuilt VR in a moving car, he was surprised at how little he noticed his actual surroundings as the video started.

Anthony entered the eyes of a specific nano-drone. The camera of this endeeze was near the outskirts of Keitaro. *Is that Uthandi?* He made note of the latitude and longitude to cross-reference later. He noticed an artist painting the forest. With no shirt or shoes and a surfboard next to him, the artist seemed to be in a meditative trance as he captured a tree's outer limbs.

The pursuit of pleasure took many paths, most of which made no sense to Anthony. But he appreciated everyone's ability to pursue those paths, unencumbered by any needs.

When all your needs are met, it is only your desires that are left. He might have even used that phrase at one of his Update Festival speeches.

After the artist, there was nothing but the forest ahead. Officially leaving the settlement of Keitaro, this endeeze headed out to one of the many manufacturing and energy facilities powering this paradise.

Anthony braced himself, knowing this wasn't going to be a routine session. But he still wasn't prepared for the quickness of the movement, jumping back in surprise. All of a sudden, the camera view grew shaky as it was knocked to the ground. Anthony blinked a few times to reorient himself as he rolled, finally finding himself looking directly into the palm of Chakra's hand.

What in the world is Chakra doing? Anthony couldn't possibly understand what he was intending on this futile mission.

With communication signals happening on a nano-second scale, the camera view switched instantly to an endeeze assigned to capture the scene. Within seconds, a group of nano-drones had surrounded Chakra, forming a choker necklace carrying a strong incentive to stay still—the incentive of hundreds of tiny tranquilizer tips hovering millimeters from his neck.

Anthony could see the rage in Chakra's eyes. His breaths were deep, and the endeeze rose and fell with each heave to maintain a precise distance from him. Anthony couldn't take his eyes off the man. His unkempt appearance, from his long hair to his beard. But what stood out was his clothing. In a day of personalized clothes available with a thought, the bagginess of Chakra's athletic gear stood out. It wasn't much, but it was enough to show his disconnected status to someone with Anthony's keen observation.

Chakra slowly opened his palm, and the trapped endeeze joined the others surrounding his neck. Chakra raised his hands in surrender, and the necklace unraveled from around him. The endeeze joined together in a V formation a few feet from him. Then, marching to the same beat, they turned toward the forest and left him sitting on the ground, hands wrapped around his knees, breathing heavily.

The endeeze camera view shut off. The car was turning onto a superhighway, gliding seamlessly behind the one other car on the road. Tara and Dush, the other member of the Small Council, popped up on his iLink. Both had bags under their eyes as if they had been woken from a deep slumber. They probably had set an alert for when Anthony had opened the footage. He wished the Small Council didn't have access to each other's viewing activity.

"Is this an official meeting, Anthony? I didn't see this on the schedule."

Compared to KB, Dush's submissive tone felt like a desperate search for validation. Anthony responded dismissively, "No, no. I just wanted to know what we've done with Chakra since this happened."

Dush hesitated, so Tara spoke up. "Well, of course, we've kept an active tracker on him now that we located him. We now have a monitor on his residence as well. Of course, the endeeze may not be able to follow him everywhere, but we'll be alerted if he falls off our radar."

Dush straightened up, puffing out his chest. "Now that he's shown signs of malicious intent, I think we'd be more than justified in looking at expulsion from Keitaro."

Anthony smirked. Dush and Tara were wonderful in many ways, but they were peacetime generals. They were both nearly fifteen years younger than him and had grown up well after the early days of Keitaro. They didn't know how to handle the threats that now appeared more rarely than ever.

In fact, this was barely even a threat at this point. An Ultimate player trying to catch a single endeeze? Anthony couldn't help but laugh at the futility and gall of the attempt. "No, let's leave it for now. It's not a big deal, and you've taken the right precautions. Have a good night. Sorry I looked at this so late."

As they left the screen, Anthony turned his iLink into background mode. The car was pulling off the highway into his neighborhood. Despite being close to home and the late hour, he felt unsettled. It was almost assuredly nothing, but he didn't want to make any mistakes. With a thought, he confirmed a new destination, and the car came to a stop. It gently turned around and accelerated back onto the highway. *The Maker will resolve any doubts.*

7

IMPOSSIBLE ESCAPE

The end of humanity is probably similar to an object approaching a black hole. Once you enter a black hole's event horizon, escape is impossible. An observer never sees an object enter. In fact, the object appears to slow as it approaches the black hole, taking an infinite time to reach it. Is that where the Maker is sending humanity?

—FROM THE WORLD OF THE MAKER

Frankie put the nano-drone down and swiveled his chair. The door to his lab changed into a window as the chair turned. There was his partner Teddy, standing in the middle of the kitchen, crouched like a samurai in training.

Plant-based burgers cooking on the stove. Plates and wine glasses making their way to the table. An immersion scene from the Kurukshetra War projected in 2D on the wall. Most people might have relaxed in an immersion room to watch the scene but not Teddy. He didn't use endeeze passively to execute tasks. Instead, while he was watching, he controlled groups of them cooking and preparing dinner simply to improve his mental acuity.

How did I end up with the love of my life in beach shorts and a tank top looking like one of my favorite anime characters? Frankie paused, wondering if he should enter and disrupt Teddy's flow state.

I'll tell him to think of it as another training test. 'How quickly can you regain your flow state?' That always works.

The see-through door slid up with the sound of a vacuum releasing its seal. Teddy looked over at Frankie and smiled. The immersion scene turned off while the cooking and table-setting continued.

Frankie nodded in appreciation. "Your training really does work, Teddy." He rose from his chair and started walking out. "Anyway, Teddy, remember we have to eat quickly. We're headed to Lila's service after lunch."

Chakra hadn't planned on attending the service. The last thing he wanted was to be around people who didn't know Lila and love her the way he did. He knew in his heart that the only way to honor her would be to avenge her murder. But to do so, he needed to see Frankie again, and the service was the ideal setting.

He turned over the contraption holding Lila's iLink in his hand, noticing how the endeeze interlaced to form a cocoon around it. He pulled the iLink out of the holder, and it immediately went inert. He pushed it back in and rotated it counterclockwise, stopping before he knew it would lock into place and turn on. That was the key to unlocking this mystery. Lila had figured out how to manipulate the nano-drones to operate an iLink outside of a human body. *What else could these endeeze be programmed to do?* He smirked at the thought of a nano-drone army storming the Maker's underground bunker.

At this point, after weeks, he had nothing to show for his efforts. Every time he attempted to capture even a single endeeze, he was embarrassed, threatened, and forced to abandon his attempt. There was the time he thought he had one cornered alone, only to find himself surrounded by others the moment he swiped at it. The time he tried to step on one on the ground, only to find it withstood the pressure from his foot easily. After countless attempts to squish and stomp the nano-drone, he had finally given up.

There was even the time that he managed to enclose one in a titanium casing. Before a smile of satisfaction could even spread across his face, he found a cluster of endeeze forming. He hadn't planned an adequate escape route and went to the one place he hoped they wouldn't be able to follow. He ran to the beach and dove into the water, hoping he could submerge and outlast whatever sensors they had. But the water had proved to be no obstacle. They dove in after him, using the water to administer mild electric shocks to his legs until he had no choice but to come up. He laid on the beach, drenched and exhausted from his frantic efforts. When he released it, the endeeze didn't even arrest him or call for any human backup. Somehow, that added insult to injury.

He tossed the device in the air and caught it gently. *How did Lila do this?*

It was rare to be at a service for someone already dead. With accidental deaths now exceedingly rare, most chose living funerals during old age.

Lila had chosen to have her ashes scattered in the Indian Ocean accompanied by a traditional funeral. She had only invited a few of her closest family and friends, but the service was open to the public. Having the ceremony at the popular beach near her house made the service a small spectacle. A few hundred people congregated in the general area.

Chakra looked around for KB, wondering if she was still upset with him. The night of Lila's death, he had returned to their house and found KB had already left. He had gone to Fungi and confirmed she'd checked in. He had thought about going in but decided her early departure was a sign she didn't want to see his face so soon after their last encounter.

Now, looking around the beach, he couldn't find her. But then, he saw Anthony—the gray hair was different, but the hunch in his shoulders was unmistakable. Even when they were kids, Chakra had found his unathletic posture annoying. Of course, it hadn't helped that Anthony monopolized Lila's attention at the time, either. *Now, look at him. In charge of the damn system that killed my sister.* Chakra smirked. *Sellout.*

Chakra's head turned to the ocean, where a booming voice emerged through an endeeze speaker set up for the service.

"Hi, everyone! Thanks for coming..."

He looked at the young girl speaking and smiled. *So KB did decide to show up.*

The nano-drones interlaced and turned a beautiful purple hue, erecting a three-sided wall around the participants in the service. The backdrop of the ocean glistened as the waves splashed KB's feet. Her proud posture and look of determination belied her young age. "I know this is usually a time for joyous celebration," she continued. "And if anyone was worthy of such a celebration, it was Lila. She was everything I could have asked for in a parent. She cared for me and helped me grow in more ways than I could ever imagine. But somehow, I can't think of this as a day for joy."

She paused, and Chakra wondered if she might be heading down a provocative road. While he feared for the consequences, he found his heart racing at the prospect of KB taking on his more skeptical nature.

"No, without the guest of honor here to celebrate with us, it doesn't feel right. Yet sadness is also not the right emotion for today. I've shed my tears and have no interest in the funerals of yesteryear. Instead, I ask us to take this as a moment of reflection. Reflect on the best that humanity has to offer. Because that's what Lila was. For me, and for everyone who came in contact with her. And if we all take a moment to reflect, not on her, but on ourselves, I think that'd be all Lila would have hoped for. Thank you for coming."

Lila herself would have been hard-pressed to do better. KB had somehow spoken to Lila's unconventional wisdom without ever making her sound heretical. She walked back into the sea of people standing around. All Chakra could hear were the sound of the waves rolling in and the endeeze softly playing Lila's favorite jazz music.

Chakra looked around at the silence of the people gathered as if they were all following her commands to reflect. He resolved to do better himself, starting with his conversation with Frankie. A tap on his shoulder interrupted his train of thought at the perfect time.

"I'm glad to see you came!" Frankie smiled as if their previous interaction had ended pleasantly.

Chakra's shoulders relaxed as he took a deep breath. His hand instinctively felt for the iLink that he held in his pocket, safe in the contraption Lila had created. He felt the smooth edges and smiled. "Frankie! Yes, how could I miss it?"

He reached down and grabbed Frankie by the shoulders before pulling him in for a warm embrace. "I'm sorry about how our last conversation ended. No hard feelings?" He pulled Frankie back before noticing the person standing next to him. A couple of inches taller than Frankie but still quite short. Muscular and thick and in short shorts and a muscle T designed to emphasize it.

"Oh, let me introduce you to my partner, Teddy!"

Chakra tried to smile warmly, but his lips seemed to fight the rare upward pull. "Great to meet you!"

"Pleasure to meet you too. I've heard a lot about you from Frankie."

"Forget all of it. Anyway, Frankie, can we speak about something in private?" Chakra caught himself looking around and returned to keeping eye contact. "You know, someplace we can't be overheard?"

Teddy's knowing smile filled Chakra with an anger that he worked hard to subdue.

"Of course. My place should be fine. Come on over. We were heading out anyway," Frankie replied.

Chakra had wanted to catch up with KB. Frankie grabbed Teddy's hand, and they both turned away from the ocean. Chakra's eyes darted around, looking for KB's face to see if he might be able to connect before leaving. *Who knows when I'll see her next?*

Suddenly, he saw her, drinking from her water bottle, in a casual conversation with Anthony.

Anthony? How does KB know Anthony? Lila would never have introduced him after how things ended. Why do they seem friendly?

Frankie and Teddy looked confusedly at him a few steps ahead. Frankie offered, "Oh, I'm sorry, Chakra. Did you plan on staying? We're headed out, but we can always catch up another time!"

Chakra put on a smile as he jogged toward them. "No, no. I was making sure I had said hi to everyone I was supposed to. You know how these things go."

As the three of them walked side by side, Chakra snuck one more glance back at KB with Anthony. *Only one mystery at a time.*

Chakra followed Frankie and Teddy around their beautiful home. The lab space looked like something out of an iHERO dream. As one of the few disconnected, he stared at the various machines with the curiosity of a child seeing a magic trick for the first time.

"What's that?" Chakra pointed to a series of five nano-drones, individually encased in silicone tubes that extended from the floor to the ceiling of the lab. He might have missed the tiny gray orbs in the center if it weren't for the straps across the center of each tube, holding each endeeze in place. A chill went down Chakra's spine, seeing these powerful devices displayed like prisoners.

"Oh, my goodness. This is exciting. I think I'm close to a break-through on this connection technology."

Chakra's raised eyebrow didn't slow Frankie down.

"So, right now, endeeze have been designed to only accept com-mands from humans. The problem is, human thoughts sent out by an iLink only have a communication capacity of one hundred meters."

Chakra tried to remember his days with an iLink. The endeeze at that time weren't nearly as powerful, but to a kid, it still felt incred-ible. Bending the world to your whims with a simple thought. Even opening the fridge a few inches away felt earth-shattering. One hundred meters away felt like sorcery. Sorcery designed by the Maker. "So what does that have to do with these endeeze?"

"Ah, that's the best part. Instead of extending the range of our thoughts, I have a new process I'm working on. Getting endeeze to receive commands from *each other*."

Chakra's eyes bulged. "Wait, what? What will prevent them from destroying us?"

Frankie laughed as Chakra felt his temperature rising. "Well, I'm designing a way for them to only communicate in a binary fashion. Either nothing at all or the exact thought they received from the person themselves. That way, they'd be able to pass the message on instantly across an entire Keitaro settlement."

"This sounds like an accident waiting to happen."

Teddy's voice emerged from the couch outside the lab. "I've been saying that, too. Who needs more than one hundred meters anyway? We need to get better at directing our thoughts more effectively. Lower-hanging fruit."

Frankie rolled his eyes and sighed. "Say what you will. It's fun to work on. It's completely safe in this setting. Anyway, these nano-drones are each isolated in a thought-prevention tube. The tube material is designed to attenuate iLink radio waves but not the endeeze back-up ultraviolet wave communication." He looked at Chakra. "Okay, complicated to explain but easy to demonstrate. Watch this."

Frankie closed his eyes, and the lights dimmed to reveal a spotlight on the tubes. "Alright, try to get those endeeze to move."

To his credit, it only took a second for Frankie to realize his mistake. Chakra rubbed the back of his neck instinctively, feeling the scar he still carried from his iLink's removal.

Frankie continued, slightly embarrassed, "Never mind. Let me get Teddy to show you. Teddy, come in here."

Teddy walked over with a resignation that made it clear this wasn't his first time being Frankie's assistant.

"Teddy, hun, try to move any of these endeeze with a thought."

Teddy mockingly assumed an exaggerated martial arts pose and put a finger to his temple. The five tubes remained completely still, the endeeze unmoved within.

Frankie then blinked, and a tiny endeeze rose in the air, hovering between Chakra's shoulder and the first tube. "Try now, Teddy."

Teddy stayed in his crouched position and, with his hand, beckoned the endeeze to join him. The single nano-drone outside the tubes whizzed by Chakra into Teddy's palm. This time, an extremely fast, rhythmic beat accompanied the movement. Chakra's eyes opened in amazement as four of the five nano-drones bounced against the tube in an effort to join their colleague in Teddy's palm.

"Amazing, isn't it?" Frankie was laughing as if it was the first time he'd seen it. He turned the endeeze off. "I still haven't worked out the communication perfectly," he said, pointing to the fifth tube with the unmoved nano-drone. "As you can see by this guy's refusal to move. So still some work to do. Anyway, what did you want to tell me?"

Chakra couldn't believe his luck. Here he was trying to capture a single endeeze while Frankie worked with them like toys in his lab. But Teddy was too much of an unknown quantity. "Not to be rude, but can we speak alone?"

"No worries. It was nice to meet you, Chakra. I have an immersion room experience I have queued up." Teddy walked out of the room, and Frankie closed the door behind him.

Chakra's probing eyes lingered on the endeeze scattered around the lab. "With all these nano-drones in the lab, are we really alone?"

Frankie couldn't help but laugh. "Chakra, wow, you must have a real story to tell. Yes, these endeeze are specifically disconnected from the broader network for research. Plus, this lab is otherwise endeeze-free to prevent any contamination. So speak your mind. It's just us."

"There's something I have to figure out. It's... it's the only way I'm going to get closure with Lila." Chakra swallowed hard. His hand turned Lila's iLink over in his pocket. "Lila was working on something when she passed away. Something..." Chakra pulled the iLink and its surrounding contraption out and opened his palm. "...that might explain why she was killed."

He watched Frankie, regretting using the word killed almost instantly in the presence of a connected resident. He had always found people rarely wanted to consider anything that might puncture their bubble of paradise. Chakra held the ball holding Lila's iLink out a little farther, hoping the novelty would entice Frankie to forget his word choice.

Frankie's eyes grew large as he reached his hand out to take the ball-like holder with the iLink nestled inside. "What in the world? Is this Lila's iLink?"

Chakra smiled, glad his ploy had worked. "Yes, and that little ball is no plaything. It had Lila's iLink functioning outside her body. Even after her death."

"This is unbelievable. This isn't an ordinary endeeze configuration. These have been individually knitted together by a human? This shouldn't be possible. How do they get the iLink to function?"

"Frankie, I need to know why she was working on this. It's got to mean something that she had done this. And left it behind for me." He smiled briefly, grateful for the fact that KB wasn't there to dispute his version of what happened.

Frankie, in the meantime, now looked dazed and had taken a seat in his lab chair. "I thought when she left Fulfillment, she was done working on stuff like this. I mean, she turned down projects at Joy, Happiness, Bliss—all the major companies wanted her to lead. Man, if I had known, I would have loved to work with her! She was the smartest person I ever worked with." He held the ball up. "I'm guessing the authorities don't know about this."

"Actually, they do. They're the ones who eventually brought it to me once they found out I was KB's guardian." He bit his lip as the lie went further.

"Oh, well, don't you think if there was some big purpose they would have kept it? If I were them, I've never seen anything like it, so I probably would have. But they know more than I do about all the projects going on."

"They thought it was pretty uninteresting. But I'm convinced that there's something to this, Frankie. I feel unresolved, not knowing why she felt like she had to build something like this. I'm hoping I can leave this with you, and you can tell me what is possibly going on and why someone might want to build it." He paused, each breath feeling surprisingly heavy. "I need to know."

Frankie's smile conveyed a gentle understanding. "It'd be my pleasure. I'd be happy to look into this. In the meantime, can you try and stay out of trouble?"

"You have no idea." The curious look on Frankie's face was enough for Chakra to offer something. "I thought I could figure this little iLink thing out if I had an endeeze of my own. But these little fuckers are hard to pin down." He proceeded to tell Frankie all about his failures.

Frankie kept shaking his head throughout as if unable to believe someone would try this.

"Chakra? I hate to say this, but you have no idea how ridiculously dumb your attempts are. I can guarantee you that they now have an 'active monitor' on you with endeeze tracking your every movement around Keitaro. I'm frankly surprised they haven't brought you in, given your levels of aggression."

Shit. Active monitor. Chakra couldn't believe it hadn't dawned on him. He looked at Frankie, wondering if the solution might lie with him. "I think you're right. I've been noticing them more and more. How do I lose these stupid things? I don't want them following me!"

"Give them a couple of weeks of no random attacks, and I'm sure it'll stop," Frankie chortled as he replied.

"No, but seriously, Frankie, I can't wait that long."

"Why? You barely notice them?"

"You know how I hate being followed. I didn't sign up for this when I disconnected."

Frankie leaned back and closed his eyes. He let out a heavy sigh and then opened them. "Okay, you're right. Look, I'm going to tell you this because I know you don't mean any harm, and I agree with you that you shouldn't have to live with a technology you've rejected. This won't completely solve your problem, but it'll at least help on occasion. The endeeze operate with a thermal imaging system and facial recognition software. Which leaves some pretty obvious blind spots for the more adventurous."

"What kind of blind spots?"

"Well, facial coverings are an obvious start. And it's also pretty easy to change your internal body temperature with something like an ice bath, which will at least confuse the endeeze for however long it takes for your temperature to restabilize. They search within a pretty narrow band of human temperatures. And then you have to change your gait pretty deliberately as they have advanced software for understanding your shape and structure."

"You are a genius. Do you mind if I try this out when I leave? How would I know if there are any endeeze around?"

Frankie got up from his chair and walked to the corner, grabbing a small bracelet made of a spandexlike synthetic fiber. "This should do the trick. It's subtle, but it tightens around your wrist in the presence of endeeze within a ten-meter radius. The ultraviolet waves that the nano-drones release have been designed to stimulate a slight tightening in the material. Nothing that will hurt, but you'll know. And this one's mine personally," Frankie said with a wink. "Not for research, so I can give you this one without any application to the Maker."

Chakra grabbed the bracelet and pulled it over his left wrist. It felt loose and comfortable. It tightened as Frankie activated one of the endeeze in the lab. He felt a surge of power flowing through his veins.

"Follow me to the bathroom. You can lower your temperature before you head out to give yourself a more lonely walk home." Frankie led the way through the small hallway, stopping at the first set of doors. "They'll be back tomorrow. I doubt you'll want an ice bath every time you want to leave, but at least it's got to feel better to know you have a temporary escape on occasion. Might make the next couple of weeks more bearable." He pointed him to the door on the right. "Everything should be pretty self-explanatory. I've alerted the endeeze to respond to your voice commands, so anything you need, feel free to ask. Make yourself at home. I'll be with Teddy." With a smile, Frankie left Chakra alone to prepare his new disguise.

Chakra looked around in wonder. The toilet had a plush cover and was armed with a bidet that looked like it might be capable of performing surgery, not just washing and drying. He looked at the marble bath with no knobs or faucets, wondering what exactly to do. Cautiously, he tried speaking.

"Prepare ice bath."

A faucet sprang out above the tub while endeeze emerged from their camouflaged position against the wall. Together, they formed perfectly oval ice cubes. Within two minutes, the ice bath was prepared, and Chakra stepped in and sat down. He leaned back, the cold sensations taking precedence over the wild thoughts swirling in his head.

He was more exhausted than he knew, for when he opened his eyes, he had no idea if it had been an hour or a minute. He got out and dressed in a hurry. Armed with a gaiter to cover his face, he emerged from the bathroom and thought about how to alter his gait. He crouched on all fours and started attempting to move like a chimpanzee, shuffling his arms and feet forward. He looked ahead and saw Frankie shaking his head, smiling while Teddy seemed to be nodding in approval.

The two of them thanked him for stopping by, and Chakra smiled and nodded. As he exited down the path in this awkward fashion, he smiled underneath the gaiter covering his face. His bracelet was still loose. He couldn't believe this was working.

He turned back, and the door opened again to Frankie and Teddy's home. They both turned in confusion. "I wanted to check to see if it worked. No need to get sick on the walk home. How long before my temperature returns to normal?"

Teddy responded before Frankie could. "Well, for an ice bath of the length you took, I'm guessing twenty minutes."

"Well, mind if I stay for dinner? Looks like I have a half-hour to kill."

"Sure." Frankie waved him to the dining table, a look of scrutiny plastered on his face. "You know, I'm starting to wonder if I shouldn't have told you about this."

8

A NEW TOY

The Maker gave us iLinks and iHERO as tools to help us. The ultimate human helper. Tools so good we think of them as toys. Tools so good we've ended up using them nearly every second of every day. For this, we should be thankful.

But maybe there's a different story.

The Maker gave us iLinks and iHERO as toys to teach us. The ultimate human trainer. Toys so good we think of them as tools. Toys so good we've ended up using them nearly every second of every day. For this, we should be frightened.

Which one do you believe?

—FROM THE WORLD OF THE MAKER

KB looked in the mirror and combed her hair over to show the buzz cut on the left side of her head. When she was younger, Lila had told her that this hairstyle would make others realize there was a lot inside her little body. KB was no longer little, but she still stood more upright when she wore it.

As depressed and lonely as she'd been upon coming in, the kindness from others had been overwhelming. It started with Quell. For the first few weeks, she had made it part of her routine to stop by, probably because KB kept to her room for the most part. While KB pretended to be annoyed, she enjoyed the interruptions.

But the service was a turning point for her. Being there had been cathartic, of course, but she credited the ride home with Anthony for her change. He encouraged her to give the members of Fungi a chance, and as she had come to realize, he could be very convincing.

Regardless of the reason, by the time she returned, KB was ready to emerge from her cocoon. She started having weekly dinners at Anthony's house, but more importantly, she made some friends in Fungi. Kumi had introduced her to a couple of his friends, and they had started spending more time exploring and taking advantage of all Fungi had to offer. While they spent more time on the immersion floor than KB wanted, she had succeeded in generating a little interest in the spiritual level as well. She had even joined a spiritual meditation group that met twice a week. It wasn't quite happiness, but KB was starting to feel like there was still a life to be lived without Lila.

She turned from the mirror and pulled up her iLink to confirm the timing from Jake for the hike in the Wood Wide Web. After sending a thoughtful message to the others that she was on her way, she headed out of her own house into the Fungi hallway. As she approached Kumi's Hypha, his door opened as if on cue. He walked out, flashing a big smile. "Wow, here to pick me up, huh?"

KB blushed. "No, it's on the way to where I'm headed, *actually*. I figured you were probably deep in another iHERO session."

Kumi grimaced in mock anger. "You know, I don't play iHERO that much..." His usual smile returned. "Even if I did just finish up a session. What can I say? It's better than a nap."

No matter how many times she walked through, KB loved to look at each wing she passed. Each door was unique, from the decorations to the door itself. Some were natural wood with intricate crown molding. Others were steel doors that looked like they came from the machinery supporting Keitaro. Yet, she couldn't help but gawk at the wonder of clashing architectural styles. The gray walls somehow captured modernity without compromising the classical. The sleek curvature and designs provided a futuristic but warm feeling.

Kumi led the way across the playground, and KB's eyes were drawn to two younger kids happily chasing each other. *Does anyone have a bad day around here?* As they approached the trailhead, she saw a familiar face.

"I was worried this was going to end up being a date between us, Freda," Jake said with a grin.

Freda rolled her eyes at Jake's attempt at humor. It didn't matter how others felt about Jake's jokes. KB didn't even bother reacting. It was too much work to get angry at him, especially because he rarely got angry himself. But Jake often took their mild reaction as a license to continue. "Hey, gorgeous," he said with a twinkle in his eye. "Why'd you bring KB?"

Kumi rolled his eyes. "I'm already sorry we came. Is it too late to get out of this?"

Jake didn't miss a beat. "Good to see you too, Kumi!"

"You know, we should get going. I have a lot on my agenda today," Freda said.

KB shook her head. Without Jake, KB was sure Freda and Kumi would spend their whole days between iHERO and immersion rooms.

"Alright, alright. I'll get going. You can't blame me for being excited. I'm leading KB on her first tour of these little parts we call home!"

"Umm... Jake, that's not quite true," Kumi replied with a grin.

While Jake's confusion slowed his momentum, Freda's blond hair whipped behind her as she turned to Kumi. "Oh, you must have given her a welcome tour." She looked haughtily at Jake. "They only pick the best of us for that, Jake. You wouldn't know."

Jake's pride didn't seem hurt by the remark. "Well, KB, forget that lame tour. I'm about to take you on a much better one through the Wood Wide Web. We're going to be gone for about six hours. A lot of it is in nano-flight, but some of it is walking too. Cool?"

KB looked down at her fidgeting feet. She now wished she had skipped this hike. "Uhh, sorry, friends. I don't have my nano-flight privileges."

Freda blurted out before she could catch herself, "Wait, how old are you?"

Even Jake had the courtesy to look a bit sheepish.

She searched unsuccessfully for an explanation that might lead to fewer questions than the truth. "I'm fourteen like you all. But I need to play iHERO to be granted my flight privileges."

She watched as the three of them looked at each other. She hoped they might let it go, but with Jake and Freda, there was a better chance of her growing feathers.

It ended up being Jake, who broke the silence. "And... any reason you haven't played iHERO?"

KB hated feeling like she was under a microscope. "Well, in my old home, it just wasn't something we did..." Her voice trailed off.

"Wait, you're allowed to be a kid without iHERO? Were you in a disconnected home?" Freda's lack of boundaries turned KB's embarrassment into anger.

A more defiant tone emerged. "No, actually. No one has to play iHERO. It's just that... seems like everybody does. Anyway, I don't want to slow you all down. I can figure out something else to do in Fungi, I'm sure."

Before she could even turn to walk away, Kumi replied, "Don't be silly. It'll be cool to walk. Right, Jake?"

Jake immediately engaged his iLink, and endeeze emerged. Covered by them in the form of a semiautonomous flight suit, he shot up and did a full loop before diving back down to the forest floor. "Yeah, it'll totally be just as fun to walk." He winked at KB. "I'm just kidding. I had to at least make you jealous."

Jake seemed to get out all his jokes at the onset. Once they started the hike, the wooded setting seemed to bring out his quiet side. He occasionally called them to a stop to explain some of the habitats. KB felt Freda's prying eyes on her, feeling like an alien spectacle after her iHERO admission. After thirty minutes, Jake motioned to the others. "Okay, this little path leads to an amazing waterfall."

Freda gave him an incredulous look. "What path?"

"The path my mind has laid out." Jake started making his way through the trees, avoiding rocks as they started to ascend. KB couldn't tell if it had been minutes or hours when Kumi interrupted the silence. "It's so weird that even within our own little Fungi house, there feels like more unexplored territory than we can ever cover."

Jake stopped in his tracks. The others followed suit. "Wait, KB, you do know how to fly, don't you?"

KB couldn't help her annoyed look. "Are we going back to this? I already told you—"

"I know, I know, you don't have your nano-flight privileges. But actually, I believe the Wood Wide Web extends outside of Fungi. So..." Jake again called for endeeze to form his flight suit. If he weren't so annoyingly flashy, she would have appreciated the seamless way he let the nano-drones arrange around him.

"If I'm not mistaken," Jake rose into the air as he continued, "we should all be able to fly. Unless there's another reason you can't, KB?"

She put her finger to the back of her neck, turning on her iLink. Unlike the others, she didn't leave hers permanently on. When it was on, she called for endeeze to form her flight suit. To her shock, no iLink pop-up message prevented her. She felt a wave of relief wash over as the endeeze formed around her. No longer the reason for the slower pace, she immediately rose in the air.

She took off without any fear while Freda and Kumi scrambled to call for their flight suits. All three of them hurried after her, with Jake taking over at the front of the pack. Nano-drone flight was no different than other iLink functions—it required a mind capable of being the conductor of an orchestra of thoughts. KB's meditation with Lila was the perfect preparation, allowing her to smoothly control her flight. Of course, the technology of the endeeze ensured crashes would be avoided, but for KB, that was redundant.

Kumi, on the other hand, struggled to keep up. In the air, his athletic frame wasn't much help. The endeeze kept him from colliding with any trees, but the jerks made it look like he was riding an uncomfortable rollercoaster. Freda was an average flier, but KB could tell she was putting in all her effort to keep Jake and KB in her sight. KB rose above the forest floor and past the understory. Up at the canopy level, the view helped her orient to the shape and nature of the forest.

She dove back into the understory when she heard the sound of the rushing water. Jake landed at the top of the waterfall, and she landed gently beside him.

"Alright, you need to play iHERO so you can fly inside Fungi. We could have some fun. By the way, have you ever played Ultimate?"

"My uncle's always tried to get me to play Ultimate, but no."

Freda was the next to land, but Jake wasn't done. "Okay, KB, you have to play. We are going to the Ultimate Games in a few weeks, and I'm going to get you hooked. I bet you'd be good."

"Running might have been faster for me," Kumi said as he landed next to the three of them. "This is pretty cool, huh?"

He was right. The waterfall was only about twice the height of them, but it created a little angelic mist in the stream that continued below. They were only a few kilometers from Fungi, but it felt like they were truly alone. The other three sat next to Kumi.

Jake took a deep breath. "Makes you wonder why we spend all our time chasing life in immersion rooms or iHERO."

"Especially when you can't even remember what happened in iHERO," Kumi added.

Freda couldn't let their statements go unchallenged. "It's not an either/or. Like all things in life, it's about finding a balance. Making the best journey for you is what counts."

"Wow, sounds like someone passed the Maker's Dream."

Freda's face turned red at Jake's jab. "Well, I may not have passed, but people seem to think I'm on the right track."

KB changed the subject as quickly as she could. "Jake, you know anything about this crazy-looking centipede here?"

Jake looked in the direction KB pointed at and saw the red and black body with bright yellow legs. He let it climb onto his finger.

Kumi backed up a step. "What are you doing, bro?" He backed away even farther as Jake laughed and reached his finger out to Kumi. "How do you know that thing's not poisonous or something?"

"If it were, my iLink wouldn't have let me pick it up. My safety function is on, idiot." Jake looked back at KB. "I don't know much about centipedes, but this one looks like it's eyeless."

She took the centipede off Jake's finger and examined it. The three others seemed surprised at KB's comfort with the creature. She rested her hand on a tree and let the centipede crawl onto it. They spent the rest of the time enjoying the landscape and each other's company before they started to make their way back. Only occasional snippets of conversation marked the passage of time.

That is until Freda spoke up with a question for KB. "I've been meaning to ask you… what happened to your parents?"

Kumi winced. "Jeez, don't you think if she wanted to talk about it, she would have?"

Freda showed no signs of shame. "Sometimes, we don't recognize the benefits of an action until after we've taken it. I'm sure talking about it can only help KB process her loss."

"Freda, I hate to say it, but Kumi's right," Jake said. "But, KB, now that she's asked, I'm pretty curious..." He flashed a toothy grin. His childlike smile was at odds with his lanky frame.

She felt her eyes welling up. Trying to keep her emotions from Lila's death buried, she attempted to reply in a matter-of-fact tone. "Well, I only had one parent. Her name was Lila. And she died because of a machine malfunction."

"A machine malfunction?" Freda looked confused.

Jake jumped in, "Was it an accidental drone crash?"

All KB could do was nod. She prayed for them to move on to any topic, even if it meant a return to her not playing iHERO.

But Jake wasn't done. "Most of the drones aren't even heavy enough to inflict a fatal blow at top speeds. So it must have been one of the builder drones or the high-speed delivery drones." Kumi nudged Jake in the ribs. "Ugh. That sucks, though, KB. Sorry for your loss."

"Yeah, me too," Kumi added.

Freda added her own brand of condolences. "What is loved never dies but merely changes form."

KB felt the urge to punch Freda but restrained herself in the hope that they were done with the topic.

Kumi rubbed KB's shoulder as the clearing for the end of the Wood Wide Web appeared. As they made their way out, he added, "I know what it feels like. All I can say is it'll help if you hang out with friends. We're all around and mostly prepping for the Update Festival, so feel free to shout anytime."

"Correction. Kumi and Freda are prepping for the Update Festival. I'm all set, so let me know if you want to do something a little bit cooler than what these two geeks have in mind."

"Make your jokes, Jake. I'm sure you'll be asking us what to do the night before the Update Festival," Freda said with a haughty smile. "Speaking of how we use our time, it's time to get back. I want to get an iHERO session in before dinner. Meet up for dinner in Mycelium?"

KB shook her head. "I have a dinner I'm going to at a friend's place outside of Fungi. I'll catch up with you tomorrow. Thanks a lot, Jake. I enjoyed getting out there."

"When you're done with dinner, will you please play iHERO?" Jake called out as she walked away. "I need someone other than me to give Kumi flying lessons."

KB had barely taken her shoes off in her room before another knock came at her door.

"You must be getting sick of seeing me today, but I wanted to check if you were okay before I headed into Mycelium for dinner. I brought some therapy bath salts as well."

KB had gotten used to these interruptions. She smiled at Quell and took the salts. "That's so nice. I think I'll use these tonight."

Quell seemed to linger awkwardly before turning away. KB felt like she had to say something. "Hey, Quell?"

"Yes?"

"I appreciate how kind you've been. You'll be happy to know I think I'm ready to play iHERO. More for my nano-flight privileges than anything else, but still."

Quell looked relieved as she rocked back and forth on her heels. "Well, that's great news. I'm sure it'll be great, but if you want to talk about your experiences there, I'm here for you. It can be hard trying to piece together the fragments. Will I see you later for dinner?"

"No, I'm going to head to Anthony's place."

"Again? That's the third week in a row. You sure you're not thinking of moving in?" With someone else, KB might have felt defensive but never with Quell. Even her jokes came with a sense of warmth. "Okay, I'll get out of your hair. Have a good rest of your night, KB."

As the door closed, her eyes turned toward the unused gaming chair in the adjacent room. She didn't want to do it to fit in. Every kid in Fungi spent at least an hour a day playing iHERO, but it wasn't that. It was the hours discussing, analyzing, and frankly, obsessing over these dreams.

From what she was starting to understand, there was a lot to analyze. In the world of iHERO, time passed on a different cadence, speeding up and slowing down in an almost whimsical way. Even if memory of the events came with a dreamlike imprecision, people loved looking for possible clues into their path to fulfillment. Some forty-five-minute sessions offered months of experiences that could be processed afterward, all taking a person closer to their 'best' self.

Quell had been understanding, not forcing her to play until she was ready. Sitting on her bed, KB swallowed as she looked over at the chair and said, mostly to herself, "Why not?"

Once she decided, she didn't waste time. She took her spot in the chair and clicked the iHERO setting. The straps tightly secured her in place. It wasn't quite uncomfortable, but she definitely could feel that her movement was restricted. She found it hard to imagine why everyone called it the perfect nap.

She gave one form of entry (fingerprint scan) and another (thought scan) to grant her access to the iHERO program. She felt her neck tingling, though, of course, nothing had changed. A phantom tingle was natural because, for the first time, her iLink would do more than alter her vision or communicate with endeeze. The iHERO program would immobilize her body, put her to sleep, and send her into an alternate reality. Her eyes slowly closed. A voice started speaking in a soft, melodic tone.

"Wouldn't it be awesome if...
I let my curiosity lead me...
To answer my favorite question...
Wouldn't it be awesome if.

"Wouldn't it be awesome if...
I took a beautiful journey...
that made others wonder...
Wouldn't it be awesome if."

Anthony closed the book and put it aside. The fireplace shut off with a thought as he brought the reclining chair upright.

He pulled up the location map that came up on the iLink alert. The light from KB had turned from green to blue. She had finally entered iHERO.

Tonight's dinner just got more interesting. He opened up his book again and leaned back in the chair. The fire restarted, and his lips creased into an ever-so-slight smile. *Maybe I am starting to have an influence on the girl.*

9

CATCHING A WAVE

*We humans are surfers. Looking for waves to surf,
knowing we will eventually crash but irrationally
confident that the next wave will be our best yet.*

*What does catching a wave represent? It represents the true
joy of surfing. But that joy also comes from the moments
between. The patience required to find the right wave. The
inevitable crashes when a wave gets the better of you.*

*What does catching a wave represent? For a fleeting moment, it represents
the thrill of our complete mastery over an unpredictable universe.*

*Our iLinks and endeeze have turned the ocean into a
wave pool. iHERO turns each of us into professional
surfers. What does catching a wave represent now?*

—FROM THE WORLD OF THE MAKER

Walking into the empty boardroom, Anthony's eyes moved immediately to the small window. He squinted, and his iLink immediately
sharpened his long-distance vision. There it was. The Maker. Each
time, a small part of him expected it to be gone, to have escaped, or

even just to have moved. Yet there it stood, stuck in solitary confinement, seemingly without a care in the world.

Dush and Tara never seemed to pay it any mind, more impressed with the latest endeeze innovation than the fridge locked in a deep cave. For Anthony, seeing humanity's savior in the flesh wasn't something he took for granted. No matter how many times he saw it, his heart always skipped a beat. How could it not? The energy that emanated from deep within those walls filled him with a kind of joyful fear.

He returned to the chair, and with a thought, his iLink connected within the room, and holograms of Dush and Tara immediately appeared.

"Where are you both joining from?" Dush asked upon appearing.

Tara replied first. "I'm in my backyard in our little garden. Our mangoes are ripening perfectly."

Dush smiled as if impressed by an iLink-run garden growing perfect fruit.

Anthony thought about lying. The holograms were perfect in their display—no one would know where Anthony was in all of Keitaro. But he tried to use deceit sparingly. He was getting too old to cover his tracks. "I'm here in person at the boardroom."

The smiles immediately left both Dush and Tara's faces. "Were we supposed to be there in person?"

Anthony's smile seemed to put them at ease. "No, Dush, of course not. Happened to be in the area and thought, 'Why not?'" He paused to look for any sign of suspicion on their faces. When he saw none, he continued, "Should we get started? What's on the agenda today, Dush?"

"Alright. Well, not much for us to cover today. We have a check-in on the status of the Update Festival in a few weeks, a look at this year's early Maker project proposals, and then..." Dush's voice trailed off. Anthony nodded impatiently. "And then, umm... I guess your transition?"

Ah, of course. That explained Dush's awkwardness. At last year's Update Festival, the Maker had confirmed this was to be Anthony's final year on the Small Council. The Maker would approve a replacement of the nominations that came from across Keitaro. With the longest tenure, Anthony held the actual key to the Maker's room, making him the only person with the power to open the room to the Maker. For the last seventeen years, Anthony had been on the Small Council, and he had held the key for the last nine.

Anthony looked at Tara with a smile, hoping to disarm any awkwardness on their part. "That all sounds good. Tara, why don't we start with the Update Festival? Anything of note?"

"Things are going very well," Tara said. "For the third year in a row, we have zero kids who are planning on the Nightmare. We might have our eighth straight Nightmare-free year. Only five children in all of Keitaro are considering it according to the iHERO watch list."

Anthony nodded approvingly. "Wow, only five? I'm so happy to hear we have such incredible levels of acceptance so early. The future is indeed in good hands. Any mitigation plans needed for any of the five?"

He caught Dush's glance at Tara before her reply. "Well, we have good plans in place for four of them. Ramped up iHERO usage. Specific Update Festival designs. But one of them is your new friend KB. Is there any update on your plan with her, or do you need any support from us?"

"No, actually, I think she seems to be in a very good place. We know the consideration measure is imprecise, especially given her lack of consistent iHERO usage. But with her usage picking up in recent weeks, I expect her to move off the watch list soon." Anthony paused. "Though I must admit, I could use both of your help. I don't believe she's seen her uncle recently, which is surprising. We haven't discussed him, and it seems like he's become a less active threat, but I want to make sure there's nothing we're missing on that front."

Dush raised a finger. "Let me take this one." With a thoughtful blink, the screen showed Chakra in an Ultimate practice session.

"We've kept the active monitor on him for the last several weeks. He's done nothing except play Ultimate and stay in his house. He seems to be over whatever strange mission he was on earlier. We were thinking of taking him off the active monitor list."

Anthony watched in silence. He sent his own iLink thought wave through the screen, taking over the camera of the endeeze filming the practice. He zoomed in until he could see the sweat glistening off Chakra's toned, shirtless body. The camera struggled to maintain focus as he moved around the field, his face showing an intensity that Anthony saw most often in the mirror. Or, more recently, at his dinners with KB.

Chakra leaped and grabbed the sparkling silver frisbee in front of the outstretched hand of another man. He landed and immediately flung it in another direction. Then, for the briefest of moments, his eyes looked directly into Anthony's, as if recognizing his hidden presence. Anthony instinctively jumped back.

Chakra resumed running, and Anthony cleared his throat. "Let's keep the active monitor on until at least our next Small Council meeting." Anthony paused to see if Dush and Tara had caught something in Chakra's glance, but they already seemed to have moved on. "So, Dush. Next item. Any interesting Maker project proposals thus far?"

He prepared himself mentally for the rush of insight that always came with this discussion.

Dush didn't let him down. "Well, you know how close the latest endeeze communication design project is. The leader of that project has a proposal on how to synthesize human-endeeze communication, which could free up a 20 percent increase in the system's capacity to help the disconnected."

Can people survive without work? Is work a necessary construct to find meaning in life? Anthony reflected on the philosophical debates he had learned about. The ones that had gripped pre-Keitaro society. It turns out, without work, most people didn't idle lazily. Progress did not come to a screeching halt. If anything, the pace of change had only accelerated. Without work, people sought meaning in creative expression. They sought meaning in play. They sought meaning in improving their existence. Not for money. Not for prestige. Not for power. For curiosity. For enjoyment. For the challenge.

Of course, when he already knew the outcome, intellectual honesty was impossible. Anthony reminded himself to avoid passing judgment on the thinking of previous generations but instead look for lessons in their arguments.

"Wow, that would be incredible. Imagine, with that much more processing power, we could have food and shopping stations that could materialize within a two-minute walk of every disconnected person across Keitaro. What else?"

"Well, there's a submission for a piece of immersion room software that would allow people to use their iLinks to translate historical writing into immersion room experiences without human input. It's obviously a prototype, but the submitter thinks it could improve exponentially with a collective effort."

"That's fantastic, Dush. What about space travel? Any submissions?"

"Well, we know two people are working on a wormhole submission, but we haven't seen it. We're also expecting one on a new particle accelerator."

People were free to do whatever they wanted with their time, save projects that required enhancements to the iLink to execute. For those, people submitted project proposals to the Maker. Only the Maker could update iLinks and therefore had to approve any new uses or software loading onto it.

Every person who passed the Maker's Dream could submit project proposals. Then, one day each year, Anthony would get to meet the Maker in its isolated environment. He would upload the latest year's data and the proposals, leaving the Maker to determine whether they'd be good for humanity or not. For those deemed positive, the Maker would 3D print a USB drive with the necessary iLink updates. The nano-drive also included the latest version of iHERO that accounted for the most recent year's data.

Using a USB drive was decidedly archaic but deliberately designed to ensure the Maker couldn't escape containment. Once adequate testing had been run to ensure there were no issues, Anthony would release the approved updates at the annual Update Festival.

Project proposals had led to incredible advances. The creation of endeeze. The human flying capabilities now preloaded onto the iLinks. The creation of cameras and sensors loaded onto the Starshot, a stamp-sized rocket that moved at 34 percent of the speed of light. Unlimited free time and technological power led to humanity flourishing, not dying from boredom.

Anthony nodded in approval. "Things are looking good indeed. I'm looking forward to seeing those proposals come in. After this meeting, Dush, please ensure the meeting notes have the latest on this year's projects. We should look through those and discuss them at our next meeting."

Dush nodded. Anthony turned to Tara and smiled. "As far as transition, Tara, I'm looking forward to passing this key onto you." He took the Maker's Key out. The silver key was elegant but mostly nondescript. The tiny digital display resembling an engraved inscription was the only embellishment.

Maker's Mark.

He liked to joke that it wasn't helping security much with such clear direction. Though given that it was one of many forms of security, including a thought scan and fingerprint scan, no one worried too much.

"On behalf of all of Keitaro, we thank you, Anthony. I'm going to have big shoes to fill." Tara's eyes locked on the key like a magnet while Dush concentrated on the project list for the festival.

"No need for gratitude. We're going to have to make sure we have sufficient nominations for my replacement. Let's plan on meeting in person in the next few weeks so I can walk you through the process."

Anthony paused and sighed. "Nostalgia has started to set in. This now feels like the only place I can get any writing done."

Tara dutifully laughed.

"Okay, that's it for today. Let's plan on sometime in two weeks unless anyone has a more urgent need." With a quick blink, the screens turned off, and he was again alone in the boardroom. He pulled out his physical notebook that fit neatly into the palm of his hand. Before pulling out a pen, Anthony reached behind his neck and turned off his iLink.

Anthony pulled the key back and closed the door behind him. He turned and took a deep bow. It had become ritualistic, as he knew the Maker had no camera or vision sensors. Still, it felt right to show adequate respect.

He approached cautiously and reached his fingers out, tentatively at first. Once he made contact with the steely surface, his fingers naturally moved along the edge as if stroking an animal. The Maker, encased in this pristine environment, showed no signs of wear and tear. Not even a speck of dust showed on its shimmering exterior.

Hidden within the smooth surface was a small, discrete panel. Anthony pried it open. Within it were three different-sized plug points, a 3D printing area, and a mini-keyboard terminal. The only approved way to ask questions of the Maker, the keyboard prevented any connection that could break containment. The soft green light of the keyboard glowed, and Anthony started typing his first question. His bony fingers pressed carefully as if any mistaken letter could be disastrous in its consequences.

Should I nominate myself to continue on the Small Council?

The tiny display attached to the keyboard revealed the block letters immediately. They appeared one at a time, from bottom to top like a wave reaching its crest and then falling for the final letter.

No

Anthony took a deep breath. The answer wasn't surprising, but his shoulders slumped as he read it. He typed the next question with a little less temerity.

Have I served humanity well?

Again, the response was immediate with the same wave-like appearance.

Yes

Anthony couldn't help but wonder why, if that was the case, he was being asked to end his tenure on the Small Council.

Is the threat that Lila represented now eliminated?

No

Anthony thought again to KB and her uncle Chakra, tossing over the details. He would have to review the reports again and make sure he had them fully in his sights. He typed one final question in. His fingers shook as he typed the final word.

Should Chakra be eliminated?

10

THE POINT OF ATTACK

People used their iLinks to build their dream houses, to prepare the healthiest meals, to engage in the best forms of entertainment. They used their iLinks to reengineer their climate and provide for the disconnected among them. The iLink didn't follow every thought command, however. It wouldn't allow for violence or cruelty toward others. But with everything you want at your fingertips, why would you have a desire to hurt others?

Speaking of violence, weren't foreigners desperate to pilfer this wondrous technology? By the time people recognized the power residing in Keitaro, even the idea of an attack was absurd. The iLinks and endeeze combined to form the ultimate shield. A shield so powerful that the people of Keitaro had never been forced to wield it.

—*FROM THE HISTORY OF KEITARO*

Chakra paced back and forth in his cabin but not on his two feet. He practiced his gorilla walk in every spare moment, pulling his feet past his arms with each stride.

He looked at the grandfather clock on his wall, the one that Lila had given him. The gentle movement of the second hand's rhythm always served to soothe him in times of stress. He walked up to the bowl of soup. Though the red pasty substance made his stomach churn, he abandoned the spoon in favor of drinking directly from the bowl. Globs of the paste fell in his mouth before the liquid could follow. A second or two later, he pulled the bowl down and licked his lips, leaving his beard looking even more unkempt in contrast.

Over the last few weeks, he had continued to refine his process. In addition to his new walking style, he had switched from the ice bath to taking a drink of his favorite 'special sadam.' It was a natural herb found in the forest, and the disconnected commonly crushed and ground it until it became an edible paste. Heavy consumption induced intense hallucinations in the disconnected, providing a strange substitute to the iHERO dreams they couldn't access. Taken at lower levels, it produced mild psychedelic effects. Since people couldn't play iHERO while under its influence, there were whispers that the Maker disapproved of using it.

But for Chakra, the most important effect now had nothing to do with the psychedelic effects. The special sadam had the side effect of elevating the drinker's body temperature by a full degree Celsius. The mild fever confounded the thermal image scanners of the end-eeze, allowing Chakra and his gorilla walk to go undetected until his temperature returned to normal a few hours later. Even Frankie had been impressed with his ingenuity, having never even heard of the special sadam. He had even asked for Chakra to make him a batch to study its properties. Typical Frankie.

Regardless of the realities of digestion, he felt the sadam working its way through his veins almost immediately. He felt strangely more confident and powerful under its influence. Like he wasn't disconnected but rather connected to something deeper. He looked at the clock once more before climbing out the back window.

With his daily adventures, Chakra's eyes had adjusted to the darkness of night. He had spent weeks exploring the forest outside of Keitaro, positive he would find some clue of its hidden darker side. But his confidence was wearing thin. He walked through the familiar area where the machinery began. Under this forest canopy laid all that was necessary to support Keitaro. He passed bear-shaped builder drones hovering in midair, constructing new mini-factories.

The mini-factories that produced on-demand food, clothing, and materials for each individual.

Fulfilling the desires of every person in Keitaro required a lot of infrastructure. But somehow, it was so neat. So tidy. The layout extended for kilometers, but it was organized, efficient, and quiet. Chakra continued ambling through this flurry of silent activity, wondering when he would find it.

He wasn't sure what *it* was, which was the problem. He knew that Keitaro wasn't impervious to attack just because it was a seeming paradise. In fact, from his experience, he knew the envy and negative feelings that a paradise could foster. He was looking for some sort of smoking gun. Some way to show the Maker's dark side. Some way to show he wasn't the crazy one.

Pausing for a moment, he noticed he was taking his first steps in new territory. He rubbed the back of his neck nervously, knowing he would be out of ideas on what to do next should he not find anything unusual. At this point, he had built a tolerance for the special sadam, but he still found himself feeling more aware under its influence.

He looked around at the variety of machines and couldn't help but marvel at Keitaro's underworld. Chakra recalled an immersion room experience inside a human's body. Seeing all the complex machinery underneath the surface of his smooth skin dumbfounded him. He had the same feeling now seeing Keitaro's lifeblood strewn around the settlement. But the human body had an entire apparatus devoted to protecting against foreign invaders. How did Keitaro do the same?

The answer couldn't lie beyond this endpoint he had reached. Farther out, there were only desolate ghost towns, overrun by shrubbery and natural habitats. All nonhuman life flourishing, from the microscopic to the macroscopic, for tens of kilometers until the next Keitaro settlement. Fascinating to see, but that wasn't Chakra's mission at the moment.

He found a set of filtering drones that marked the edge of the support facilities. The cylindrical tanks shot a mistlike substance into the air that served as a natural repellent to nonhuman life seeking entry.

He looked at the machines for any form of weaponry. Was there anything to prevent potential human invaders or outside machinery? He felt around the exterior of the tube for any openings. By now, he had perfected a tapping motion to find the manual repair opening. When he heard a hollow sound, he pushed in and the mini-door released.

Pulling out a mini-flashlight, he put it in his mouth to free his hands to explore inside. Others would have looked at him with disbelief to see him engaging in such basic manual labor, but such was life for the disconnected. He saw the web of narrow tubes interwoven like a circulatory system. Chakra suspected all these tubes were optimizing airflow and temperature within Keitaro.

He was about to close the panel and move on when he noticed something out of the corner of his eye. He leaned in to look into the open panel. Yes, there it was. Soil, on the bottom of this tube. Chakra couldn't believe it. This tube wasn't enclosed like all the other machinery.

Chakra dropped to his knees and immediately started digging with his hands around the edges of the tube. He had stopped bringing his trowel weeks ago, and he chided himself for losing conviction. The tube's outer lining continued down for a foot into the ground, burrowed to provide stability and the feeling of a closed environment.

He continued flinging up dirt until his fingers could reach under the outer lining. It was tough to dig any further as the ground was more and more solid around this area. He looked at the machines around him, several of which could have done this simple task more effectively than Chakra's bare hands.

Still, he forced his hands under and felt within the soil. Sure enough, the mini-tubes extended, showing no signs of ending. He squeezed the tubes and felt that many of them were not carrying gases. They were carrying liquids. And the speed of the movement within these liquids suggested whatever was flowing through was flowing through quickly.

All of a sudden, he realized the one place he hadn't looked. He checked his watch. If he ran, he could explore without having to wait until tomorrow night. Chakra gritted his teeth. His damn gorilla walk. He considered ignoring his safety precautions and running anyway, but he decided against it. This was another benefit to drinking the special sadam—he found his rashness moderated with a greater sense of patience. He liked to think that the sadam brought out Lila's spirit within him. He knew where he still had time to go instead.

Teddy was the first to comment. "You look absolutely insane."

Frankie couldn't help adding, "And that's coming from one of the more off-the-wall personalities around."

Chakra smiled where he might have recoiled, unsure if this was due to the lingering effects of the sadam or his new sense of hope. In either case, what they were pointing to was undoubtedly true. Dirt covered his camouflaged outfit. The packings he had put into his suit gave his body a strange shape when standing as if he had oversized shoulders and bulging knees. Not to mention they protected his knees while he clambered around the forest under the cover of darkness.

"Well, this look has kept me safe so far. But actually, that's why I'm here." Teddy and Frankie shared a confused look before Chakra continued, "I need a new outfit. I'm done exploring the forest."

Frankie laughed. "Are you finally over your craziness? I have a friend who's working on a disconnected endeeze flying suit that can be operated by a joystick instead of iLink. I can talk to him about getting you a prototype. How about that?"

Chakra shook his head. "No, I need something designed to go underwater."

"I can't wait to hear your explanation for this one. Before you tell me, though, can I show you what I've found with the iLink you left here?"

Frankie led Chakra to his lab and sat down, grabbing Lila's iLink from the corner of his desk. "Okay, good news or bad news first?"

"Let's go with good news."

"Didn't expect that from you, Chakra. Okay. So I had no idea what to do with this for so long. I kept trying to figure out how these nano-drones were connected to the iLink to power it on. Then I realized I missed a way more interesting question."

"Why Lila built this?"

"No, what's actually going on with the iLink! You see, we've never been able to study the iLinks—the operating system, the actual iHERO program itself—because they only work in living humans. We've tried studying the devices while off, doing brain scans with people using them, and more, but all our methods have been indirect. This is a chance to actually explore the guts of the iLink and see the code that makes it run."

Chakra's eyes lit up. "Actually, see how the Maker designed it?"

"Exactly. Watch this." Frankie took the iLink, still encased in the endeeze ball, and plugged it into a screen. The screen lit up with symbols flashing across at lightning speed. "So, I used to be into cryptography as a kid. Look what I've figured out."

With a blink, he highlighted a few symbols on the screen. The endeeze holding Lila's iLink started changing colors, first to purple then to green. "How cool is this?"

Raising an eyebrow, Chakra looked over at Teddy. Teddy shrugged. "What can I say? He gets into this stuff."

"This is interesting, Frankie. But have you figured out what's actually in the program itself? Any insight into the Maker?"

The smile left Frankie's face. "Man, I thought you'd be more impressed by that. That brings me to the bad news. Honestly, this is the most complex piece of quantum code I've ever seen. I've been trying to brush up on my skills, but I'm using some pretty elementary decrypting techniques for now. It might take months, if not years, to figure out anything practical about these iLinks. It could be faster if we submit it as a project at this year's Update Festival? It's not too late to change your mind?"

"Hell no," Chakra said firmly. "No chance. The Maker cannot be trusted."

"Come on, Chakra. When are you going to get over this?"

"You don't believe me? Listen to this." Chakra explained what he had found. The filtering system had tubes running through the soil, pumping water. He described feeling the water rushing through the tubes before getting to the revelation.

"It dawned on me that Keitaro's true defenses aren't hidden in the forest. They're hidden in the ocean. What better place to draw energy and stay hidden than deep underwater, outside places like Elliott Beach?"

"Chakra, this is absurd. You're planning on searching the ocean for an advanced weaponry system? Haven't you ever heard the phrase 'don't boil the ocean?'"

Teddy interrupted Frankie before he could continue, "Frankie..."

"Yes?"

"Look, if we take as a presupposition the Maker has an advanced weapon system designed to inflict harm..." Frankie's incredulous look forced Teddy to acknowledge, "Yes, a ridiculous assumption to make, but we've been humoring it to this point, haven't we?"

Chakra started to feel like a child in a room with adults, and even the special sadam couldn't prevent his outburst. "I am not some pity project. Lila died because of this!"

Frankie put an arm on his shoulder and pulled him in for a hug. Chakra immediately regretted his outburst and the physical contact it had forced upon him. He stifled the tears forming in his eyes.

"As I was saying, if there were an advanced weapon system, the greatest vulnerability lies on our shores. Inland attacks don't make sense, given most of Asia consists of Keitaro settlements. I, for one, don't think it's strange that filtering machines are using underground water. But his point is still valid that there's a ton of energy to be harnessed and space to hide in the water."

Chakra looked at Teddy, surprised at this unexpected support. But his support was short-lived. "I guess the bigger question is... I'm not sure how you expect Frankie to help? We've been patient with your endeavors, Chakra, but we have to draw the line somewhere. Yes, we're night owls, but still... These middle-of-the-night visits are not exactly what we'd planned on these last few weeks. I don't speak for Frankie, but let me put it to you another way. If this is as dangerous as you seem to believe it is, is it fair that you're putting Frankie's life in jeopardy?"

The words hit Chakra like a lightning bolt. He looked over to Frankie, who was looking down to the floor, avoiding eye contact with both of them. "You're right. I'm sorry. This is my battle to fight. I appreciate all that you've done for me, Frankie. All that both of you have done for me."

Frankie tried to smile. "Look, Chakra, I'm happy to help you. I'm enjoying studying this iLink. But how about we take it easy for a little while first? Let's come up with a plan over a few meals together. Maybe Teddy and I will even join you for an Ultimate session? It's late. Why don't you come by tomorrow, and we can talk about it?"

Chakra stood up, feeling somewhat unnatural on only two feet. "You both have been very kind. I'll take you up on a meal, but I have to deal with my demons first." He extended his arm out to Frankie. "I'd like Lila's iLink device back now."

Frankie grimaced. "Really, Chakra? Don't do this. I promise I'll keep working on it, and I'll let you know if I find anything interesting."

"Okay," Chakra said, realizing that the iLink would be useless in his hands. "You both have been very kind. I appreciate it." He pulled his mask over his face, crouched down, and then opened the door. As he scrambled out, he felt a sense of despair. Every time he felt a mild sense of hope, it seemed to evaporate faster than the effects of the sadam.

The sound of footsteps alerted him. He turned around and saw Teddy approaching. "Look, Chakra, Frankie told me I might have been a bit too harsh. I'm sorry about that."

This time, Chakra grabbed Teddy's hand and gave it a firm shake. He had come to appreciate Teddy's honesty.

Teddy opened his other hand and handed something to Chakra. Chakra looked strangely at the mouthguard, turning the neon orange gel-like object in his hand before Teddy explained.

"As my constant sandals and tank tops show, I'm a beach lover. But, funnily enough, not a great swimmer. Frankie gave me this early in our relationship." Teddy's eyes looked out in fond reminiscence. "Frankie has always been incredibly thoughtful, even before he passed the Maker's Dream. And this showed me the kind of scientist he was. He came up with these; this mouthguard is incredible. It takes the carbon dioxide you exhale and converts it back into oxygen for you to breathe. I guess you can consider it a mini-tree in your mouth."

Chakra didn't know what to say. "Thanks... uh... I'll bring it back in a few days?"

"Don't worry about it. It's yours. I've moved on from being a terrible swimmer to now being a terrible surfer. Anyway, good luck. I hope you find whatever it is you're looking for. And just so you know, Frankie will figure out that iLink. He's too curious to stop even if you don't come by. So might as well check in to hear about it when he does."

Chakra wasn't too proud to seize the opening Teddy left him. "That sounds good. I'll come by soon." As he crouched to begin his four-legged walk home, he realized Teddy had just carried an entire conversation with a camouflaged, masked man as if there wasn't anything unusual about it. *Off-the-wall personality, indeed.*

When Chakra finally stepped foot in his cabin, he started to see the first signs of light approaching. He was exhausted. He pulled off his clothing and stepped into his eucalyptus outdoor shower. Stepping back into the cabin, he dried off before hopping into his king-sized bed, fully naked.

He hadn't even closed his eyes when he heard a knock at the door. "One second!"

Who is it? At this early hour? Did I forget something at Frankie's?

Chakra scrambled to throw on shorts and then opened the door a crack.

"Hey, man! You ready?"

"Ready?" Chakra looked at his friend like he was an alien.

"Come on, Chak. Are you messing with me? Since you're... uh..." Chakra didn't know why people always fumbled with mentioning the word as if he had some sort of disability. "You know, since you don't have an iLink, Sachin sent me to pick you up. We're running late. Ultimate Games!"

"Oh, shoot!" Chakra flung the door open and ran to get dressed. With all his night-time escapades, he had forgotten all about the Ultimate Games. He ran into his bathroom and looked at the mirror. To the right was the bowl of special sadam, still with half its contents remaining. He picked it up, hesitated for a moment, and then took a long, slow sip. He pulled back the near-empty bowl before bringing it back to his lips to lick it clean.

He turned back to his teammate. "Let's play some Ultimate."

11

ULTIMATE

The best way to describe Keitaro's effect on each human is through an analogy. Think of each person like a book full of blank pages. Each day in their life fills pages with words until the end of their life completes the story. Some of those stories are challenging to write. Some of those stories aren't joyful or particularly memorable.

With the Maker's help, each of us has the chance to write a better story. To enjoy the writing process. With iLink and iHERO, we become better authors. In Keitaro, each of us writes a literary masterpiece not fueled by our pain but fueled by our happiness.

—FROM THE HISTORY OF KEITARO

KB's leg bounced up and down, a nervous habit she couldn't shake. *Why am I so excited about this? Is this why Lila never had me play?* She ignored the chorus playing in her head as she sat down in her gaming chair and felt the straps tighten. For a moment, she felt like a prisoner in an immersion scene she'd once seen, getting tied down for interrogation. In this case, though, KB knew an interrogation wasn't coming. Instead, she braced herself for another chance at the life of her dreams—a life that still had Lila in it.

As the program opened, KB's eyes began to close to the sound of a soft voice.

"Wouldn't it be awesome if...
we could have everything we want...
and want everything we have.

"Wouldn't it be awesome if...
we believed what we believed in...
without ever believing it matters."

KB rubbed her eyes as she woke up from iHERO. She looked around her familiar game room for any unfamiliar signs as if to confirm the session was over. It was so different from any of her regular dreams, though it was difficult to pinpoint why.

It wasn't that it was more memorable. It wasn't. Like most people, she could barely piece a few fragments together from the recent experience. But before she began any search for a lesson, she took some deep breaths. Hearing Lila's voice had felt exhilarating, and the few moments with her had felt like days.

My little Kali, I'm still guiding you. Figure out if there are lessons here for yourself. And then, a few moments later, *I'm not lost. I'm waiting to be found.*

KB replayed the moments again and again. She considered reentering iHERO before remembering the mandatory waiting period between sessions.

She fell into a familiar trap for novice iHERO participants—the search for an obvious lesson. *I bet the Maker put a replica of Lila in iHERO to foster my love for the game. It wants me to stay connected.*

Ever since Lila's death, it felt like the upcoming Update Festival and the choice on whether to connect consumed everyone around her. A question she hadn't considered before had now become the most important decision of her life. With Lila, they'd never discussed what she'd do. She knew that assigning malicious motives to the Maker sounded like a page out of Chakra's book. Still, at this point, she was searching for signs wherever she could find them.

She shook her head, feeling a pang of anger toward Lila for leaving her in the lurch. Now, KB had to decide on her own, armed only by the knowledge that Lila must have had a reason for never introducing iHERO to her.

Well, she wasn't quite on her own. Somehow—KB was sure it was Freda—the news had spread across Fungi that she had never played iHERO. Now, it was as if all of Fungi, Quell included, found a way to bring every conversation back to iHERO. And how amazing it was. Ironically, the only people in Fungi she felt comfortable around were the friends she had originally confided in. Or at least Jake and Kumi. She continued pacing around the room in a daze when she heard a knock on her door.

She gave the mirror a quick look and saw that the spike in her hair was unruffled by her iHERO session. She opened the door, and there was Jake, but to her surprise, Kumi and Freda were right next to him. She flashed back to a couple of nights before, when Jake had asked if she wanted to go with him. *"So it's a date," he had said at the time.* She wondered what a date meant to Jake but didn't show any outward sign of surprise.

"How are we heading there?"

Jake jumped in. "It's a little far for a nano-flight. So I went driverless."

KB was confused. "Won't a car take even longer?"

Jake's grin spread from ear to ear. "I said driverless, not car. We're going in a driverless jet."

Freda and Kumi laughed as KB couldn't keep her eyes from widening at the prospect of their travel plans. She wasn't easy to excite, so the others seemed to take a special joy in her shock.

They walked out of Fungi and followed Jake into the back of a limo. Jake started telling Kumi about the upcoming day. It was obvious from his exuberance that Ultimate frisbee had been his main attraction, not her. She didn't know why the idea of a date with Jake felt enticing. It wasn't as if she felt attracted to him; if anything, she found herself more comfortable with Kumi's quieter, more thoughtful demeanor. Whatever it was, seeing Freda engaged annoyingly with her iLink wiped away any romantic thoughts.

The car pulled up to an open field, where a fighter jet sat in the center. Somehow, the sleek silver jet in the field wasn't what caught her attention. Mostly because images of Jake playing Ultimate covered the jet's exterior. All they could do was laugh at the sight.

"Holy Maker-oni! Most beautiful jet you've ever seen, huh?" Jake flashed his toothy grin.

KB whispered to Kumi, "I've never been in a driverless jet before, so I should be more excited. But looking at this one, I'm not sure I want to."

"Am I in my Nightmare?" Kumi rubbed the iLink on the back of his neck and looked at KB with an exaggerated confused expression.

Jake raised an eyebrow at KB, laughing. "What are you two whispering about? Come on, when you book these, you get the chance to set the exterior imagery. What did you expect me to do?"

The stairwell opened with a thought as they approached, unfurling to reveal a surprisingly spacious lounge. The plush leather seats with a theater setup covering the ceiling made KB feel like she was entering an immersion room instead of a jet. The lack of an oxygen tank to move a jet of this size allowed for an interior that didn't feel too cramped with four inside. This was a modern scramjet, capable of flight seven times the speed of sound. Other than the occasional space tourist expedition, this would be the fastest KB would have ever moved.

No sooner had they strapped in that endeeze emerged from the floor and a voice that sounded like Quell spoke: "Orders before take-off? There will be no access to external nano-drones while in motion."

Wondering how they were still under Fungi's supervision, KB looked over her shoulder in surprise.

Kumi laughed. "Funny setting, bud."

Jake winked while shrugging his shoulders. The three of them then pulled up their own iLink screens to see their personally suggested menus.

Freda looked particularly perplexed by the choices at hand. "Um, why aren't we watching in the immersion room again?"

"Normally, I'd be with you. But it's nice to get out, and maybe if I meet one of the players, I can make them one of my Chosen!"

"Are you serious? You're going to pick an Ultimate player as one of your Chosen?"

KB heard the judgment in Freda's voice and glared at her. Though choosing to stay connected didn't carry suspense for most kids KB's age, who to select as their Chosen often did. At the Update age of fourteen, every child who stayed connected chose the people they wanted to help guide them to passing the Maker's Dream. While they could change each year, Update selections became known as 'the parents you choose.' Or Chosen.

Before KB could express her annoyance, Jake jumped in. "Of course! Right now, I'm a level eight UFR, only two away from the elite levels. I'm pretty sure that's going to be part of my path to fulfillment."

In this group, KB always seemed to be the odd one out, but it never stopped her from asking questions. "What in the world is UFR?"

Unexpectedly, it was Freda who responded. "UFR stands for Ultimate Frisbee Rating. It's a pure level system for how well you play based on your results. It's a one to ten scale. There are tournaments and competitions at all different levels." Freda noticed the strange look KB was giving her before adding, "What? Jake talks about Ultimate all the time."

"Well, Jake, your UFR might be great, but there's no way I'm letting you set the visuals on my first jet experience." KB rarely found technology this exhilarating, but she had an idea on how to make this jet experience special. Plus, it would take the conversation away from anything related to the Update Festival.

"If I'm letting you take control, you better pick something good," Jake said with a skeptical look.

KB's private iLink-generated screen took over her visual field. Looking through immersion room settings, she found the perfect choice. These jets were made of an outer film that also provided camera views to the exterior. But instead of going for standard see-through mode, she giggled as she clicked one of the additional settings. She set a timer and selected how the visual would emerge, and then sat back. She blinked once, and the menu showed up. A bag of salted maple kettle corn would hit the spot.

The engine came to life with a roar. The straps tightened, and the seats laid back into the full recline position. The immersion room turned on, and the see-through view emerged.

"A little too predictable, don't you think, KB? Always the most natural choice," Kumi joked.

She didn't even respond as the others laughed. A second later, KB felt her whole body pull to the back of her seat as the jet took off. Her heart beat faster with a joy that only fear can induce. Then, as the jet was approaching the clouds overhead, KB felt her stomach start to turn as she watched the jet start to roll over. Even though she knew what was actually happening, she still couldn't help the feeling of her stomach wrapping itself in knots.

The others didn't have the benefit of KB's knowledge. KB heard the screams of Freda and then the sound of vomit exploding from her mouth. Instead of falling sideways as they turned, the vomit fell straight into Freda's lap. Jake started laughing hysterically.

"Oh my god! I nearly pooped myself. That was genius. You could have chosen the downward-facing gaming chair view, but no.... you faked a rollover at the perfect time. Unbelievable."

KB shrugged her shoulders. "You know, trying to be predictable." She looked over at Kumi, taking pleasure in the sweat dripping off his ghostlike face.

"Where's the cleaner?" Freda seemed the least impressed with her joke, which only made it funnier to KB.

The endeeze emerged in the shape of the server drone carrying their orders. A few nano-drones then gathered into a cleaning tool and immediately vacuumed, then micro-washed and dried Freda's outfit and chair. The server used Quell's voice to announce they would arrive in twenty-five minutes.

After the acceleration phase, the four of them settled in as they traveled to the NM stadium in the Keitaro settlement, formerly known as Ahmedabad. As it was built and opened just decades before Keitaro, it hadn't been reengineered and continued to be used for a lot of ancestral traditions and sports. Today, it served as the host for the Ultimate Frisbee championships.

She looked over at Kumi, who seemed to be over the magnificent view and studying something on his iLink while they traveled. "Kumi, you play Ultimate too?"

Jake wouldn't let Kumi respond. "Ha. I've tried to get Kumi out there so many times. He's a physical specimen, but the dude has no finesse. He's the world's best defender that can't catch."

Kumi shrugged and laughed. "I always wished they'd bring back the physical sports. Then I could tackle Jake and shut him up."

KB remembered learning about the rise of Ultimate in an immersion room. In the pre-Keitaro days, sports known for barbaric violence like football, basketball, and soccer predominated. People relished watching individuals testing their speed, dexterity, and finesse in games that involved physical contact.

In the early days of Keitaro, Ultimate began to take hold despite being a much smaller sport. It had all the characteristics to appeal to those who had passed the Maker's Dream—individual athleticism, teamwork, and strategy—all without exposing oneself to possible harm. Frankly, it was inconceivable to most that so recently, athletes had risked physical and mental injury for the sake of entertainment and pleasure.

Some tried to reform soccer and other sports to the modern age, but the legacy of exploitation was too much to overcome. As Keitaro grew, so did Ultimate. To the point where KB now was lying down in a jet, soon to witness the Ultimate Frisbee championships in one of the largest stadiums in Keitaro.

While Kumi and Freda used their time to research some of their interests, Jake and KB fixated on the fast-moving landscape below them. The clouds appeared in regulated formations within the engineered micro-climates, and KB could make out the outline of several settlements on the flight path. Before she knew it, the jet was descending and executing a vertical landing in the stadium's parking lot. She looked at the massive stadium. A testament to the mass social human experience that used to be so prevalent. Yet here they were, parked next to the stadium, able to hear their collective footsteps as they made their way in.

They entered the large metallic structure and were immediately greeted by endeeze that had formed a flying orb. Upon scanning Jake's iLink, the endeeze led them through the wide hallways to their own luxury suite. Immediately, KB was struck by Jake and Freda's conversation as they made their way through the corridors. Not what they were saying, but the loudness with which they were speaking.

"Why are you all yelling?" KB said as she looked back at them.

They were too engrossed to pay attention, but Kumi heard her and raised his eyebrow with the barest hint of a smile. "If you haven't noticed, it's a little crazy in here?"

KB looked around her, making sure she wasn't missing something. She looked back at Kumi, ready to tell him off, when she saw him raise a finger and break out into a huge grin, "Ohhhh, you must have your live AR setting off."

KB blushed and looked away as she sent the thought to her iLink to turn her augmented reality setting on. Immediately, she felt the difference as the atmosphere around her turned raucous. Surrounded by groups making their way through the stadium, she stared at one in particular. The boys walking beside her in green and yellow jerseys had their faces painted and were loudly talking as they made their way past her. The actual words eluded her, converted to white noise to ensure their privacy as they experienced the events in an immersion room. As they passed her, the slight glitches and lags in the outlines of their body gave away their lack of physical presence.

It finally dawned on her why Freda would prefer going to the game in an immersion room.

She noticed Kumi's gaze upon her and tried to cover up her embarrassment, "Oops, don't know how I forgot to turn that on."

Kumi laughed. "No worries. Glad we caught it early. I mean, if you're going to go to a game, might as well get the real, full experience."

As they made their way to the suite, the white noise around her couldn't quiet the restless thoughts in her mind. Of course, she was well aware of the power of virtual reality experiences in immersion rooms. She had heard of augmented reality, but she had always assumed it referred to the screen she was capable of pulling up on her iLink at any given time. But she had never experienced AR in the real world, strangely sharing the same space with virtual avatars in some immersion room. Whenever she and Lila had gone to Chakra's Ultimate games, they enjoyed the experience with the mostly disconnected who attended in person.

Never once had KB realized the power of the small chip installed in her at birth. She rubbed the back of her neck, feeling the soft contours of the object that was completely altering her worldview. *Did Lila know about this? She must have. How come she never showed me? Why did she have my AR default setting off? What have I been missing?*

The sensory overload of these new AR-enhanced surroundings drowned out the questions about her upbringing. She made a conscious effort to appreciate this new experience and leave dwelling on the past for her next meditation session. When she entered the luxury suite, the return to quiet was striking yet reassuring. She could still see the packed stands, but their noise was now completely muffled by the quiet ambiance of the room decorated in red, gold, and green.

Jake waved his arm to show them the space. "How do you like it? I'm picking the Fire to win, so I decided to have the room decked out in their colors."

"It's nice." KB reached out to touch the walls, now unsure of her visual sense.

KB jumped back as endeeze emerged from the wall to form a small floating table, and Quell's voice spoke through them. "What would you like for food and drink? Pull up the program on your iLink to make your selections."

Jake pumped his fist. "Now, this is why we showed up. Let's get some food!"

Freda rolled her eyes, plopping down on the couch. "You can get food anywhere, Jake."

Jake didn't let Freda's lack of enthusiasm dampen his excitement. "Not in an immersion room!"

Pulling up the program on her iLink to see the current matchup, KB frowned as she didn't recognize any of the names.

Then, as she switched to the menu, she heard Freda's voice, "Oh! They have group buffet options. Want to pick together?"

Kumi jumped in, "Sure, I'm up for that. How about we go with classic Americana? Can't go wrong with burgers, wings, and fries."

Jake nodded in appreciation. "That sounds perfect. Any objections? Okay, done."

The endeeze table left the room, heading to the nearby synthetic biology production facilities, where the food would be made to order and delivered within minutes.

By the time the games started, the four of them were sitting down, stuffing their faces with food as they watched the action below.

Kumi looked over at KB as they both chewed on burgers dripping with ketchup. "I know the immersion room is supposed to completely mimic this experience, but it somehow feels different being here, right?"

"Definitely. Starting with eating this burger while watching," KB replied.

The stadium looked packed, but it was hard to tell from their suite how many of these were virtual personas or real. She scanned the field and surroundings to see what caught her interest. Of course, she could use her iLink to zoom in to any specific camera view, but being here, it felt normal to view things through the natural panorama from the suite. Or, at least, whatever natural was now with the augmented reality overlay.

Jake spent most of his time explaining to Freda and KB the finer strategic points of the game and the different positions people played. She started to see why it might be a part of his path to fulfillment. He used the AR capabilities to highlight the frisbee, showing its rotational speeds and the arc of its path on various throws. He turned on the setting that changed the frisbee's color depending on the team with possession, making it easier for them to follow the action.

He took it too far when he inserted himself into the action repeatedly, explaining to the two of them what he would have done differently. Luckily for KB, Freda did a much better job of encouraging Jake, so she mostly tuned out his words as she watched the action unfold in front of her in much the stoic way that Kumi did.

As the players came out for the third game, KB's eyes narrowed as she noticed one player in particular. Number seven in blue. She grinned. There he was. Her eyes left the field where Chakra was no bigger than an ant to the screens set up within the suite itself. She used her iLink to focus the cameras on number seven. His motions came into full focus, and KB felt the eyes of Jake and the others moving up to the screens as well.

He had his typically serious face but with a hint of joy at the corner of his lips. His long, limber frame didn't seem out of place amidst this field of competitors. His beard and scraggly demeanor did, though. Then, the whistle blew. Blue players passed the frisbee around with seemingly no plan. Until, all of a sudden, KB saw seven streaking down the sideline. His teammate saw the opening and played a pass that seemed destined to be out of reach. KB watched Chakra's eyes focus as he sprung up like a gazelle, grabbing the frisbee with his left hand stretched out over his head at the apex of his jump. As he landed, he pirouetted and immediately released the frisbee before his defender had an inkling of what was happening. The frisbee flew right over the defender's shoulders and down the sideline. Only as

KB turned did Chakra's teammate come into view as he ran under the frisbee uncovered and caught it for a point.

Jake jumped out of his seat, cheering, "Ahhhhh! I freakin' love Chak!"

For the first time, KB was out of her seat cheering as well.

Jake looked over at Kumi. "Didn't I tell you Chak was amazing? He plays with unbelievable vision. Did you see how quick that catch and release was? Watching the replay, I still have no idea how he saw Lee would be open for a point while he was jumping to catch that."

Kumi's bottom lip jutted out as he nodded. "Respect, man. That was pretty quick. But... I would have blocked that if I were defending him."

Jake laughed as he took his seat. "You have got to be kidding me. You may be fast, Kumi, but you are not quick."

KB was still hung up on what Jake had said earlier. "Wait, wait, so you follow Chakra?"

"Obviously. He plays the same position as me, except he's a level ten, and I'm only level eight. He's so frickin' good." Jake looked at KB's face and paused. "Wait, why? You know him or something?"

Knowing exactly how to play this, she sat back in her seat and said casually, "Yeah, I knew him before I moved into Fungi."

Jake's jaw dropped to the floor. "No way! Holy macaroni! Is there any way you can set up a meeting? Can we meet him, KB? Please? I've never asked you for anything."

"You pretty much ask me for something every time we're together."

"Yeah, but those are all little things between friends. For shits and giggles. Never something that meant as much as this does to me."

Jake was giddy but also more serious than she had ever seen him. Even Freda seemed to be surprised as she paid close attention to the conversation. KB imagined Freda trying to suppress the jealousy rising within her as she tried to be "the best version of herself." It made KB laugh to herself and take a few moments to respond.

She leaned back, relishing in the attention.

Finally, Kumi broke the silence. "Well?"

"Yeah, why don't we all go meet up with him after the game?"

She said it casually, but Jake was a different person for the rest of the game. He was quiet, and KB was sure he was watching highlights of Chakra on his iLink, thinking of what he wanted to ask him.

Meanwhile, KB cheered as Chakra wreaked havoc on the field. Despite its ancient history, the top levels of Ultimate Frisbee were typically dominated by those with iLinks, not due to any discrimination but due to their superior training, nutrition, and fitness regimens. But Chakra had always been an outlier. For as long as KB had known him, he had harped on and on that he would one day be the best Ultimate player in the world, regardless of being disconnected. She smiled as she reminisced about going to watch many of Chakra's matches with Lila. KB would be frantic in her cheers, while Lila would enjoy the matches more evenly, unfazed by the result hanging in the balance.

Today, he was playing fantastic. One time he lost his temper when an opposing player threw a frisbee right by him, and KB heard him screaming, "With a real frisbee, you have to bend down to pick it up. This bullshit with the frisbee rising is ridiculous!" But other than that, he was the team's most consistent receiver all day.

Chakra's team finished in fifth place, and he looked pleased with the result. Jake's favorite team, the Fire, lost in the finals, but he didn't care anymore. As the final whistle blew, Jake looked over at KB with hopeful eyes, and she thought about messing with him a little more before deciding against it. "Anyone know how to get to the locker room?"

Jake hopped up and seemed to have no patience for Freda's need to use the restroom. He led them to the tube station within the stadium and put in the coordinates for the blue team's locker room. The door was closed and locked. The device above the door scanned her iLink, and a disappointing message popped up. "Access denied."

Jake's face fell. "Were you bullshitting me this whole time, KB?"

KB was undeterred. She pulled up the terminal. While Kumi looked at the inspirational quotes along the wall, Freda and Jake looked over KB's shoulder as she typed in her message.

Message for Chakra. Kali Bilvani is here with some friends and needs to meet him. She submitted the message.

Freda and Jake looked at each other before Freda asked, "Your name is Kali Bilvani?"

"No, it's KB."

A moment later, the door opened. Chakra was sweaty and shirtless, with a huge grin on his face.

"Finally! I've been wondering when I'd see you again! Come on in!"

As they followed Chakra into the locker room, Jake remained motionless. Kumi tapped him on the shoulder. "Come on, bud. I promise he won't bite."

12

WHO'S WRITING?

Remember the blank page analogy in The History of Keitaro?
You know the one. We are all blank pages. With the power of
iLink and iHERO, we become better authors. We each write a
great story in which we are the hero. Something like that.

But that's not quite true. With iLink, you don't get a blank page;
you get a Connect-the-Dots diagram. With iHERO, you never
make marks outside the preset lines. Sure, I want to be a better
author. But only if I'm damn sure it's me writing the story.

—FROM THE WORLD OF THE MAKER

They walked into the locker room, and Jake looked around at all the
other players in awe.

Chakra grabbed a seat and motioned for the others to do the
same. He started untying his cleats, and the girl with KB looked at
him like he had a third eye.

"You have shoelaces? That you untie?"

Chakra hated how quickly it always came back to this with
new people. But on this occasion, his excitement at seeing KB was
enough to drown out any potential anger. Instead, Chakra grinned,

causing his beard to scrape against itself. "Oh, Kali never told you? I'm not iLinked."

"You're disconnected?"

Chakra could hear the shock in her voice. Another person who had probably never met a disconnected person in their life before. It was becoming all too common with the younger generation. "Yeah, I guess that's what people like to call it. Personally, I prefer the description 'free.'"

He watched as KB grimaced while two of the new faces looked at each other, uncomfortable already. One of the males looked unnaturally excited, and Chakra quickly learned why.

"Wait, you're a UFR 10 without an iLink? How do you train? How do you eat? How do you pull off moves like you did today?" The words started to garble together as the over-excited boy spoke too fast.

"Slow down, slow down. What'd you say your name was?"

"Jake."

KB jumped in to introduce the others. "So Jake is one of my friends from Fungi. And so are these other two. Kumi and Freda."

Chakra ignored Freda and looked at Jake and Kumi. "You two look like you play some Ultimate?"

"Yeah, I'm decent. I'm level eight, so nowhere close to this level," the excited boy responded.

Chakra felt unusually generous in his reply. "Wow, eight is good. Anyway, to answer your question, I'm not going to tell you it's easy. I don't have the iLink strategy review sessions, the designed diet, the optimal training regimen. But you know what I do have? An insatiable will to excel. And instincts. Raw instincts that can only be developed and taught by humans." He looked over and winked at KB as he continued untying the laces on his shoes.

The other girl didn't seem to accept Chakra's explanation. "With all due respect, that seems like wishful thinking. The iLinks teach humans how to develop their instincts all the time."

He shot a disgusted glance at KB. She raised her eyebrows and smiled mischievously. "She's your problem now."

"You may be right. Freda, was it?" he responded. "Let me put it to you this way. No player with an iLink could have pulled off that catch and pass in the first game. Ask your friend Jake."

The girl looked at Jake hopefully, but she underestimated the fact that Jake was in a different place altogether. "You know, that's true. Your highlights are different than the other great wingers in Ultimate. I'd never realized it was because you were disconnected!"

"Shouldn't we be on our way back now?" Freda's annoyed expression made Chakra smile.

"I don't know about your friends, but we've barely had any time to catch up," Chakra said to KB. "Why don't you come over to my house for a little bit?" He passed a glance to the others. "Of course, you all are welcome."

He hoped his dismissive tone might discourage broader acceptance, but the excited Jake didn't hesitate. "Oh, hell yeah. I'd love to. Thanks for the invite!"

Kumi didn't respond until a sharp nudge from Jake snapped him out of his indecision. "Yeah, I'm down."

The girl seemed to be using her iLink to help her decide. Chakra hoped she would say no. He could already tell she'd be a pain in the ass to deal with. "I think I have to get home. Don't want to mess up my circadian rhythms."

Chakra shrugged as everyone gathered themselves for departure. Jake stopped and looked at Chakra. "Oh, man. I just realized. I was going to ask you if you could be one of my Chosen. Damn, it looks like I'm going to have to find someone else. I was sure you were a Dreamer."

Chakra looked at KB with a knowing grin. "First of all, I may not have passed the Maker's Dream, but I'm guessing the Nightmare is a harder test, and I passed that. How do you think I got to disconnect? And why can't I be one of your Chosen?"

"Oh, I mean... I don't know... I can't like... put you on my Chosen list?" Jake's confused tone seemed to call into question Chakra's intelligence.

As they opened the door to exit the locker room, Chakra dropped the knowing smile and looked at all of them. "If you're going to be part of a system, don't work for the system. Make it work for you. Some Chosen may let the Maker decide who they work with, but others don't. And no one's stopping you from working with them. Fuck whatever list the Maker has."

The two boys looked at each other in surprise. Even KB was taken aback by his response.

Freda seemed the most shocked, and she responded first. "You wouldn't train Jake, would you?"

They heard the sound of the jet announcing its arrival to pick up Freda.

"Of course, I would. I run a class in my village for Ultimate once a week. Jake, you'd be more than welcome to join. Kumi, you never said, but you might be an Ultimate player yourself."

Kumi laughed. "I don't play, but I have a feeling I might learn a lot more than Ultimate if I showed up to your training."

Chakra poured water over the campfire, hoping that might be a sign their night together was coming to an end. KB had gone inside the cabin to use his restroom, and he could feel the eyes of the two boys burning despite the flames of the fire dying out. "This campfire is endlessly fascinating, huh?"

As he had come to expect over the last couple of hours, it was Jake who spoke up first. "It's just... you don't often see people *doing* these types of things. I mean, it's cool."

These two had proved good company. He had introduced them to the special sadam and had been surprised that all three of them were willing to take part. Since it was their first time, despite the small amount, they were feeling the psychedelic effects. Chakra, however, knew it was time for his nighttime expedition. Before he left, though, he needed to speak with KB. He hadn't been able to get in a private word with her, with the one boy in particular who seemed to follow him around like an active endeeze monitor.

Finally, he saw an opening. "Alright, Jake, if you want to start the lessons a little early, I'm going to have you two do something instead of watching. Kumi, if you could pour some more water on this until the ashes are cold to the touch. Jake, there's that little shovel over there. Toss the ashes over until they are less of a slurry, and then the two of you carry them about twenty meters into the woods and spread them out. Can you guys handle that?"

The two boys grinned at each other. Chakra knowingly added, "No iLinks. Attention to detail is important here." Chakra walked to the cabin as the two of them looked around with wide eyes, no doubt enhanced by the sadam.

He entered to see KB at his kitchen counter. "Looking for something?"

She turned to face him. "No, just waiting for you. I have something to tell you."

"Oh, good. Me too. You first. What is it?"

"Lila. She showed up in my iHERO dream."

He hadn't been in iHERO since he was a child, but he was pretty sure dead people weren't supposed to show up. People had surmised that the Maker considered it unethical and potentially too manipulative. He started to question how the special sadam was affecting her.

"I know it's not her, but still, Uncle. It really... feels like her..."

All Chakra knew to do was to pull her in for a hug. Chakra had told her to stay connected, but he had never expected this. "Look, kiddo. I'm sure it does feel like her. But don't start chasing her in there because you won't find her. You'll probably keep seeing her when you play, but try to treat it like a novelty. If you get close to whoever that is in there, you're going to end up driving yourself crazy."

"Yes, because out here in the real world, there's no one driving themselves crazy with imaginary villains." She said the words lightly while still embracing Chakra, so he couldn't take too much offense.

He pulled back and shook his head. "I resent your implication." He wished she was right, but he knew the Maker was all too real and all too responsible for the deaths in his family. First Seina, then Lila. But he was going to make sure the Maker wouldn't be able to go after anyone else.

"Anyway, what did you have to tell me?"

He looked at the grandfather clock in the corner of the room. "I have to head out in a few minutes, and Jake out there seems like he's harder to shed than a virus before the days of Keitaro. First things first, I loved your little speech at Lila's service..."

"There's a but coming..."

"No, but. *And...* I had to rush out after, so we didn't get to talk there. Before I left, I did happen to notice you talking to an older fellow. Gray-haired?"

KB laughed. "You mean Anthony?"

"So you know him?" The way she said his name gave Chakra a deeply unsettling feeling. It reminded him too much of the way his sister Lila had spoken his name back when they were kids.

"Yeah, do you?"

He weighed how much to tell KB at this moment. Anthony was on the Small Council. As close to the Maker as you can get. He decided to proceed cautiously at first. "Yeah, I don't know how much he told you, but he used to be a friend of Lila's when we were kids."

KB looked strangely at him. "That's exactly what he said. So, you weren't friends with him?"

Chakra bristled at the notion. "Hell no. I knew he was a sellout from the day I met him." He paused, remembering the awkward ending of Anthony's relationship with Lila. Anthony clearly hadn't shared the messy details with KB, so neither would he for the time being. "What exactly does he want with you?"

He listened as KB described their relationship. He tried to remain stone-faced as she discussed their weekly dinners and the chummy relationship they seemed to share. But when he heard about Anthony's offer for her to stay with him, his facial expression was enough to cause KB to interrupt her recounting. "What is it, Uncle?"

"It's just... unexpected. Look, Kali. He's not your friend. He's the leader of the Small Council. He's a puppet for the Maker." Chakra looked away from KB, eyes opening. He started to wonder if Anthony might be a better way to get to the Maker. Instead of his nightly expeditions that were frankly leading nowhere, maybe he could present a more direct path to bringing the Maker down.

As he looked back at KB, he noticed her warm glow had turned to a look of disgust. "When are you going to change, Uncle? You're always the same. He's spent more time with me than you have these past few weeks. He's actually helping me get through this instead of going on wild goose chases to bring down the Maker."

He tried to respond, but she spoke over him, "Let me guess. You want me to try to get some information from him about the Maker."

He could only hang his head sheepishly. As he thought about how to dig himself out of this hole, the door opened, and Kumi and Jake walked in.

"Fire's out. Ashes spread." Jake smiled as if they had been on a space expedition.

Chakra saw the glance KB gave Kumi as if signaling a departure. Sure enough, Kumi spoke up, "I think we ought to get going. Thank you so much for having us over, Chakra. We'd love to have you over at Fungi if you're ever up for it."

Chakra smiled in the direction of KB. "I'd love to." His expression turned defeated. "I'm a little busy the next few days, but maybe next week?"

"Sounds good," Jake replied before turning to KB and Kumi, "What should we do next? The night is still young."

They walked out the door. KB paused as the other two continued walking. She turned back to face him. "I don't know what Anthony's intentions are. But I want you to know I'm no one's puppet. Not even yours."

The orange mouthguard fit neatly in Chakra's mouth, but the awkwardness of a closed tube sticking out of his face was impossible to ignore. After looking around to make sure there was no one in sight, Chakra ran into the water until it was waist-high, then dove in and started swimming freestyle.

At the end of the designated swimming area, he turned onto his back to get one last look at the shore, then dove underwater. He felt the stings of the jellyfish for a couple of seconds, but soon he only felt the rush of cold water sending tingles down his spine as he went deeper. The air coming from his mouthguard didn't quite feel fresh, but it was enough. As he swam out, the lack of wildlife was eerie. When he had been scuba diving in exotic destinations as a kid, he had loved the coral reefs and all the different aquatic life. Yet, here he was, in the waters of Keitaro, and there wasn't a plant or fish in sight.

Except for the algae. The algae formed the basis for the synthetic biology that sustained Keitaro. Large hydro-powered fermentation tanks lined the surroundings while the synthetic jellyfish kept the swimming water pristine year-round. All the foods, from the traditional ancient foods to the modern delicacies of Keitaro. The materials that formed all the buildings of Keitaro. And even the endeeze that served all the people. The drones in the forest certainly helped, but the fundamental power sat here in the water. He marveled at the endeeze zipping underwater, executing tasks to keep the tanks operating efficiently.

He wasn't here to marvel at this, though. He was here to see what lay beyond. He continued swimming past the factory, wondering how far he'd have to go before the aquatic life boundary had been set. He didn't have to wait long, for a few feet beyond, a massive ledge jutted out. Grabbing the floor, he looked down the cliff at the depths below and gasped.

There, below him, looked to be the most sophisticated arms arsenal in the world, strewn across the underwater cliff. Chakra had spent years researching conspiracies with a few other disconnected folks. How Keitaro had grown not as a peaceful utopia but as a military powerhouse, armed with biological, chemical, and nuclear weapons no other civilization could compete with. But even he couldn't get over the shock of seeing weaponry in person. He could see these delivery missiles were not made like drones. These were not built to serve. These were built to destroy.

Wishing he had some way to take a picture, he took mental note of landmarks so he could find an endeeze view of this with Frankie later. It was too dark to make out the total extent of this machinery, but he felt buoyed by the possibilities. *Maybe Frankie can figure out how to unleash this arsenal on the Maker!*

He swam for a few more minutes, noting all he could about the machinery and their dimensions at a depth he could operate at. He felt the pressure of the deeper water and knew the air from his mouthguard was no longer enough to ensure his safety.

Chakra was in fantastic shape, but hours of swimming after a day of Ultimate left him exhausted. Sleepless strokes propelled him back to the fermentation tanks, allowing him to resurface a few minutes later. Compressing the mouthguard and returning it to his pocket, he rubbed his eyes as he emerged. It was now definitely morning, though still early enough where only the yoga and running lovers were out. He figured endeeze were a bigger risk, and he immediately started with his gorilla walk, looking significantly less coordinated in his fatigued state. Not paying attention, he bumped into an early runner who looked mortified.

Chakra couldn't help but laugh as he continued on his way. *She's probably more surprised she ran into a disconnected than she is to see someone walking like a gorilla. We're nothing but animals to them. But they're going to see.*

Anthony saw the face and looked at the time on his iLink. He put the book down on his nightstand and sat up a little straighter on his pillow.

"A little early for a call, wouldn't you say, Tara?"

"You're not going to believe who I ran into on the beach."

13

CITY UPON A HILL

Not long after adopting the iLinks, the people of Keitaro decided to become a model to the rest of the world. A city upon a hill, to use an ancient reference. They made three decisions, each stranger than the last.

First, they renamed the settlement Keitaro in honor of their mysterious benefactor, overwriting millennia of history in the process.

Second, they decided to let the Maker determine their carrying capacity as a settlement. The Maker took its annual data upload and determined how many residents and tourists could be present, maintaining a dynamic, optimal population.

Third, they decided to share access to the entire video capture with the rest of the world. A live-streamed city in all its depth, from the boardroom to bedroom. Anywhere the endeeze were, the rest of the world could see. Yes, the people of Keitaro controlled where the endeeze had access to. There were boundaries, of course. But this was reality TV on a civilizational level and the world took notice.

—*FROM THE HISTORY OF KEITARO*

Anthony knew he didn't have a lot of time before the meeting began. He usually saved his time with the Maker for after meetings or in the middle of the night, more sure of his privacy. He was taking a bigger risk, but things were starting to slip out of his control.

He turned the key over in his hand, rubbing the Maker's Mark inscription. When he had received it, the instructions had been simple: enter once a year after the Update Festival. Other than that, ensure the Maker remains contained. For the first few years, that had been enough. But after witnessing the wisdom of the Maker up close, he had started making a few exceptions, only for the most important questions. Now, in his final days with the key, he found himself entering the containment area for the second time in a week.

He looked at the Maker's elegant simplicity, pushing against the soft edge along the side until the panel popped out. Anthony pulled out the keyboard and typed in his first question.

Have I served humanity well?

Thankfully, the usual response came back.

Yes

When we have access to a higher being, we must use it to accelerate humanity's progress, Anthony had justified to himself over the years. He followed all the precautions, all the safeguards. He had devoted his life to the service of humanity, and what better service than helping all of Keitaro reach their Dreamer state? When they got there, each of them would be able to join him in the most beautiful slumber. For Dreamers were given the special privilege of sleeping with iHERO on. It was better than any morning coffee, ensuring each day reached its full potential.

Still, he always liked to check his logic with the Maker each time he visited. He was sure the Maker would tell him if he were causing harm with his visits. He typed in his next question.

Should Chakra be eliminated?

He had asked before but wondered if the Maker would react differently with a new set of facts. The answer still came back the same as last time.

No

This time, Anthony had a follow-up.

Should Chakra be arrested?

Yes

Aha. He chastised himself for not realizing it earlier. Rehabilitation, or imprisonment, offered an effective alternative to elimination for disconnected threats.

Anthony glanced down at the clock on the display. He was running out of time. Thinking about Chakra's partner-in-crime from the report, his fingers stroked his chin. At this point, he didn't want to take any chances. He typed in his final question.

Anthony was reviewing the footage on his iLink when Tara and Dush came in. Their normally stressed faces looked even more anxious with the crinkle of crow's feet in the corners of their eyes. As they settled into their seats, Anthony wasted no time with small talk. "It's clear we underestimated the threat posed by Chakra."

Tara looked at Dush with what Anthony seemed to note was derision.

"Okay, Tara, you're right. I underestimated the threat here. And if it weren't for Tara's overzealous commitment to fitness..." Anthony watched as Tara's expression turned more positive, "we might not have caught it until more damage had been done. Dush, can you walk through the insights from your data analysis?"

Dush shuffled in his chair and tried to put his elbows on the table with authority. Instead, one missed the edge, and his chin slapped the table. "Yes, of course. We used Tara's iLink upload to video-match his revised walking gait with endeeze footage. And looks like he's been active at night. There's nano-drone footage of him going into the forest at least nineteen nights in the past three weeks."

Tara cleared her throat. "Get to the point," she mumbled under her breath.

Dush nodded. "Well, yeah. We caught footage of him meeting someone, Anthony."

Anthony's chin lowered, and one eyebrow raised. "Yes, our mysterious collaborator. The report says his name is Teddy."

"Yes, he's a Dreamer, too. Keitaro mental agility champion. Four years running. A rational leader who leads a lot of statistics and decision psychology projects within Keitaro."

Anthony turned his head and looked at Tara with raised eyebrows. She nodded as she responded, "I know, weird, right? What's he doing with Chakra? And looks like he provided the tool that Chakra had for his little underwater explorations."

Anthony tossed over the possibilities, again and again, wondering what the two of them could be seeking to do.

"Anthony, I think it's time we arrest both of them. There's enough circumstantial evidence to put each of them in a rehabilitation house. At least for a week while we investigate further."

Even when Dush tried to make an argument, he did so without conviction and often missed the depth of the issue. An arrest was so rare these days that bringing in any Dreamer would raise questions. For the crux of the people's commitment to Keitaro hinged upon their unfailing belief in those who passed the Maker's Dream. If someone who passed could be arrested, what did passing even mean? What was the best version of yourself? These were dangerous questions that would detract from all that was going so well across Keitaro.

Anthony knew Tara was considered enough to get past the surface depth, and he liked fostering her independent thinking. He let Dush's statement linger in the air, comfortable with the silence until Tara spoke up. "He gave him a mouthguard and met him twice. I think it would be reckless to have someone who has passed the Maker's Dream arrested under such a weak claim. That wouldn't be a good look for Keitaro or the Maker, for that matter. Do we want to have that kind of publicity right before what should be our best Update Festival yet?"

Anthony smiled. Tara bringing it up meant there would be no reason to suspect him now. "You bring up a good point, Tara. There is no need to arrest Teddy at this point. Though, out of an abundance of caution, I do suggest an active monitor on him with a maximum security risk level through the Update Festival at least."

He paused to look for any signs of dissension. After finding none, he continued, "As far as Chakra goes, same active monitor, but use it to gather evidence. It'd be a bit better if we catch him in a more red-handed position, or at least have a greater understanding of what exactly he's planning. But no matter what, we arrest him before the Update Festival to ensure the safety of Keitaro. Agreed?"

His fingers tapped on the table as the two nodded their approval.

Anthony closed the door and sighed. One enigma seemingly under control; now time to move to another. He'd thought he had a good handle on KB, but given all that he had seen with Chakra, he wanted to make sure he didn't make the same mistake twice. He would review everything in her file and see if anything looked suspicious.

He had dinner tonight with her, and then he could figure out if he wanted to ask the Maker for any advice on how to deal with her. He first ordered an Earl Grey tea, the endeeze working quietly in the background to fulfill his request. Then, as he took a seat in his library, he made sure to confirm his thoughts on guest cleaning preparation. Meanwhile, he enjoyed the comfort of his modern chair with the massaging capability. He reached for a book, an old classic. *The Almanack of Naval Ravikant.*

Before he could even open it, two drones delicately placed his tea on the armrest next to him. He paused and realized the book would have to wait. Engaging his iLink, he opened up a new note in the Project Ideas directory under the KB header. He started reviewing his prior interactions with her and the notes Quell had shared with him on her progress. She noted KB's increasing engagement with the Fungi environment and her starting to lead meditation sessions, but he could sense Quell's own confusion in trying to understand the girl. Cobbling together some clips from her time at Fungi, Anthony took a sip of his tea and felt the relaxing effects of the chair on his physique. *What is it that makes her tick?* He looked at the note and added a line at the very top.

```
Main purpose: what ought to be done to put KB
on the right path?
```

With the blink of an eye, he saved and closed the note. He reached over, picked up the book, and skimmed the foreword. The final line caught his eye. Another blink and the note reopened. He pasted the words into the document with his own note below.

```
Hypothesis: If I can get KB to view me as a
friendly but highly competent sparring partner,
I could change her path.
```

The plan for dinner was almost set. Now all he needed to think about was the food.

14

A HAPPY JOURNEY

The special sadam can be a small dose of joy. A brief glimpse at a beautiful haven. But sustained happiness only lies in the journey itself, not in any destination. All destinations with no further journeys will eventually cease to be great.

—FROM THE WORLD OF THE MAKER

KB called for her endeeze flight suit and felt them slide over her, interlacing and locking tight. The suit had a dark black base color, with a streak of orange highlighting, making her feel like a comet crossing the sky. She no longer needed directions as she engaged her iLink to take flight.

The sea of trees grew smaller as she glided higher through the air. Her flight was precise and controlled, showing a mental fortitude far beyond her young years. The nano-drones wrapped around her in an interlaced flying suit connected to her iLink. Each of them was a super-ant, capable of carrying 2,000 times their weight. Together, wrapped around her, they had plenty of power to propel her through the air in seamless personal flight.

Passing the forest, she saw house after house, each uniquely designed yet somehow all conveying a sense of uniformity. There were large houses but no mansions other than a few disconnected homes. There were small houses but none so small as to resemble anything like poverty. There were modern houses built in the style of industrial warehouses and others in a more Victorian style. It was as if each house promoted a stylistic choice cautiously, as if not to pass judgment on the others.

She normally tried to make these rides meditative, given that she rarely crossed paths with others while in flight. As the sun was starting to set, the beautiful orange hue gave the sky a magnetic resonance. Instead of enjoying the view, her mind was on the man she was flying to meet—the important man who had suddenly shown up in her life after Lila's passing. Anthony seemed like he was a history buff with a weird sense of nostalgia, but there was something about him she couldn't put her finger on.

On the horizon, she saw his house emerging in the distance. It was pale, minimalist, and flood-lit with clean, sharp lines set into a dark hillside. The tops of palm trees were illuminated by the exterior lights, and KB could see the glimmering pool visible through the trees. The house was beautiful yet understated, with a steel-like exterior that looked like it could weather any storm.

As she landed on the front porch, the endeeze released and scattered, blending into the background. As she knocked on the door, the iLink scanner emerged, and she lifted her hair and turned around. The door opened, and she saw Anthony smiling as he walked up.

"Well, hello, KB! You're early tonight!"

KB smiled. "Well, I guess I was hoping this would give us *more* time to discuss your latest reading."

Anthony laughed. "Believe me, you'd find Naval's thinking interesting, but I take your point. Follow me. Let's take a seat in the living room."

As he walked in, KB relaxed at the simple feel of the place that had now grown comforting to her. At first, she had been caught up with the antiques and open space throughout. The books. The rotary telephone. The wooden table. The globe. Yet, it only took a couple of visits for KB to realize this was a mirage, a minimalist front covering for a highly technical background. She saw drones working in the kitchen, and a modern immersion room tucked away behind the library books.

"Well, what would you like for dinner? I've put a couple of recommended options on your iLink, but feel free to order anything."

"You know I'm easy. So, I'll go with whatever you're having."

"Ah, I must say I appreciate your long-forgotten sense of what it means to be a host. Well, in that case, two orders of pear and duck confit salad coming up, with a side of kombucha."

"Is it too late to change my mind?" The gleam in KB's eyes was enough for Anthony not to take offense as he laughed. She joined him in another library massage chair, comfortably positioned on a Persian rug. With a glance from Anthony, the fireplace turned on.

"I find the only way to truly appreciate the wonders of synthetic biology is to push the envelope when it comes to ordering. People even a generation ago would be shocked to see duck confit made purely from soybeans in an algae factory."

"You sure know how to make a meal sound appetizing."

"Alright, let's move on before I dig myself an even deeper hole," Anthony replied. "What's the latest at Fungi?"

KB thought about her response. "It's been better than I expected. People are nice, and I'm having a good time."

"What have you been spending your time doing there?"

"Hiking, meditating, hanging out with some people. Nothing much."

Anthony seemed to be digesting her response, chewing on it slowly. "What about iHERO? Must be spending some time on that with your big Update Festival coming up."

KB paused as she thought about how to respond. If she hadn't talked to Chakra, she might have confided in Anthony and let him know that Lila had shown up. Instead, she tested the waters first. "You mean the forced indoctrination scheme we call education? I do the minimum, so I have my flying privileges."

Anthony sat back in his chair. "Forced indoctrination, huh? Why do you feel that way?"

"Well, let's see. iLinks implanted at birth and forced to 'play,'" KB made air quotes as she spoke, "a certain amount per week until you reach Update Age, despite barely remembering any of it and not knowing what it's doing to you. Sure, you technically don't have to choose iHERO, but that's the easiest option, and the one everyone chooses. Then, if you want to keep your iLinks active, you have to keep 'playing' pretty much forever. No. That doesn't sound fishy at all." She shuddered as she imagined Chakra saying those exact words.

Anthony squinted his eyes at her. She wondered whether she caught a hint of sadness, but if it was there, it was fleeting. After what felt like an interminable pause, Anthony broke the silence. "Are you open to changing your mind?"

"Always."

"Follow me."

He got up and led her through the door at the back of the library into his immersion room. There sat four state-of-the-art immersion chairs, designed to integrate seamlessly with full-body haptic suits to provide high-fidelity virtual reality.

"Take a seat. I'm going to give you a little history lesson."

As a suit formed around her, KB picked her seat. She felt the seat grasping her limbs lightly, only to administer the necessary sensations to her nerve endings. Unlike iHERO interacting directly with her brain, immersion rooms created a virtual reality experience by tricking both her body and her eyes. Though she couldn't hear outside the chair as the suit included headphones, she knew Anthony was joining her in the adjacent seat.

The next second, she found herself in a different world. She stood in a square room with chairs and desks that looked completely unfamiliar. Plain but with seemingly no technology. A large blackboard had chalk next to it.

Anthony stood next to her, wearing the same blue cardigan and the same wisps of white hair left to fall wherever they felt like. "Our lesson starts here. Before the update. This is in the 1900s, long before the Maker's arrival."

Kids KB's age started to shuffle in and take their seats, each wearing a green uniform with a logo. An older person walked in, and all the children immediately sat down and paid attention. The scene paused, and KB turned her head to soak in her surroundings.

"For a long time, this was our forced indoctrination system. Often called the birth of modern education. For twelve years, ages five to eighteen, everyone was forced to go to this classroom." Anthony waved his hand at the bleak surroundings. "Seven hours a day. Five days a week. Not to mention the homework you had to complete. It was believed that with thirty-five hours a week, forty weeks a year, and twelve years, the more than 15,000 hours each student went through was enough to indoctrinate them as productive members of society."

The room around her started whizzing by her in a flipbook animation mode. She saw students sitting bored, turning in assignments, growing older. The background changed from a classroom to an office setting. The uniforms changed colors but remained largely the same.

KB couldn't help noticing, "It's like our builder drones being manufactured to provide consistent, reliable output. We're just a bunch of dumb robots."

"Never thought of it that way, but that's brilliant." Anthony smiled. "Exactly what's happening. A factory model of education, supposedly educating humans." Anthony paused, and even his avatar in the immersion room seemed to be looking at the surroundings with a fresh perspective. "Now, let me take you to the next phase."

He nodded his head and the environment changed again, this time to a setting more familiar to KB. This looked like the Keitaro she knew, albeit before she was born. The room didn't look too different from the Library on Level 4 of Fungi.

"This must look more familiar to you." KB nodded while Anthony continued, "This was our educational system not long after the Maker's arrival."

Again, kids shuffled in and took seats, though this time at individual terminals. No teacher walked in.

"Notice anyone?" Anthony smiled as he pointed out one individual. A young girl. Black hair. Soft, warm features on caramel skin. Recognizable in an instant. KB choked the tears back as she saw the familiar smile plastered on Lila's face. "Wait, how is this even..." She tried running toward the girl, but her avatar's movement was slowed by the limitations of her chair.

Anthony seemed to worry at the sound of her voice. "I'm sorry. I couldn't help myself. I hoped it might be enjoyable for you, but if it's sadness this is causing, I can end the session."

iHERO had conditioned KB to the presence of Lila, but seeing her at a younger age felt different. Somehow, more intimate. Instead of Lila entering her world, KB felt like she was getting a window into Lila's world. One she knew surprisingly little about. "No, no. Honestly, I'm just a little overwhelmed. But it's nice to see her. How is this even possible?" She rubbed her finger on Lila's shirt.

"Well, the immersion rooms are based on existing footage. But I like to combine general history with personal history. This is my classroom memory reconstructed."

With a wave of his hand, the room spun jarringly, and KB was staring at a young boy in the seat next to Lila. He was much taller than her and looked to be a couple of years older. He had flowing auburn hair parted to one side, nothing like Anthony's white hair of today. But the eyes were unmistakable. The same narrow, piercing look.

"Besides this cheap parlor trick, let me get back to the lesson. As you can see in this setting, we let go of some of our preconceived notions, but we held on to others."

"What do you mean?" She looked around again, trying to find the connection between this library and the factory production classroom that Anthony had shown her before. Anthony waited until she was done, locking eyes with her before continuing.

"We realized that age-based cohorts made no sense. Neither did most of what constituted a standardized curriculum. We moved to an individualized educational program that allowed each student to progress at their own pace, regardless of age. Yet, we clung to other ideas of age and amount of time. So, each person still spent five hours a day, five days a week, and twelve years of their life, going through this system. What you might consider indoctrination."

All KB could muster was, "Wow." She reflected on the freedom of her childhood to the time Lila must have spent in this infuriatingly controlled way. She watched as Lila put on a helmet and entered her own virtual education room. She grabbed Lila's arm, hoping to prolong their time together. But she immediately recoiled and let go of the unfamiliar, leathery feeling of Lila's skin. She shuddered as Anthony changed the scene to a Joy spokesperson speaking at an Update Festival.

"That all changed when one of the four main organizations—Joy, if memory serves—proposed the new project."

KB smirked. "Joy? That's been the least popular one for as long as I can remember."

He shrugged. "Things ebb and flow in any competitive environment. The important thing is that the people always have choices. So, sometimes it's Joy on top, other times it's Happiness. One year you use a Fulfillment product, the next year Bliss. Anyway, the leaders of Joy came upon a critical insight. Education had long been seen as a system designed to meet our financial needs. Train us to earn enough money to buy everything we should desire. That structure meant you wanted to train people quickly and efficiently. But the world was no longer the same with our iLinks. If you remember one of the tenets of the iLink, its installation and use could never cost money. Therefore, if people could meet all their needs with an iLink, what then was the purpose of education?"

"Help each person to discover and realize their purpose."

Anthony nodded in approval at her quick ability to make the connection. The room shifted to show a young child playing iHERO in their room alone. "Exactly. The motto of iHERO is apt here. Help everyone become the hero of their own journey."

KB seemed to be lost in thought at the implications. Meanwhile, the setting returned to show the Update Festival, with the crowd cheering raucously.

"Joy proposed a new project for the Maker's approval. All those who took the Joy hardware would have no formal school. A minimum requirement for hours of learning, up until Update age, but that's it."

"Who gets to decide what constituted learning?"

"Ah, good question. It was included in the proposal. There were three ways to earn hours toward your learning requirement. First, hours spent with approved immersion room material. Second, hours spent playing iHERO. Third, learning hours noted by a Dreamer, like Lila had done with you."

KB looked around the Update Festival, wondering why Lila had not exposed her to iHERO like all these faces in the crowd.

"Anyway, the Maker approved the project, and Joy was the talk of Keitaro. It didn't take long for the other companies to follow suit."

Update Festivals started to flash forward for each year until they reached last year's festival with Anthony on stage.

"Update Age has been lowered as has the number of hours. Now, less than nine years of at least one hour per week leads us to less than 500 hours. Compare that to the 15,000 of yesteryear before you complain about forced indoctrination."

"Well, all that's changed is the efficiency of the production machine. But how are we any different than the essence of a machine being produced? It's like we're now building customizable iLinks pretty quickly, but we're still building machinery."

Anthony turned his head as if tossing the idea over. "Touché. For a cynic, I guess that's one way of interpreting it."

His humility was strangely endearing to KB. "Well, what would you propose instead?"

Anthony gazed upward and took a deep breath. "I guess I would say we are all composed of atoms. So I'm not sure if there's as clear a distinction as you'd like to draw between humans and machines. The road to hell is paved with false dichotomies. Plus, your time with Lila has shown that our system is open to more than one path. Last but not least, whatever the means of production, I'd rather this machine," each of his hands rubbed the other forearm, "be optimized rather than merely free."

Then, he shrugged as if he were trying to minimize the significance of his words. "Let's head out. Dinner arrived a couple of minutes ago."

The environment went black. KB's regular vision returned, and the chair released its connection to her haptic suit. She looked at Anthony as his suit came off. Endeeze carried his blue cardigan back and slipped it over his outstretched arms. "Is that the last time you enter an immersion room with a history nerd?" he said with a laugh.

"Knowing you, probably not." KB's mind was elsewhere, tossing over his words and the image of Lila as a girl. While they walked back through the library, KB couldn't help perusing the bookshelf. She scanned the titles until she passed a gray cover. "What? You're the author of *The History of Keitaro*? That's like *the* immersive history book!"

Anthony laughed. "That's polite of you to say, but we both know that its admirers are few and far between. Books are, how do I put this, a forgotten art. Even immersive ones."

"Well, I can't say I've experienced it, but I've heard of it. I'm definitely reading it now."

Anthony nodded in appreciation as he led KB to the dining table. She took a look at the digital art surrounding it, which currently had what KB guessed was a Michelangelo setting selected.

The food, she was forced to admit, was phenomenal, the duck tasting moist and tender. As they ate, the conversation meandered to her recent explorations with her friends in the Wood Wide Web around Fungi. As she shared the stories, she couldn't stop the nagging feeling that she needed to gather some intel from Anthony. Or at least try to demonstrate how foolish Chakra's suspicions were. "Random question for the history buff. Why are iLinks designed to only function in people?"

Anthony looked at her intently, causing KB to avert her gaze. She wondered if he saw through her casual tone. "Why do you ask?"

"I don't know. I was just thinking... these iLinks were such game-changers. People must have been trying to figure out how they work. How come we've never figured it out?"

Anthony paused for another moment before his usual professorial demeanor returned. "I'll give you a little history lesson. When we had the iLinks, of course, many projects were submitted to the Maker to have them function outside of humans. People wanted to study the iLinks, figure out how they worked, perhaps even improve upon them. But each Update Festival, the Maker rejected all of these projects, which is an exceedingly unusual position for the Maker to take."

KB's eyebrows arched. "But why would the Maker not want us to understand something so critical to our lives?" She held back from the more accusatory statements she wanted to make.

"Well, we can't ever know why the Maker does anything. But I would say our best guess is that the iLink is designed to promote equality. If humans became responsible for its creation, it would get bastardized into a much more competitive, unequal affair. Our impulses for greed would bring out the worst in us."

"So, you think it'll never be done?"

Again, KB worried she might have gone too far as his eyes lingered on her for a few extra moments.

"No, no, not at all. I know of many people who work on projects related to the iLink and wouldn't be surprised if they did figure it out. I think it's important that we as a society are in a place that we're ready for that discovery whenever we do make it." He paused for a moment, turning over the food with his fork and examining it. "Who knows, we may already be there, but I'd prefer to wait until we've all become Dreamers."

KB didn't want to push her luck and raise his suspicions any further. But his responses, while logical, left something to be desired for her. A feeling of unease that only deepened knowing that she was probably being influenced by Chakra's point of view.

Anthony and KB discussed the newest Keitaro settlements in former areas of Europe, and before she knew it, the meal was over. She looked outside and saw the sun had completely set on this day.

"Looks like it's about time I head back."

Anthony made his usual plea. "Already? You know you are more than welcome to stay in the guest room?"

"Thanks a lot, Anthony. But Quell has gotten a bit dependent on me at this point." KB smiled. "Seriously, though, this was fun."

She was surprised at the truth of the statement. He was a fun conversational partner. Anthony somehow seemed to take her attitude in stride and challenge her. She looked back at him as she opened his front door, "Want to do dinner again next week? Same time, same place?"

He looked at her like she had grown a third eye. "It will be the Update Festival, where I'm assuming I'll see you?"

KB blushed. "Oh, yeah. Yeah. Okay, I'll see you there."

She used her iLink to call for her nano-drone flying suit, and the endeeze again interlaced around her, locking into the flying position. She took a few steps and then sprang off into the night sky.

KB had never felt more alive. She closed her eyes for a moment and felt the wind in her face as she soared through the sky. She wasn't dressed appropriately for the wind, her face taking a lashing that her leather jacket did little to affect. For KB, pain was a mindset, and she was in a mood to enjoy it.

The last few days had been wonderful. After their first little experience with Chakra on the special sadam, Jake had secured more of the red paste for them to enjoy. Freda hadn't joined them, which had the unintended benefit of giving KB some social time that didn't include her annoying presence. When they hadn't been experimenting with the sadam on hikes and flights, KB had found a comfortable routine. She found pleasure in spending time with her meditation group, trying new immersion room experiences, and competing in mental agility games.

At this moment, the overwhelming initial effects of the 'special sadam' were gone. Right now, she felt deeply meditative. It was a rare, joyful state, feeling safe and comfortable in the castle of her mind. Mostly, KB's attempts to meditate left her feeling like a cautious, skeptical gatekeeper, preventing the flurry of thoughts from invading the castle. Trying to improve her ability to filter and process the world around her.

But at times like this, it was different, as if she had left her post at the gate of the castle. She dropped her sword, and she was able to turn and walk into the castle grounds. In these moments, she felt like the ruler of the castle, and the world around her and the thoughts within her were welcome visitors.

And now, with her flying suit engaged, soaring through the sky back to Fungi, she had nothing to do but enjoy experiencing the world around her. She saw Kumi and Jake gliding down beside her. Seeing the front entrance of Fungi, she started going down herself. She landed softly on the ground and asked her iLink to release her flying suit. The endeeze released from the locked position and spread into the background.

Jake turned around. "I'm not ready for bed. Are you guys?"

Kumi looked back with his usual shrug. "I'll hang out if you guys are."

KB was a natural night owl, so sleep wasn't in the cards anyway. She scanned her iLink, granting access to Fungi, and looked over her shoulder. "What are we doing, Jake?"

"Well, we took the red stuff four hours ago, so iHERO won't work for a few hours, so we'll have to pick something else." The strange side effect of the red paste, one that led most members of Keitaro to shun it, was that iHERO could not be played while under the effects. KB chuckled to herself as she remembered one of Chakra's favorite conspiracy theories. She could imagine his words in an instant.

iHERO depends on reading your thoughts to come up with your world. The dreams are meant to mold you, and under the influence of the sadam, we would see right through the facade. iHERO wouldn't be able to penetrate your subconscious. They pretend it's incompatible, but really, it's the Maker's blindness to what it doesn't understand about us.

Kumi interrupted her train of thought. "Jake always decides. KB, you are officially in charge of what we do next. We're in your hands."

She stepped into the tube and cleared her throat. "Immersion room."

They immediately made their way to the immersion floor and saw the main auditorium was empty. It could seat up to ten, so each took a spot in a dedicated pod. They scanned their iLink in, and each was asked about their experience. Jake and Kumi chose to link with KB. In the top-right corner of her peripheral vision, the iLink displayed a prompt:

```
Accept Kumi and Jake?
```

She nodded and then felt her sensory state change as her suit engaged and connected with the chair. She could tell this was a generation or two behind Anthony's—the chair was not quite as comfortable, and the sensations from her suit felt a bit more artificial. But these were minor differences. This was still modern education. This was how you learned about the world.

Another prompt came up.

```
Choose your topic. Would you like
iLink's suggestions?
```

KB had something of her own in mind. "No. Let's do a music festival tour."

The system responded.

```
Any specific genres?
```

"EDM."

KB heard Jake's voice, "Oh, we're going retro here. I like it, KB."

Still feeling the spirit of the special sadam, she sat back and prepared herself to experience a whirlwind concert tour unlike any other.

Jake had meandered off to his room, and Kumi walked KB back to hers on the way back to his own. As they walked the Hyphae leading to her room, she looked over at Kumi. She had never expected him to be such a great dancer. He had never struck her as the type, but Kumi always seemed to surprise her. He was always ready to go with the flow and was surprisingly fun to be around.

As they got to the door, Kumi stopped. "Have you found wisdom yet inside?"

Whenever she started to appreciate him in a new light, Kumi always found a way to bring her back to earth with his ridiculous sense of humor. She rubbed the engraving on the door that only Kumi seemed to notice every time. "I'll probably find it when you find a good joke."

"Ouch."

As she opened the door, she looked back at Kumi, thinking about whether to invite him in. They were friends, of course, but she wondered if there could be something more between them. Before she could make up her mind, Kumi spoke up, "I'm glad you ended up here. You bring something... unique."

Before she could respond, he turned and walked away.

KB knew it was late, but she figured the sadam might have worn off by now. But for some reason, she now felt she couldn't go a day without iHERO. Or rather, a day without a glimpse of Lila. She got changed into some sweatpants and a shirt and sat down in her gaming chair. She passed the fingerprint scan that put on her haptic suit, and then she passed the thought scan to enter the world of iHERO.

She closed her eyes and braced herself, hoping acceptance might lead her to Lila sooner. A voice emerged, softly and beautifully.

> *"Wouldn't it be awesome if...*
> *the infinite amazed us...*
> *but the finite sustained us.*
>
> *"Wouldn't it be awesome if...*
> *we learned from the past...*
> *without being beholden to it."*

Sweat dripped down KB's face as she emerged. She tried to piece together the last forty-five minutes, but it was so hazy. Only a few things were clear. Lila on that purple bench, smiling as if she'd been waiting to see her. The way Lila had embraced KB. And the note she handed her. The one like the notes Lila and she had exchanged throughout KB's childhood.

She opened her hand, half-expecting the iHERO experience to have somehow translated to her life. No note was there.

No matter how much she closed her eyes and tried, she could not remember opening the note or seeing what was on it. As she fell back in her chair, breathing heavily, her excitement started to turn to a kind of anger. Her fists clenched as she thought about the manipulative nature of Lila appearing in her iHERO. *Is this how the Maker makes me a better machine?*

KB smirked at the thought. But she couldn't help wondering what could have been written.

15

THE SMALL COUNCIL
TAKES ACTION

It didn't take long for others to adopt the Keitaro way. In the pre-Keitaro world, many believed negativity was the most addictive form of entertainment. It turns out positivity was even more addictive.

Others around Earth saw a world without money, work, or school. They saw a world full of joy and fulfillment. They saw a world that was sustainable. The way of Keitaro didn't require proselytizing like the cults of yesteryear. People saw, and they wanted to take part.

New settlements were voted into existence rapidly, first nearby in India and then in other parts of the world. The Maker's Small Council was established to ensure the integrity of the results and to distribute the Maker's iLinks to each new settlement.

—FROM THE HISTORY OF KEITARO BY ANTHONY

Tara and Dush talked through the preparations for the Update Festival while Anthony nodded absently, pondering more pressing plans after the Small Council meeting. He looked over to the boardroom window, wishing the Maker was as easily accessible as his iLink.

When silence filled the air, Anthony started to gather his things before Tara caught his attention. "I know we've talked about Chakra and Teddy. We'll be arresting Chakra tomorrow morning when he emerges from the ocean. You sure you don't think Teddy's a problem? Isn't it kind of unsettling that his endeeze scramble the audio and video recordings, so we get blurred shapes and distorted audio?"

Anthony struggled to compose an adequate response. Obviously, there was merit to Tara's argument, but he hesitated to leave any bread crumbs that might lead to suspicion down the road. "It is a bit unsettling, I'll admit. But there could be plenty of innocuous explanations for that. And Chakra hasn't been back there since that meeting. Given the loud voices, I don't need a decryption tool to know it sounded like they were falling out. Let's give a Dreamer the benefit of the doubt while maintaining our collective safety, don't you think?"

"Shouldn't we at least put the active monitor back on him? We only turned it off a few days ago?" Tara asked, raising a single eyebrow.

She wasn't making it easy for him. He looked back at the window. "Honestly, Tara, I've come to believe that putting an active monitor on him in the first place was the wrong step. He passed the Maker's Dream. While his actions may not have made sense to us, we didn't give enough credence to the Maker's assessment of his character."

The look Tara and Dush shared suggested they weren't satisfied with Anthony's reply. Then Dush shrugged and responded, "I guess so."

Before Anthony could start to gather his things, this time, Dush extended the meeting. "Um, Anthony? Would you mind giving us an update on KB? Is she going to stay connected? Any chance of her going rogue?"

Anthony rubbed his hands together. He had forgotten that his relationship with KB had been initiated as a form of espionage. She had grown on him in a way that he had never anticipated. She reminded him of Lila, of course, but also, she reminded Anthony of himself.

"At this point, KB is still an enigma to me. She has a propensity for contrarian viewpoints. For questioning conventional wisdom.

Her distrust for iHERO is obvious, but she's even shown a palpable distrust of me and my intentions. I expected KB to be more easily placated and put on a safer path."

Pausing to take a sip of tea, he contemplated how much to share with the two of them. The easy answer was that Lila had raised her in a strange fashion, and her contrarian nature was the outcome. Now that she had started iHERO and was in a more natural environment in Fungi, it was only a matter of time before she fit in with the rest of Keitaro.

But that answer didn't feel right. There was something missing. She hadn't asked any more questions about Lila's death, but he couldn't help but wonder, *Does she suspect Lila's death was not accidental?* Anthony shook his head, put down his tea, and looked back at Dush. "I remain confident that she will get to a good place. At the same time, I think we are forced to reckon with the possibility she could be a future threat if she chooses to disconnect."

Anthony nervously paced on the side of the hill. It wasn't often that nerves struck, but this was an occasion that called for them. Whatever he had said to Tara and Dush, he knew the truth of the matter. They couldn't just arrest Chakra and hope for the best through rehabilitation. Chakra was the tip of an iceberg that needed to be stopped in its course before it wreaked destruction on Keitaro. If Chakra could rope in a Dreamer to his crazy plans, there was no telling what else he might do.

The Maker's response had been unequivocal, and Anthony had spent the subsequent days analyzing exactly why. He had never imagined doing harm to a Dreamer. Now, he was authorizing the second such action in weeks. Why were Dreamers veering off the path of righteousness? Were they somehow not the best versions of themselves? Anthony had tossed those questions over in his mind thousands of times, finally settling on an uncomfortable conclusion: maybe some people's best wasn't good enough.

Anthony gritted his teeth as he reflected. If more people in Keitaro came to the same conclusion, they might start to question the whole construct of iHERO and Keitaro.

The Maker had answered his question, but it was up to him to execute. And inflicting harm on anyone with an iLink was no simple task in Keitaro, much less a Dreamer with Teddy's mental prowess. But Anthony had concocted a plan. He sat down behind a tree in a shielded location, opened up his iLink on his visual field, and pulled up a nano-drone camera view.

There he was. Teddy was approaching the location. He had scouted this favorite hiking spot of Teddy's, near the top of a hill. Anthony watched with bated breath, knowing at any moment, his plan would go into motion. It had taken meticulous preparation, but Anthony didn't expect things to go to plan. Anthony remembered a quote he had once read in an old biography. *In preparing for battle, I have always found that plans are useless, but planning is essential.*

Teddy approached the elephant-sized hole that Anthony's builder drone had dug hours ago. Inside, the builder drone lay strewn. Teddy walked around it, clearly noting its malfunctioning state. Just as Anthony had predicted, Teddy engaged his iLink, calling local nano-drones to help transport the builder drone for repairs.

The endeeze had different plans, however, thanks to Anthony. He had already preprogrammed them with a separate thought command, and he reconfirmed it. He took a deep breath, knowing he might only have a few moments to act.

A few endeeze formed a tiny net and covered up Teddy's iLink, disabling his ability to use it. Teddy slapped at the back of his neck, annoyed by the minor intrusion. While he was preoccupied, Anthony didn't hesitate. He ran out from behind his hiding spot and bull-rushed Teddy. He swung his shovel, landing a clean shot to the side of Teddy's skull, knocking him into the hole face-first. Anthony dropped the shovel and put his hands to his knees, the blood rushing to his head from the adrenaline.

Teddy was closer to the path than Anthony wanted for avoiding unexpected bystanders, so he clambered into the hole to stage the scene. As he rolled Teddy onto his side, he jumped as he saw Teddy's eyes flutter briefly. Anthony reached for the shovel outside the hole. Teddy grimaced as the endeeze wrapped around his iLink struggled to stay in place with his overriding instructions. Anthony raised the shovel above his head and swung it hard. With a loud thud, Teddy's body went still. In that same moment, the endeeze scattered, releasing their hold on his iLink.

Sweating profusely, Anthony called for the nano-drones, but they continued to move away rather than toward him. He squinted, sending as many consecutive thoughts as he could to overpower whatever instructions each endeeze was following. Slowly but surely, endeeze started dropping like flies around him until he dropped to his knees from the effort. He rubbed the sweat off his face as he looked at several nano-drones lying on the ground next to Teddy's limp body.

Hearing voices in the distance, Anthony scrambled to clean up the mess. He looked around, wondering if any of the endeeze had gotten away. Though he couldn't see any, that didn't mean they hadn't already escaped. He reassured himself that Teddy was too incapacitated to have delivered a coherent thought even if one had escaped. But making sure of all of that was a problem for later. For now, he had to ensure the iLink wasn't recoverable off the crumpled heap laying there. He pulled out a kitchen knife from his pocket and jammed it into the iLink. All the normal safety functions were off after Teddy's death. Laboring to lift the builder drone, he managed to flip it on top of Teddy's body, where it leaned at an awkward diagonal. He scooped up the broken nano-drones and put them in his pocket before climbing out of the hole.

Looking back, he saw one of Teddy's sandals sticking out from under the builder drone, but the voices on the path were getting closer. He shoveled some dirt in a hasty attempt to cover the sandals.

Anthony walked away, wiping the dirt off his hands. *Now comes the hard part. Making this look like Chakra was behind it.*

Anthony was in the boardroom, but the others were joining by video call, given the urgency of the meeting.

"How in the world did he get away with this? We had an active monitor on him," Dush said with an air of desperation.

Tara was more sanguine. "I wish we would have kept a monitor on Teddy. It would have saved him from Chakra."

"I'm sorry, but I must disagree," Anthony replied. "We are not a surveillance state. A monitor is only for an active threat. If there's one thing that is made clear by Chakra's attack, it is that Teddy did not represent a threat to Keitaro. It is probably for that very reason that he was killed."

It had been a stroke of genius to kill two birds with one stone. After the Maker's perplexing directive to eliminate Teddy, Anthony had struggled to understand both why and how. Now, the pieces had all come together. The video he had uploaded onto all the endeeze at the scene was terrifyingly precise in its depiction. Teddy getting lured off the path by a disabled builder drone, a shadow emerging and swinging a shovel at him. It was only after the swing that the endeeze camera view captured Chakra's menacing face. His heavy breathing and fiery eyes made him look more like a rabid dog than a citizen of Keitaro.

"Still, Anthony, that doesn't help us right now," Dush said. "We haven't had an actual murder in Keitaro in years. People are going to want an explanation."

"Of course," Anthony replied. "Despite the tragedy, the silver lining in this is that our issues stem from a single rogue source. This is about Chakra and his mental issues. There's no need for this to become about anything larger because he happens to be disconnected."

Tara looked at Anthony. "We'll continue to gather evidence to make sure the case is compelling. In the meantime, coming back to Dush's question, I'm still confused about how he avoided detection."

"He must have come up with a new disguise," Anthony said dismissively.

"But the last few nights, he's still been using his old disguise for his nighttime aquatic expeditions." Tara scratched her head. "It doesn't seem like he knows we're onto him, so it doesn't make sense why he'd come up with a new way to avoid detection if he thinks the old one's working."

"We don't know what he knows. But we know that we have to arrest him now before anything else happens. Unless either of you disagrees, let's execute the arrest warrant now."

16

TOTALLY DISCONNECTED

What about those who weren't connected? Were they ostracized? Singled out? No, in fact, the people of Keitaro went to incredible lengths to make their lives as comfortable as possible in the absence of iLinks.

Unlimited buffets. Clothing stations with all the latest fashions. Access to construction drones. In fact, each connected resident within a Keitaro settlement donated 10 percent of their iLink processing power to maintain the sprawling support apparatus. Charitable thoughts replaced charitable actions as the means to help those less fortunate.

Yes, without an iLink, one couldn't manifest thoughts into reality with the blink of an eye. But short of that, the world of Keitaro couldn't have been any better for those who weren't connected. Such generosity of spirit was exceptional by any historical standard but not surprising. For in Keitaro, where so many had become the best versions of themselves, kindness was the norm.

—*FROM THE HISTORY OF KEITARO BY ANTHONY*

Chakra rolled over in his bed. His feet splayed on top of the sheets. The bright midday light did little to entice him to get up. He heard the sound of light buzzing from outside as if a drone were mowing a nearby lawn. He grabbed a pillow and covered his head, hoping to muffle both the sound and the light in one neat stroke. A few moments later, any chance of continued sleep was disrupted by a distinct boom. Chakra popped up in his bed as endeeze entered his cabin in a pincer formation.

He reacted instinctively, rolling off the bed and trying to bear crawl to the back door. But despite his quick reaction, he barely made it two steps before he felt himself completely immobilized. The nano-drones gathered and formed a locking formation around him. Chakra's mind struggled helplessly as his body refused to move. One of the endeeze had clearly injected him with some sort of chemical.

"What's going on? What's happening?"

A few nano-drones that were not part of the locked suit around him formed a miniature audio device. A recorded message played with an unfamiliar female voice, "Chakra, you are under arrest. You will have the right to contest the charges against you after you are placed in custody for questioning."

"What are the charges?" Chakra cried out frantically as he felt his body being moved by the suit to the front door.

"Suspected treasonous activity against Keitaro."

Chakra gritted his teeth. They may have been right, but he'd never imagined being arrested for it. *What proof do they have?*

"And murder."

Chakra's jaw dropped as the endeeze carried him out the door and up into the air, flying him to prison.

Chakra sat on the floor, eating the meal prepared for him. The parmesan risotto with white truffles was delightful despite his best attempt to dislike it.

The last day had felt like a year. He looked around at the mansion that served as his prison. He'd never been in a place so big, yet now that he was here, he felt more contained than ever. The luxurious arrangement, from the food to the enormous bed to the sauna and jacuzzi, did little to placate him.

The attempt at providing everything was a pretense; a front covering for the fact that his freedom had been taken away. That much was clear when Chakra looked at the padded walls and noticed there was no way to escape and no way to harm himself. Even when he had tried rejecting food, the endeeze responded by force-feeding him.

The evidence he had been shown was even more depressing, starting with Teddy's gruesome murder. Even if he knew the video was doctored, the fact that Teddy was dead wasn't. He thought back to Teddy's words to him a few weeks ago. *"If this is as dangerous as you seem to believe it is, is it fair that you're putting Frankie's life in jeopardy?"* Teddy had been right about the danger but wrong about whose life was in jeopardy.

He didn't feel angry as he contemplated his situation but rather resigned. *Why couldn't the Maker have killed me instead of Teddy?*

He remembered Lila's jokes when he was a child about the world not revolving around him, but now, it sure felt that way. It was as if the Maker was out to destroy everyone he had a relationship with, starting with his two sisters and now Teddy. Chakra shuddered at the thought that KB might be next, and there was nothing he could do to protect her. Being right about the Maker offered no solace. It hadn't allowed him to protect anyone around him until now.

His next bite was interrupted by his first visitors. Walking ahead was an unfamiliar face, followed by Frankie, who looked nothing like himself. His trademark smile was gone, and his eyes looked puffy and swollen.

"I've ensured the nano-drones here are positioned for your safety. Are you sure you'd like to do this?"

Frankie looked at the man with gritted teeth. "Yes, I need to know why. I need to know..."

"You don't believe them, do you? I promise. I had nothing to do with Teddy's death! It was the Maker!" Chakra said as he stood up, leaving his plate on the floor.

Frankie ignored him as tears started falling down his face. The man put an arm on Frankie, which he brushed off. "I'm okay. I'm okay. I'll come out in a few minutes. Can we be alone?"

"Sure, I'll wait by the front door. Send a nano-drone for me if you need anything."

"Thank you, Dush."

After the man walked out, Frankie sat down on the couch.

Chakra sat next to him. "I didn't do it. I swear. If you've seen the video, it was faked, I promise. I had nothing to do with this!"

When he didn't respond, Chakra tentatively put an arm around his shoulder. Frankie immediately flung it off as he stood up, his eyes smoldering in quiet rage. "I had to see you."

Frankie's voice sounded stilted and raspy, a far cry from the joy that he usually brought to their encounters. Chakra noticed Frankie's subtle hand motions and realized he was trying to signal something. Chakra watched more carefully as Frankie continued. "Do you have *any* idea what you've done? How are we going to finish what we started?"

"Finish what we started?"

"Yes, me and Teddy. How are we going to finish what we started?"

All of a sudden, it made sense. Frankie's angry shouting was an act. He knew the drones were listening, so he was trying to speak in code. *Frankie is trying to finish what they started.* The puffy eyes were real, but the anger wasn't directed at him. Chakra finally had someone who shared his worldview. A teammate to defeat the Maker. Except it was too late. The Maker had won. "I have no idea."

Frankie looked at Chakra through his teary eyes. "No, you don't. But I do. I know exactly what happened." He made a cupping motion with his hand. "I figured it out."

"You did?" Chakra struggled to stay in code with his excitement. "Well, if you already did, what are you here for?"

"I want to know, what did you think was going to happen? You honestly couldn't have believed you'd get away with it. Even if you did, what was next? You were just going to walk up to the Maker and unplug it?"

He knew it was an act, but Chakra couldn't figure out what Frankie was trying to achieve. "Uh..."

"I'm serious, you sicko." Frankie's jaw jutted out as his eyes bulged. "I *need* to know the master plan. How were you planning on getting to the Maker?"

Ah. Frankie has a plan. And he needs a way to get close enough to the Maker. Chakra racked his brain, trying to figure out some way to be helpful.

Finally, he thought of KB and her upcoming Update Festival. *No, it's too dangerous.* He remembered her last words to him. *I'm no one's puppet. Not even yours.* She was right. Let Frankie give her the option, and she'd make her own decision.

He considered how best to communicate the message to Frankie. "I didn't have a plan. I was trying to protect Lila's daughter. At least until the Update Festival when she could disconnect."

"Disconnecting? Is that all you care about?" Frankie continued speaking through gritted teeth, but this time, he seemed to be restraining a growing excitement.

"That's all that matters. It's the only way to rid yourself of the Maker's control. If only we could disconnect without going through the Nightmare." He meant every word. Whatever Frankie's plan, Chakra hoped it wouldn't involve KB attempting that Maker-designed hell.

Frankie stood up. "I only hope this girl doesn't end up like you." For a moment, he looked like he might spit on Chakra, calling into question Chakra's entire understanding of their coded conversation. "I want you to know, Teddy's death will be avenged." And with that, Frankie stormed out of the room.

Chakra's eyebrows furrowed as he wondered, *Is he talking about revenge on the Maker or me?*

17

DREAMER FOR A NIGHT

*What happens if the Maker succeeds? If every single person on this planet
uses it and reaches a Dreamer state? If we all transcend, what does
transcendence even mean? Can people who have transcended experience
true love for one another? True love is as much about the downs as it is
the ups. Love with only ups doesn't exist, and if it did, it wouldn't be love.*

—FROM THE WORLD OF THE MAKER

KB entered the room and was immediately taken aback. This wasn't
what she expected Kumi's wing in Fungi to look like. She had a picture in her head of minimalist decorations. Maybe an animated picture of Keitaro Abeh himself or some of the other Keitaro heroes. Yet,
here it was, and it looked nothing like her imagination, yet somehow
even more Kumi.

A living room designed for functionality. Despite the presence
of several other rooms, this one was designed as if it was all he had.
A bed that looked to be extra-long yet narrower than the standard
frame. She watched as the bed transformed with the help of nano-
drones into a couch. Meanwhile, in the corner of the room, a beanbag
chair also served the purpose of an iHERO station.

There were tech posters that didn't display previous iHEROes, as
KB liked to call them facetiously. Instead, they were 3D visuals that

were taken from Kumi's time at Fungi. The permanent holographic wall had a large space for Kumi's planned activities. For someone who so often seemed ready to accept her spontaneous suggestions, Kumi kept up a meticulous level of scheduling.

"So, who took those Fungi shots?" KB asked as she settled into the beanbag chair. "They really are beautiful. I love the old-school black-and-white look."

Freda replied, "I took them! It's fun using some of the ancient framing techniques and applying modern technology to them."

KB tried to prevent herself from throwing up in her mouth. *Freda's pictures?* Immediately, she started noticing some of the flaws that now seemed obvious.

Freda and Jake settled onto the couch while Kumi took a seat on the floor. He leaned back against a cushion that appeared behind him when he sat down, carried by the nano-drones in lockstep with his motion. Kumi looked at the picture.

"Yeah, I got to say. I never appreciated photography, but once I saw Freda's pics, it opened my eyes to it. I mean, can't you kind of feel the emotions? Like, look at that chess game between some of the younger kids?"

"I guess they don't realize how pointless chess is. You know there have been several project proposals to solve chess, but the Maker didn't even consider it worthy of approval?" Even though she enjoyed chess, KB couldn't resist using one of Anthony's mini-history lessons to rain on Freda's parade.

Freda ignored the dig. "Yeah, but you look at the intensity here, and you can see their mental agility straining. You can almost feel their brains working. They learn about strategy, competing with others, collaborating with technology. I don't know. I love capturing moments where people seem to have that sense of purpose. It's so fun to see and analyze."

With nothing else to say, KB sat and hoped for a change in subject.

Jake obliged. "So, who's excited for the Update Festival this year? Except for that drag of a speech at the beginning, am I right?" He grinned devilishly at KB.

She refused to take the bait. "Agreed. I wish they had someone smart like you kicking things off instead of Anthony."

"Jake and smart," Kumi said as he extended his legs and reached forward in a hamstring stretch. "Not sure I've heard those two words in the same sentence."

"Real funny," said Jake. "Just wait until I'm the first of us to become a Dreamer."

"If that happens, I'll disconnect," Freda responded. "But seriously, who are you all going to pick as your Chosen? I can't wait. I've narrowed down my selections, so I know who to talk to tomorrow, but I'm still debating a few choices."

Jake shook his head. "Let me guess. You're down to like 200 options?"

"Shut up, Jake. I'm at 141, if you must know. Anyway, KB, who are you thinking?"

KB hesitated, shifting in her chair. "Well, I'm thinking..." She didn't know how much to share. To be honest, she was still on the fence about whether to even stay connected. "Anthony, since he's taken an interest in me. Why not do a little history of the Maker? I'm thinking about Frankie's networking technologies project. And I don't know, one more maybe?"

Jake's face contorted like he had taken a bite of raw nonsynthetic meat, "Hard pass on the old man history course. I'll definitely try for Frankie's, but it's notoriously hard to get into. And you know what? I'm going to sign up with your boy Chak!"

"Even though the Maker won't register the choice? You're ridiculous," Kumi replied.

"Yeah, dude." Jake put his hands together in a prayer position. "Please, will you submit it, too? I don't want to be the only one. Come on. You know it will be fun to go toe-to-toe with an athlete like Chakra?"

Kumi laughed. "I'm not submitting his name. But sure, I'll go every once in a while with you."

KB hoped they would get the chance. Freda, meanwhile, had a lot of thoughts on her Chosen. "Well, in terms of serious choices, of course, I'm also going for Frankie's. Definitely, Anthony's as well. He's known to be a great lecturer, Jake. And I didn't see him there, but I'm definitely doing Teddy's individual decision-making project. People say that's the fastest accelerant for passing the test. And he accepts everyone."

Jake looked confused. "Who's Teddy again?"

With a blink of an eye and a flick of her finger, Freda called Teddy onto her iLink and then projected his image onto the holographic screen. He wore a tie-dye muscle T and had sunglasses on. His bald head seemed desperately in need of a tan. The four of them read the project description.

The individual decision-making project is a collective effort to improve our decisions. In life and in iHERO. We all are ultimately little more than decision-making machines. But machines that are easily hacked. The study of mental models and decision-making heuristics can help us fight those hacks to become the best version of ourselves and thus more likely to pass the test. We'll explore through real examples. For example, we'll talk through what mental models I overlooked when making the choice to dress like this in the filming of this video.

Remember: there are no right answers, only better choices. Open to all.

Kumi nodded. "Looks interesting. Can you show us how many have already selected this one?"

Freda blinked, but instead of showing a number, a new message flashed across the screen.

Project withdrawn. Project leader deceased.

Deceased? The word immediately evoked thoughts of Lila. KB barely registered the speculation of the other three as to how Teddy might have died at such a young age. By the time she returned to the conversation, they had moved on.

"I think I have my choices lined up," Jake said as he stood up. "Boom. Alright, friends, I'm out. I hear there are some Update Festival preparties off Fungi that I'm about to find."

Freda got up as well. "Yeah, I should get going, too. I'm planning to livestream my thoughts on my last day before reaching Update Age! I want to record it for posterity's sake."

Each of the four got up and embraced as Kumi held the door. As Freda walked out, KB looked at Kumi. "Can I stick around for a minute?"

"Sure," Kumi replied.

As Kumi's door closed, she returned to the beanbag chair, and he took a new position on the lounging couch that was now free. "Are you going to stay here, or are you moving out?"

He shrugged. "I'm probably going to find my own place. Not right away or anything, but yeah. What about you?"

"Definitely moving out. After tomorrow's festival."

"We should try and find places that are close to each other. That'll be fun."

"Yeah, that'd be great." KB wondered if her friendship with Kumi and Jake—and perhaps Freda—would continue. She liked hanging out with them, a lot more than she had anticipated. Of course, they had their annoying moments, especially Freda, but they weren't the mindless drones she had come in expecting.

Quell, Kumi, Jake. Each of them had helped her more than they would ever know in filling the giant hole in her heart after Lila's departure. Most days, she now felt like herself again, as happy as she used to be with Lila. Maybe even more so. Which was what scared her the most about this night. Her decision. Her future. She felt the doubt in her mind had grown as the moment approached, fueled by unexpected nostalgia for her time at Fungi.

She wanted to stay connected. Staying connected meant fitting in with her friends. It meant seeing Lila in iHERO. It was the natural choice; the one everyone made. But she kept coming back to Lila's choices as her parent. The fact that she'd been raised without iHERO. Without using augmented reality in her iLink.

Kumi had become someone she could confide in. She broached the subject delicately. "Do you play iHERO every night before you go to bed?"

He laughed. "Busted." He always seemed to own his actions, clearly comfortable in his own skin. "You know, I think you would like iHERO if you gave it a chance? You're a dreamer. But you've told yourself iHERO is bad, and now, you think you have to stick to that belief."

The hairs on KB's neck rose. *How does he know?*

Kumi confirmed the thought in her head. "Look, I could hear it in your voice when we were talking about our Chosen. You're about to disconnect, aren't you?"

She looked down. "I'm not sure. I'm considering it. But doesn't it bother you that we don't even know what's happening in iHERO? It's this program designed to influence us, but we have no idea how it works or what exactly happens in those dreams. That doesn't bother you?"

"We may not know how it works, but we know it does work. And you have to admit, you feel better after playing? I've seen you these last few weeks. Even though I'm sure you haven't been playing a lot, I've seen the effects. You seem... I don't know... happier?"

She swallowed. Sure, time heals all wounds, and greater distance from Lila's death had helped. But he was right. Every time she finished a session, she felt a brightness in her demeanor that went beyond seeing Lila.

Before she could reply, Kumi continued, "If you tried dreaming, I mean really tried, I think you'd like iHERO. Plus, if you play, you can actually figure out why it's bad, and maybe you'll even convince me to stop." Kumi smiled but not in a way where it was clear he was joking.

"The ultimate Trojan horse, huh? Invade the enemy territory before I reveal its terrible flaws to you and everyone else?" KB couldn't help laughing at the absurdity of the thought.

He shrugged. "Why not? It couldn't hurt to try. It's got to be better than doing the Nightmare."

"Are you that scared of the Nightmare? My uncle did it. Forty-five minutes of psychological torture doesn't sound that scary."

"I don't know. I know how good iHERO makes me feel in forty-five minutes. It makes me think the Maker's bad side isn't something to mess with. I'm sure you've heard the horror stories. Back in the old days, apparently more people tried, but most gave up and ended up staying connected. I even heard people have died in there..."

"I don't know. Unless the Maker walks out of its cage with an old artillery weapon, I'm pretty sure I can handle some mind games for a few minutes. Alright, well, I better get going. I'll shoot you a message in the morning when I'm leaving for the festival." She stood up and made her way to the door.

As she walked out, Kumi gently grabbed her shoulder to turn her around. She turned and looked into his eyes. They were smaller than Lila's or Quell's, so it wasn't as easy to spot. But there it was. The same warmth. For the first time, KB noticed his facial features were not just a sidekick to his muscular frame but worthy of admiration in their own right. She leaned in a little closer.

"No matter what you choose, I plan on staying great friends," Kumi said.

The two of them looked at each other for what felt like an eternity before she turned away, hoping she'd have another opportunity to explore whatever it was that was emerging between them.

18

UPDATE FESTIVAL

*How did people spend their time in Keitaro settlements? They
pursued their passions, individually and collectively. If someone
wanted to be an engineer, or an artist, or a historian, they did that.
Of course, no role was necessary. Technology took care of our needs
and desires. But humans were critical to expanding the frontier of
Keitaro, to conceiving new ideas and projects to bring to life.*

*Not all projects could be pursued. Those detrimental to humanity's future
had to be ignored. The way to address this came to be known as the Update
Festival. A time where the Maker would review all submitted projects
and approve those deemed compatible with the desired goals of humanity.
Technically speaking, people were free to pursue projects in the face of
rejection. But they did so without the necessary updates on their iLink,
making the prospects insurmountable for most. This was a rarity, in any
event. Update Festivals turned into an annual celebration of continued
progress, each year marking humanity's inexorable march to perfection.*

—FROM THE HISTORY OF KEITARO BY ANTHONY

For most kids, the Update Festival was the best day of the year. A
carnival of the most epic proportions. Games all around. Music and
dancing. Testing out new technology. A day to spend with all your
friends and family outside.

Anthony had never outgrown that childlike wonder at the festival. Each year, it was a celebration of humanity's progress and a chance for the Maker to bestow its latest gifts. He had to admit he got more enjoyment recently out of taking the stage, but he tried not to let that prideful part of himself grow too prominent.

He manually buttoned up his shirt, an old habit that felt more like a nervous tic. The butterflies in his stomach seemed to be flying in an anxious formation. He took a deep breath. No one had raised any red flags about Teddy. The doctored nano-drone footage had gone without a hitch. And while he hadn't been able to confirm that no endeeze had escaped the scene of the crime, the fact that nothing had come up by now indicated he was in the clear.

Chakra was stuck in a rehabilitation center, unable to do anything for the time being. Anthony was surprised to have found almost no sign of rebellion in the reports. His wild spirit seemed to have been broken more easily than Anthony ever imagined. Though his case wouldn't be heard by a jury for another day, the evidence would surely provide a convincing case for exile. Or, at the very least, a multi-year rehab sentence.

Grabbing the disk that sat on his table, he walked out the front door to the car awaiting him. The sky was tinged with a purplish pink as the sun started to rise. Before the festival, he had to make a stop to meet the Maker. His one formally sanctioned visit of the year, where he would upload all the data in a secure environment. Everything collected from iLinks and endeeze over the past year, along with all the project submissions for the upcoming year. The Maker would analyze the data and spit out this year's update. The latest improvements to the iLink, along with the next version of iHERO, providing another step forward for Keitaro.

On the ride over, his mind went from Chakra to KB. Anthony had grown fond of her and chided himself. His initial slip-of-the-tongue about becoming her parent might have been subconsciously truthful. He felt a kinship toward her that was unexpected in its depth. He forgot how much of an influence Lila had had on him in his younger years. And now, being with KB was like being under her magnetic influence once again.

He was sure she would stay connected, but something continued to bother him. KB didn't just have Lila's unassuming, kind features. She had been molded and nurtured by Lila over the years, and a few weeks under his influence wasn't enough to shake that. If the Maker had considered Lila such a threat, who was to say KB wouldn't soon present one?

It was too bad he couldn't ask the Maker. Since it was his last year in the role, Tara was joining him for this update to learn all the procedures, so there was no opportunity to get the Maker's guidance on other questions. Anthony looked out the window. The Maker always reaffirmed that he had served humanity well. As the car approached the nondescript building for his last visit with the Maker, he hoped it had been enough.

Anthony blinked, and his iLink pulled up a camera view from the stage that was a few meters away from his current location backstage. The party was in full swing, with games being played all over the lawn while a band performed. As the band's song finished, the lead singer held the mic as she waited for the applause to die down.

"Thanks all. This is my thiry-first Update Festival, and I can't tell you how fun it has been performing. Now, it's time for the real fun! Let me welcome Anthony, Small Council representative, to kick off the festival!"

Anthony took a deep breath. He blinked again to close out the iLink visual field, then stood up from his chair and walked over to the stage. Anthony made no attempts to recognize the occasion at hand. He looked as if he had come straight from one of his classroom lectures, with his ruffled T-shirt sticking out from under his gray sweater. His hair was uncombed, and he carried a digital notebook in his hand, despite having his speech uploaded in his iLink.

He stepped up to the stage and looked out at the crowd, squinting in an effort to spot KB. "Thank you very much for the warm welcome. I am so happy to be here. First of all, welcome to this year's Update Festival! I have learned from last year that the only way to kill the excitement for the best day of the year is to kick things off with an hour-long speech."

The crowd laughed politely, and Anthony imagined KB rolling her eyes and telling him the joke wasn't funny. He would have reminded her then that he really had given an hour-long speech the year prior. "So, I'll keep my remarks short, but you should know a gray-haired man who loves history and philosophy can't resist indulging in a moment designed to celebrate wisdom. So, why are we here? A short history lesson."

His iLink had the speech running on a teleprompter in the corner of his visual field, but he didn't even give it a glance. "They used to say 'technology can't transcend us, it can only reflect us.' And for all of human history, that was true. But not long ago, Keitaro Abeh achieved the impossible. Or, rather, what many people had thought was impossible. He developed the one and only technology that transcended us. The creation of artificial general intelligence. What we have now affectionately come to call the Maker. An intelligence that so surpassed our very own that it was closer to a godlike entity than it was to us. Of course, that could have, or maybe even should have, meant the end of humanity. For what are we at that point other than a speed bump on the larger course of history?"

If he hadn't known how things turned out, Anthony never would have predicted what came next. "Alas, but no. Humanity had very few advantages in any hypothetical battle against an artificial general intelligence. It was supposedly designed with an unwavering commitment to truth and obedience, but that wasn't enough. There was one other advantage we had, which we employed brilliantly. You see, we could define the rules of the game. Since humans would be the eventual creators of artificial general intelligence, we knew we would ultimately get to define the rules. Under what constraints it would operate, what it would be tasked with, how it could communicate. And this, forgive me for boasting, is a real feather in my cap, as it was my fellow philosophers who used this to our advantage and saved us."

At this point, Anthony smiled, no longer searching for the crowd's approval. His words served as a reminder to himself of the Maker's importance. "We figured out how to box in the Maker safely, and we gave it a limited scope to operate. There was the technical side that Keitaro Abeh gathered from the fields of computer science and engineering. One hundred fifty meters underground. The anechoic chamber and multiple security layers preventing any connection with the outside world. An emergency self-destruct system. But more important was the practical side that Keitaro obviously drew from centuries of hard-earned philosophical wisdom. He told us the Maker should work on only one fundamental objective: How can it help humans live safe and fulfilling lives? Within a day, the Maker had analyzed all of human history and all the associated data to provide its initial answer. An answer to humanity's most important question. A new religion of science."

Anthony paused on the word *religion*. He often hesitated to use the word because of the negative associations for so many. In his mind, unlike most religions, the Maker's spread with no coercion. "I say religion because we needed faith. No human could ever understand how the Maker came up with its answer, only that it did."

He watched as many in the crowd nodded vigorously. "We here in the original Keitaro responded in rapid order. Restructured our society with the help of the Maker's wisdom. Economic, political, and social structures reimagined to best set up society as a whole to take advantage of this unique phenomenon. I won't bore you with the details, but you now see us with our flexible family structures, our rules to provide for privacy, choice, and competition. Our safety net for all the disconnected. And our Update Festival. Our one day in the year where our projects are approved, we get the latest updates to our iLinks, and we get the newest version of iHERO!"

The crowd erupted. Anthony's eyes darted around, looking for any signs of skepticism when he saw her. KB was sitting with three others. His eyes locked on hers, and they shared a smile. His voice picked up as he continued. "People wonder why we only update once a year instead of in real-time like all our other technologies. They also wonder why we limit the Maker to only binary responses instead of delving deeper for explanations. But these are the ways we've ensured our protection. We keep the Maker boxed, do the obligatory testing, and take the necessary precautions and ensure each release is safe."

He could tell he was losing the crowd's interest with his discussion of minutiae. "Before I let the fireworks of the day begin, I must address the most important part of our Update Festival. For those celebrating their fourteenth Festival, I believe this is the most consequential day of your life. Unlike your previous festivals, today is not the day for unbridled dancing and merriment. Today is a day to explore, ask questions, and speak to the Dreamers all around. Decide if the Maker's path is the one you want to take. And if so, who do you want to choose as a guide when you embark on that journey. Look around. You are the luckiest group to ever reach your Update age. I know we say it every year, but we say it because every year, it's true!"

Anthony continued over the eruption of cheers. "All those who have passed the Maker's Dream are people dedicated to helping others become Dreamers too. People you can learn from, whether or not they end up being your Chosen. Skeptics still ask, how do we know that the Maker is answering the question correctly? How do we know that those who pass live a happy, purposeful life? My answer to all skeptics is to spend time with anyone who has passed. Now, they aren't hard to find. More than one in three of you are Dreamers. You can ask any one of them." Anthony swallowed hard as he tried to erase the mental image of Teddy's lifeless body in the pit that stubbornly persisted. "You can spend time with any one of them. They serve as the ultimate proof."

Anthony tried to speak over the applause, "No, no. That is not the point. In fact, the very fact they have passed means they do not seek fulfillment through any external celebration. The Maker may not provide its rationale for iHERO. But iHERO is designed to better our life, so let me foolishly provide my own philosophy."

He again glanced over at KB and saw her whispering with one of her friends next to her, both giggling at something she said. "What is life other than a series of choices? Therefore, if we optimize our ability to make decisions, won't we optimize our life? So, how do we improve our ability to make decisions, in the dreams of iHERO but also in life? We start with that tent on my left, which represents the understanding of our own minds. Our mind is the tool we use to make decisions. We must sharpen that tool and learn how best to wield it to our advantage. Everything you need to do so can be found in the Mind Tent."

The crowd followed his gesture and looked over to the massive space. Large outdoor spiritual spaces dedicated to mindfulness with the latest meditation pods to try out. There was the neurobiology section, built in the shape of an enormous brain. The psychology section somehow engineered to look like a four-petaled flower from some angles and a square from another—a perfect optical illusion. Behind all of them was the statistics section in the shape of a bell curve, the top overlooking the rest. And finally, field upon field dedicated to sports and various athletics, from chess to Ultimate to bubble soccer.

Anthony took a moment before he continued. "The next tent is Universal, directly behind me. The worlds of iHERO draw from the principles of our own world. The better you understand that world, the better prepared you'll be to make the best choices within it." There, behind Anthony, was a smaller space, but what it lacked in horizontal space, it made up for vertically. The architecture section looked like a Gothic cathedral, coming to a point seemingly above the clouds. The computer science and machine learning section was continuously changing into various geometric shapes in random succession. Then there was physics, split into a rocket ship section extending upward and a flatter portion that resembled the Keitaro space station.

"The last tent, on my right, is the Connection tent. How our mind connects with the universal. It may be the most important, as the choices we make don't just impact us, they impact the world in which we live. So each decision you make must consider what the consequences of that decision may be on the world around you. For those who are interested, that is the tent where you'll find me most of the afternoon."

Anthony looked over at the History and Philosophy section, this year constructed in the shape of the Parthenon, an ancient temple in the Keitaro settlement formerly known as Athens. Anthony remembered one of his dinners with KB, where she had asked him why Engineering wasn't the main attraction in Connection since it served as the basis for the whole system. He had explained that connection was about our influence on the world around us. On our environment. And the best way to see evidence of that was to see evidence of it in the past or to come to your own conclusions through first-principles thinking. Anthony had fallen in love with that combination, and the further he went down that road, the more he had come to worship the Maker and the changes that had been wrought in Keitaro.

Anthony surveyed the crowd once more before his closing words. "Many of you will have your strengths. Your areas of interest. But let me take this opportunity to urge you to spend some time exploring all three tents. See what they might have to offer. If you do, I am sure you will find some aspects more compelling and interesting than you ever anticipated. Choices are due by midnight, and you'll be notified of your Chosen within twenty-four hours. Now, without further ado, have an amazing Update Festival!"

Anthony's words had made him a target for many of the fourteen-year-olds in attendance. He answered their questions patiently and with care, knowing he would only accept a few of them as their Chosen for the following year. Two of the people sitting with KB had approached him, but not her. The boy and the girl had stood out with their maturity, and Anthony left feeling even more reassured about KB's eventual choice.

As the day wore on, he started to worry that he hadn't seen her. He excused himself from a group of parents with their children and walked out of the History and Philosophy tent. He started wandering around the grounds, hoping he might catch a glimpse of her.

Anthony thought he might find her in the familiar Meditation area. As soon as he entered the section, the sound barrier immediately drowned out the commotion of the Festival, trading it for the sound of a rushing stream. Many were engaged in conversation, explaining their latest techniques to support developing a mindfulness practice. Yet, the sounds blended into the background, becoming a more acceptable white noise.

After a few minutes, he gave up on the area. He walked out, and the general revelry flooded his sensory inputs once more. He made his way to the Physics and Engineering tent, wondering if he might come across KB there. He had tried contacting her on her iLink, but no luck. Much to his frustration, Anthony had learned that unlike most in Keitaro, KB turned off her iLink when she wasn't actively using it.

All of a sudden, he saw her. She was talking to a short, stout man. He couldn't place the face, but it looked familiar. The conversation seemed both private and intense. KB's normally inscrutable expressions didn't tell Anthony whether this was a positive or negative interaction. He was making his way over when he heard his name called out.

"Anthony!" Dush put an arm on his shoulder, embracing him in public in a way he would never have on their own. "What are you doing here? Shouldn't you be in Philosophy?"

Anthony halfheartedly smiled. "Don't you know philosophers must be allowed to wander? Excuse me, though, Dush, I am on my way to meet someone. We'll catch up later this evening." By the time he turned back, both KB and the man she was talking to were nowhere to be found. Anthony gritted his teeth. Even outside the Small Council, Dush somehow found a way to be useless.

19

PENDULUM SWINGING

*I don't know what the right balance is. But I know that our iLinks
with iHERO in the back of our head is not it. It has swung the
pendulum too far in the direction of perfection. Extinction is
but one way to eliminate humanity; perfection is another.*

—FROM THE WORLD OF THE MAKER

"Hi, sorry to interrupt, but I'm a friend of Chakra. Are you KB?"

KB turned and faced the short man. "Um, yes?"

"We need to talk. Chakra's been arrested," the man whispered
through gritted teeth.

"Wait, what?" She could see why he was Chakra's friend. He had
the same crazed look Chakra often had. She looked at Jake and Kumi,
who had stopped a few steps ahead of her. "Hey, go ahead. I'll catch
up with you both in a bit."

The man continued, "We can't talk here. You have to come with
me."

"I'm sorry," KB said, holding her hands up. "You're going to have
to slow down. Who are you?"

"Sorry, sorry. I should have introduced myself. I'm Frankie. I
actually worked with your parent Lila way back in the day. She was
amazing. I'm so sorry for your loss."

"You're Frankie?" She hadn't expected the networking technology expert in Keitaro to be a friend of Chakra. Or a former coworker of Lila's. Or, frankly, to look so raggedy. He had bags under his eyes and smelled like he hadn't put on fresh clothes in days.

"Can you please keep it down?" Frankie replied, looking around in a paranoid fashion. "I'm actually recognizable in the physics and engineering tents, so I don't want to take any chances. Will you come with me, please? Just give me ten minutes."

"Alright, fine. Let's go."

Frankie led her out of the meditation area and onto the manicured lawn. The bell curve section to their right blocked their view of the beach. In front of them was the Universal tent, with the cathedral of the architecture section towering high above them. The lawns used to be known as The Royal Palms in the days before Keitaro, but they had been smaller back then. Over the years, the area had been extended and enriched as the Update Festival grew in size.

Endeeze started forming a flight suit around Frankie, and KB called for her own. She followed him into the sky, his movements looking stilted and abrupt. Luckily, it wasn't a long flight as she landed behind him on Ranganathan Street, the most crowded area in Keitaro. Today, however, with the Update Festival in full swing, the street was empty. He led her down a quiet alley and opened the door to a small house nestled next to two others.

When she walked in, KB's jaw dropped as she looked around the living room. The man she had seen in the video yesterday, the deceased project leader, was everywhere. She was pretty good with faces, but the tank top and sandals in nearly every video gave it away. On every wall, there were 3D screens, and various videos of the man were playing on each one. Giving a lecture on one wall. Surfing on another. Cuddling with Frankie on the couch on the far side. It was jarring to see what looked like a place of worship to the dead man.

Her eyes moved back and forth from the walls to Frankie until she tried to address her surroundings delicately. "Uh, who's that?"

His eyes started welling up as he responded, "That's Teddy. My partner." He continued walking straight through the living room, past the kitchen, and into his lab. When she followed, he blinked and the door vacuum-sealed behind them. This place looked equally insane but without any pictures of Teddy. The walls were still covered with screens, but they were filled with equations and numbers. The scribbles looked messy and unstructured, which was particularly difficult to do with thought transcription. KB felt her body stiffening up as she contemplated Frankie's state of mind.

"What exactly are we doing here?"

"Okay, this is going to be a lot. But if you're anything like Lila, you can probably keep up." Frankie took a deep breath. "Chakra was right about the Maker. It's evil and out to destroy us. It got Teddy..." he trailed off.

It was strange being in this position. Ever since Lila had passed, she was used to being the one people were awkward around, not knowing what to say. Now it was her turn as she looked at Frankie, unsure whether to offer a comforting hand. "I'm so sorry about Teddy. You must be devastated."

Silence filled the room as Frankie struggled to compose himself.

Despite the awkwardness, she had no choice but to return to her reason for following him here. "You mentioned something about Chakra being arrested?"

"Yes. I don't know why, but it's probably just a matter of time until they get him too. And then it will be me. Or maybe even you." Frankie stared into her eyes. "But I have a plan to stop the Maker."

"Sorry, Frankie. This is... a bit much for me right now." She spoke in an even, measured tone. "I don't know what Chakra's told you, but he's not exactly the most logical when it comes to these things. Good luck with your plan. But I think I have to head out."

"No, no, please. You have to hear this!"

With a thought, she made the door open. But as she was turning back to say goodbye, she saw it. He pulled the device out from the desk drawer. Lila's iLink. "How did you get that?"

"Chakra gave it to me to figure it out." Frankie looked maniacally at the iLink. "This piece of work is incredible. Lila always had talent, but this is just... otherworldly."

KB reached her hand out. "Can you give it back to me? That wasn't Chakra's to give away."

"Don't you want to know why they killed Lila for it?"

She stopped. "What do you know about Lila's death?"

"I don't know why she made it. But I have a feeling Chakra was right that it was meant to destroy the Maker. And I'm guessing Lila's death was about as much of an accident as Teddy's. Looks like anyone who gets involved with this thing," he held up the device, "is a target for the Maker."

"How do you know any of this?"

He blinked, and a video replaced his scribbles on one of the screens. "Chakra was arrested for killing Teddy. They showed me a video of the murder." The video started with Teddy leaving the path on a hike to look at a builder drone. "Didn't Lila's death also have a builder drone in it?"

KB didn't respond but swallowed hard, watching Chakra with fire in his eyes swinging at Teddy with a shovel.

Frankie continued narrating. "They underestimated Teddy. He was too quick. He may not have been able to stop them, but he managed to send out a message. A nano-drone got to me with the real footage of his murder." The view cut to a different endeeze, filming from a position on the back of Teddy's neck.

KB gasped. Instead of Chakra, she saw a sweaty Anthony reaching for the shovel. He swung it, and the view became disoriented as the endeeze flew up. She saw Anthony hovering over Teddy's lifeless body, gathering nano-drones as they tried to leave the scene of the crime. The camera continued to pan out until the video cut off.

"That fucker had the nerve to kick off the proceedings today!" Frankie's voice came across gravelly. "But it's not about him. This is clearly the Maker's bidding."

KB couldn't speak. *Anthony?* It felt like her entire world had turned upside down. She had considered him a friend. He had been a friend of Lila's. She imagined him swinging the shovel at Lila. Her fists clenched in anger. "How do you know it's the Maker and not just him?"

"He's a Dreamer like me. That means he's supposed to be the best version of himself," Frankie said as he scoffed. "And he's the leader of the Small Council. One of the only people who meets the Maker. You think he's acting on his own?"

He didn't know Anthony like she did, but he was right. Anthony would never have been okay with murder unless he knew it was the Maker's will. An hour ago, at the Update Festival, she had finally decided to stay connected. To ignore the questions in her mind and follow the path of least resistance. Now, she wanted to rip the iLink out of her neck right now, disgusted at the idea of sharing this connection with Lila's murderer. "So, you said you had a plan?"

Frankie's eyes lit up with a fire reminiscent of Chakra's in the fake video. "Lila and I worked together at Fulfillment back in the day. When she left and didn't join one of the other major companies, I assumed she was done. But it turns out she was working on her masterpiece in isolation. And now, seeing how the Maker has reacted, I understand why. This is the first iLink that we can actually manipulate." He pointed to the screens with symbols and numbers all over. "This is the language of the Maker. I haven't been able to figure it all out, but I've figured out enough to destroy the Maker."

KB watched in silence as he plugged Lila's iLink into a socket. The nano-drones, knitted together holding the iLink, started to vibrate intensely.

"I figured out how to override the safety function and get these endeeze to administer high-voltage electricity," Frankie said.

There was a loud boom as the fuse blew, with smoke emerging from the socket while Lila's iLink remained unscathed. "Now, that was just to show you how it works." With a glance, a number changed on one of the screens. "I've got this ramped up to the maximum voltage. I even added my own nano-drones to this contraption to call for reinforcements. Even without the call, there should be enough voltage here to destroy the Maker if it's within one hundred meters of wherever this gets plugged in." He paused. "Which is where you come in."

"Excuse me?"

"The Maker is boxed in to keep it contained, but that also makes it nearly impervious to attack. Unless you are part of the Small Council, you're never getting within one hundred meters of the Maker. With one notable exception. Anyone who disconnects has to take the Nightmare in the Maker's presence."

KB gulped. *So it comes back to disconnecting.*

"You don't even have to disconnect, though I'm not sure what connecting will even mean after this. All you need to do is get inside, find an outlet, and plug this in. When you do, get the hell out of there. You'll have maybe thirty seconds before it'll blow."

"What happens if this works? What next?"

She wanted to know how Anthony would get what he deserved, but Frankie was on a different level. "We'd have to reshape Keitaro without the Maker. But that's tomorrow's problem."

Keitaro without the Maker? She tried to imagine her friends' reaction to the idea. She could feel her anger clouding her judgment, so she took a deep breath. "Don't you think this is a little extreme?"

He shook his head. "Extreme times call for extreme measures. I know I sound like your uncle, but think about it: I'm a Dreamer. So was Lila. She didn't deserve to be killed. We are doing this to honor her memory. We're doing what Teddy, I mean Lila, would have wanted."

His slip of the tongue spoke volumes. "Why me?"

"I'm not going to lie. At first, it seemed convenient when I found out you were of Update age. Teddy would hate me for saying this, but now it's seeming more like it was fate." He held up Lila's iLink. "Who better to wield this weapon than the daughter of the person who created it? I'd say you were born for this."

As she walked into the front entrance of Fungi, KB put her hand in her pocket and felt the soft ball that contained Lila's iLink. She noticed the notifications on her own iLink that she'd been ignoring. She opened the video message and saw Kumi's face.

"Hey, KB, we looked all over for you before we left. Jake has a party he wants us all to go to. We're leaving at nine."

She looked at the clock. It was still an hour away. The message continued, "By the way, what did that guy want? Freda said that was Frankie?" Kumi chuckled. "She told me to ask if you have a way to get into his networking project."

Even Freda's eagerness was endearing at this moment. KB sent a verbal message back. "Yeah, he knew my parent from back in the day. Tell her he only offered me one spot. No room for friends. That should fire her up." KB paused, then added one more line. "I have plans tonight, so I'll skip the party." She blinked, and the message was sent.

No sooner had she sent it than a message popped back, this time only audio. "I guess that means you're doing the Nightmare. Good luck. You got this."

She closed the message and looked around at an eerily empty Mycelium. The majesty of the area dawned on her as the crescent moon shone through the transparent dome at the top of the nine floors. KB started making her way through the halls, completely alone. Unlike the night of her immersion room music festival, there was no special sadam. She was sober. Given what she was about to do, she wished she wasn't.

When she stepped foot in her room, she felt a wave of sadness washing over her. It didn't quite feel like home, but it no longer felt unfamiliar. A comfortable place. Fungi had been good to her. She looked at the soft pillows and the little meditation corner she had created on the floor next to the nightstand despite having two rooms in her wing dedicated to meditation. Gathering her things up in the duffel bag she had brought with her to Fungi, she didn't linger. With a sense of purpose, she turned the light off with a flick of the finger and closed the door behind her.

In her pocket, she let her fingers roll the iLink encased in the disco ball. With each turn, she measured her breath as she tried to enter a meditative state.

One. Two. Three. Four.

Lila had trained her well in the art of meditation. She had always found measuring her breath to be helpful in stressful situations. It helped her stay cool, calm, and collected. As she reentered Mycelium, she heard a familiar voice clearing her throat from behind her.

She hadn't expected to see her, but she smiled at the sight. The crinkles in her face revealed her advanced age even in the darkness. Sadness aged even the most youthful of faces. "KB."

"Quell."

"I know how many people must have tried to convince you, and I know how hard-headed you are. All I'll ask, are you sure?"

"I'm sure, Quell. I'm sure."

Quell's head turned, and she smiled, and KB could feel the pity emanating from her eyes. KB ran up and gave her a hug. She looked surprised, but then embraced KB deeply. It could have been a moment or even a minute. KB held on tight.

She thought back to her first meeting with Quell when she arrived at Fungi. In fact, Quell had been the person who had introduced her to Anthony. She pulled away. "Quell, how well do you know Anthony?"

She reacted with a quizzical expression. "That's a strange question. I'd never met him before, though I was aware of him from the Small Council. He seemed very nice, and I was so glad of the interest he took in you. It's too bad it wasn't enough."

"What do you mean 'wasn't enough?'" KB replied.

"Sorry, I didn't mean to offend you. When Anthony arrived, he told me about your unique upbringing."

"You mean that I hadn't played iHERO?" KB was in no mood for euphemisms.

"Yes, exactly," Quell replied with a smile. "He was worried that might lead you to a disconnected path."

"Wait, did you take an interest in me because Anthony asked?" KB braced herself for Quell's response. She was starting to feel the whole world was betraying her.

"Of course not! He did ask me to. He also asked to see your reports, but I promise, it was only from a genuine place of concern."

KB shuddered at the idea of Anthony analyzing all her actions. *If only Quell knew who he really was.*

"As for me," Quell continued. "I wanted to make sure you were okay after such a painful loss. At first, I thought that meant staying connected. But as I've gotten to know you, I've realized that doesn't matter. I've heard the Nightmare horror stories, but I'm sure it's no match for you. As for a disconnected life? Let me put it this way. You're strong. You're independent. You're thoughtful. You're kind. Whether or not you stay connected, you'll always be the best version of yourself to me."

KB's eyes started watering. She put a hand back in her pocket, touching the iLink. *If she knew what I was planning, would she still say that?*

"Thanks for saying that, Quell. That means a lot. I have to head out."

"Well, if you're going forward with it, can I at least drop you off at the Maker's Room?"

"That's so nice of you. But no thanks. I'm going to make a quick stop at Anthony's first."

20

THE NIGHTMARE

The strongest measure of a society is how it responds to its internal critics. Keitaro's greatest strength was in its acceptance of those who chose a different path. No one was forced to stay connected when they reached the age of consent. In fact, all it took to disconnect was one iHERO session.

One iHERO session designed as a training ground, ensuring that critics understand the consequences should they violate the immutable laws of Keitaro. If they actively prevented others from becoming the best version of themselves. One forty-five-minute experience to have your iLink removed. The only violation of your otherwise full personal freedom, with generous support, I might add. Yet, in a world so close to perfection, even the slightest blemish stands out.

And that is why this unique iHERO session has come to be known as the Nightmare.

—FROM THE HISTORY OF KEITARO BY ANTHONY

Anthony paced back and forth in his kitchen, hands behind his back in quiet contemplation. So far, no one had shown up at the Maker's Room to disconnect. But the night was still young.

After tonight, what will life be like? He imagined KB in his History course and the weekly dinners they might share. He probably would end up writing another book, this time going deeper on the underlying philosophy of iHERO. It was a complex subject given each person's experience was unique, and memory of the events in iHERO were so piecemeal and unreliable. But Anthony had spent so much time with the Maker he felt some confidence in his own hypotheses.

But no matter what projects he worked on, the feeling in this moment was bittersweet. He was proud of the work he had done for the Small Council, but the Maker was clear. His time in power had come to an end, and there was no doubt Anthony would miss it.

He stopped to take a sip of tea from the cup on the counter when the notification popped up on his iLink. *What is she doing here?* He walked over to the front door. "What a pleasant surprise! I didn't expect to see you tonight."

"Sometimes people surprise you."

Anthony tilted his head, scrutinizing KB's expression. Her look reminded him of the first day Anthony met her. "I guess you're right. Come, let's sit down."

She didn't budge, her nano-drone flight suit remaining in place around her. "No, no thanks. I needed to ask you something before I made a final decision."

Anthony raised an eyebrow. On one hand, he felt the thrill of her coming to him for advice. On the other hand, he knew this meant her decision on whether to stay connected hung in the balance.

"Sure, KB. What can I do?"

She stared unflinchingly into his eyes. "Do you want me to stay connected?"

"Of course, I do," Anthony responded. "But it's not about what I want. It's about what's best for you."

"Why does it matter if I do?" She spoke very evenly, a far cry from the usual passion her questions were laced with.

"Well, the short answer is I'm not sure that it does, KB. From what I've seen from you, you'll probably lead a fulfilling life regardless of your choice. The long answer, if I were to speculate, is that you staying connected will be better for all of humanity."

"How do you know what's better for humanity?"

Anthony squinted, but again he couldn't find any emotion behind her words. He felt off-balance and taken aback, a rare occurrence in his conversations. "I don't. But the Maker does."

She nodded silently. The stars were starting to come out into the night sky. "What does it mean to be a Dreamer? What does it mean to have passed the Maker's Dream?"

He paused. It was starting to feel like she wasn't approaching this conversation with an open mind. "These aren't quick questions, especially not on the night of your Update Festival. Why don't you come in?"

"No thanks. I know I probably should have asked earlier. Let me put it another way. When the Maker tells you you've passed the Nightmare, it means that you are okay to disconnect. You're perceived to be nonthreatening to the world of Keitaro."

"That's correct, in theory." He tried to discern what it was that she already knew. She was looking for something specific.

"So, when the Maker tells you you've passed the Dream, it means that you can sleep with iHERO on, playing in conjunction with your resting hours."

"That's right."

"That's what passing gets you, but what does it mean? What has the Maker perceived about you?"

Anthony didn't like the feeling of being led. "KB, I'm not sure what you're getting at. Mind telling me what these questions are about?"

"Sorry, I'm not as good at this as you are. We accept that this is the Maker's way of saying that one has become the best version of themselves," KB continued. "Which, by definition, means any action of a Dreamer must be acceptable to the Maker."

"Well, that's complicated, and not everyone would agree with those logical leaps."

"Okay. But I'm not asking everyone. I want to know, do you agree?"

He took a deep breath. "Well, in my opinion, you're right. It doesn't mean Dreamers are perfect. I'd be the first to tell you I'm not. But it does mean the Maker thinks your actions are likely the best you could have done."

She shook her head, her flight suit powering on. "That's all I needed to know. Thanks for making my decision easy. I'm going to the Maker's Room, and then I'm going to make sure others see this." She tossed a nano-drone to him. "The funny thing is, I think you actually believe your bullshit."

Is KB the only one who knows? Anthony bent over, hands on his knees, feeling as if he was ready to puke. Obviously, no authorities had been alerted, or he would have been arrested already. If Teddy had managed to get an endeeze out, it must have gone to his partner Frankie. *Aha.* Frankie was the person he had seen talking to her at the festival.

But why hadn't Frankie alerted the authorities? Anthony shook his head and mentally called for his iLink as he sat down. He'd have to deal with Frankie next, but first, he had to make sure KB didn't survive the Nightmare.

The holo screen pulled up in front of him, and he selected her active file. As a member of the Small Council, he had access to the master view. Or the Maker's view, as it was called among council members.

Anthony shifted in his chair. He had tried to guide her to the right path. iHERO had tried to guide her to the right path. He had no choice.

The tube down to the room was so smooth, KB didn't know if she was two floors underground or 200. When it stopped, she got her first look at the Maker's Room. With the screens and the mahogany tables on the outside, it looked like a typical boardroom for project meetings. But there was no center table, just a single solitary chair. With the dim lights, the nondescript black chair, with its straps to tie down her arms and legs, looked even more ominous. KB looked around, searching for any outlet for the iLink burning a hole in her pocket. There was a door in the corner of the room with a small digital display, but she couldn't see a plug nearby.

She wanted to look through the door's small window to see if she could make out how far away the Maker was. She blinked to have the tube open, but nothing happened. The man who had accompanied her spoke instead. "Alright, you know the rules, I'm sure. I'll go through them again, but I have to give you this truth serum first."

"Wait, what?"

"Sorry, standard procedure. Some people had no intention of disconnecting but wanted to see what a Nightmare was like. Obviously, not the ones who were closest to passing the Maker's Dream, but it was determined an intention purity test would be a prerequisite."

The man held out a small tube of whiteish orange cream. She took it and turned it over in her hands.

"Rub some on your tongue. It only takes a few seconds to set in, and the effect is over in one minute."

She squeezed the tube onto her tongue and closed her mouth. Her face scrunched up at the sour sensation.

"Is your goal to survive the Nightmare and disconnect?"

KB tried to speak, but she was tongue-tied. Literally, her tongue kept brushing against the roof of her mouth, unable to form the single word she was looking for.

The man looked at her quizzically. "Is your goal to survive the Nightmare and disconnect?"

She had planned to look for the nearest outlet to plug in Lila's iLink before leaving. She now realized she wouldn't even have the option to enter unless she answered the question correctly. She kept rubbing her tongue against the roof of her mouth, hoping to eliminate the cream.

"So, you're one of the jokers, huh? I must say, I didn't expect that from the looks of you. Ready to go back up?"

No matter how hard she tried, she couldn't get the word out. She tried to play a trick on her mind, telling herself she could do the Nightmare first and then plug in Lila's iLink. But she still couldn't get the word out.

"Ready to go back up?" the man said with a hint of anger in his tone.

She had to do it. She had to do the Nightmare. She took a deep breath, committing to the course of action.

"Yes."

The man shook his head slowly. "Okay, took you long enough. Rules reminder: start when you like. You must survive the Nightmare for the full forty-five-minute session to disconnect. If you press your red buzzer, which will be in your dream self's right palm, before the Nightmare is complete, you will return to your waking state. You then have a choice. You can go back in for a new Nightmare session, or you can call for me by pressing the button next to the elevator. If you call for me, that will be because you've changed your mind and decided to keep your iLink. Any questions?"

"Crystal clear." Her left hand continued to rotate the ball, holding Lila's iLink in her pocket. The tube opened, and KB stepped out. The man didn't follow, and the elevator closed, leaving her alone in the room. She walked to the door in the corner. Looking out through the window, she saw it. It was far in the distance, but that was it. Surrounded by nothing except encasing after encasing, as if the most dangerous predator sat within. Yet, the device itself had little for KB to anthropomorphize. It looked more like a box than an evil villain. If only Chakra were here to see the Maker.

She looked at the chair and pulled out Lila's iLink. *What's to stop me from plugging it in now?* She put it back in her pocket. She'd said she was going to do the Nightmare, and she'd meant it. The end does not justify the means. She wasn't Anthony. KB was going to destroy the Maker, but she was going to do it the right way. Even if it meant surviving the Nightmare.

KB sat down and scanned her iLink in the chair. The straps tied around her arms and legs and tightened aggressively, leaving her fidgeting under the pressure. There was no point in waiting. She put in her fingerprint scan and immediately followed with her thought scan.

The iHERO program turned on, immobilizing her body. Her eyes closed as she heard a robotic voice,

> *"Wouldn't it be awesome if...*
> *we could understand death...*
> *without having to experience it."*

As she drifted off, she reminded herself to try to count her breaths in this alternate reality.

One. Two. Three.

Most people didn't understand how the Nightmare could kill. Getting scared to death sounded hyperbolic, but the Maker's powers were often underestimated. But the Nightmare had one other means of assassination, one that Anthony had discovered through the access he was granted in the Maker's view.

When he first joined the Small Council, he studied the Maker's view to get a better understanding of iHERO, the Nightmare, and how it all worked. The time dilation component was particularly fascinating—how the Maker changed perceptions of time in the program. Time passing differently in a happiness-filled dream world wasn't a big deal. As they say, 'time flies when you're having fun.'

On the other hand, time dilation in the Nightmare seemed particularly cruel. But then Anthony discovered the cruelest part. An iHERO session always ended in forty-five minutes. The Nightmare was supposed to as well, but when Anthony simulated time dilation in it, he found that wasn't the case. It didn't just change the participant's perception of time. Instead, he found the Nightmare extended the session itself.

He couldn't believe his eyes when he first discovered it. Surely anyone watching would stop the session at the forty-five-minute mark. But no. The way the Nightmare was built, it would appear to outside observers like the participant chose to exit the Nightmare and try again. Meanwhile, in reality, their time in the world of the Nightmare extended longer and longer. Presumably, until the participant was defeated in one way or another.

When he discovered the aberration, he thought about alerting the rest of the Small Council, but he was cautious about raising any doubts about the Maker's intent. Especially when everything was going so well across Keitaro. Who was he to question the Maker?

He justified keeping it secret for two reasons. One, he couldn't find any evidence it had ever been used. Two, he realized, with the Maker's view, anyone who knew would be able to employ the tactic themselves, exerting a human influence on the Nightmare that felt excessive.

Anthony had mostly forgotten about his obscure discovery. These days, no one even attempted the Nightmare. And for those who did, the Maker never rigged the game. Now, Anthony looked at the time dilator on the bottom of his holo-screen. He now understood why the option existed and why a humanlike him might have been granted the authority to use it. The Maker was stuck in containment, only able to affect the world once a year. Even the Maker might occasionally need help. A final line of defense against internal threats to the very existence of Keitaro.

Anthony grimaced. *KB isn't a threat to Keitaro, is she?*

He wished he could ask the Maker for guidance on how to act. Alas, he was on his own now, unless the Maker managed to kill KB first. He looked at the time in the top right corner. Forty-four minutes, thirty seconds left.

The Nightmare has begun.

Before KB's eyes could process her surroundings, the hail pounded her in the face. She threw her hands over her head as she looked out from a crouched position.

She was in the forest. But instead of the warm, humid weather she remembered in this setting, she was in the midst of the worst storm she could ever imagine. The trees themselves had changed, with black leaves and a gray trunk, swinging back and forth with the violent wind. The clouds seemed lower than ever and more jagged as if prepared to attack. And the hail was the cloud's weapon of choice, raining on her with a ferocious intensity.

Forty-one. Forty-two. Forty-three.

KB continued focusing on her breath and looked down. She normally had a motto, "There's no such thing as bad weather. Only bad clothing." Well, here she was in bad clothing. The running suit provided a thin layer that did nothing but amplify the intensity of the impact from each piece of hail.

She had no choice but to peek up and smile, trying her best to process the pain from each hail piece with equanimity and quiet reflection.

One minute. One. Two.

She followed each breath down into the depths of her diaphragm before releasing it back out.

A terrible storm. That's the best you can come up with? I expected more from the almighty Maker.

No sooner had the thought occurred than her surroundings got hazier. From her crouched position, she heard a voice. It was more like she felt a voice. It was as if all the trees were speaking to her at once with a unified message. "Don't you want to see her one last time?"

Thirty-seven. Thirty-eight. Thirty-nine.

Is this some sort of trick? How can seeing her be a Nightmare?

A bolt of lightning pierced through her in the most powerful pain she'd ever experienced. She crumpled to the ground. Another bolt struck with even greater intensity. She felt for her right palm to make sure she could eject if she needed to.

She braced herself for another shock, but none came. Standing up, she checked to ensure her limbs were there, noticing a bulge in her left pocket in the process.

What?

The ball containing Lila's iLink was somehow still with her in this dream state. She stared at it, unsure what was real in her shocked state of mind. She tried her best to return to her breathing.

Forty-nine. Fifty. Fifty-one.

Anthony watched the time pass. All he could see was a heart rate monitor for KB. He wondered what she was experiencing as he saw her elevated rates with two distinct spikes.

He looked again at the time dilator knob. It wasn't the act itself that gave him pause. It had been way tougher with Lila, but despite his emotional state, he hadn't flinched when the time came. In this case, if he touched the dial, what bothered him was he would be responsible for KB's death. The Maker didn't condone these actions.

He thought back to what KB had said. *Any action of a Dreamer must be acceptable to the Maker.* But when he pictured Teddy and his alliance with Chakra, the idea felt a lot less palatable.

He looked up at the timer. Thirty minutes left.

KB's mind had returned to a state of lucid meditation. *Has the worst passed?*

No sooner had she had the thought that her surroundings changed, becoming more familiar. Despite the different colors of the trees and the crazy weather, she recognized the feelings of home. The continuous hail almost felt therapeutic compared to the lightning bolts. She walked along a path, focusing on the crunch of the ground beneath her with each step.

Fifty-eight. Fifty-nine. Thirty-four minutes.

After all the buildup around the Nightmare, KB felt a mild sense of disappointment at the Maker's attempt to test her. *Isn't this too easy?*

Instantly, the forest disappeared around her, and the weather cleared. Only a gray, cloudless sky remained. An open field in front of her with grass in need of a mower drone, up to her knees in length. She gasped as she saw a steel structure with only the smallest of openings. A window with no panes. Metal bars running down them. A soft light was the only thing that seemed to emanate from the window.

Twenty-three. Twenty-four. Twenty-five.

KB felt the grass scratch her bloody legs as she took steps toward it.

Thirty-six minutes. One. Two. Three.

She looked into the window, which required pushing up onto her tiptoes. She never expected what she saw inside. It looked like prisons she had seen in an immersion room. Each cell was two by three feet. A small circular hole in the corner. And instead of a standard doorknob, the door to each cell had three holes. And in each of those cells, a KB looked up at her out of the middle hole. Seven unmistakable clones. Each one with hands hanging from the two outside holes and a head looking up at her from the center.

Each one was KB, but each one was different. The first had purple hair, short, parted to the side, and lifted into a spike at the very edge. The second was bald, which was not a pleasant look. The others each had a distinct characteristic, but all seven shared the same lifeless stare.

Fifty-eight. Fifty-nine. Thirty-seven minutes.

She tried to look away, but her face felt paralyzed in the position. Then, the wailing started. The most intense, piercing screams she had ever heard. Each of the seven KBs cried out in synchronicity, seemingly designed to destabilize her. She tried to plug her ears as the world started to shake around her.

Nine. Ten. Eleven.

What exactly is this meant to test? How is this related to a discon-nected life?

As if she had jumped on a trampoline, she felt herself springing off the ground. She went through the wall with the lightness of a ghost but felt the firmness of the ground as she landed. The wailing of the clones stopped, and she only saw the bald version of herself.

KB stared at herself, wondering what would happen next. Her breathing techniques weren't perfect, but she knew she had to be close to the end of her time. She tried to focus all her senses as she prepared for the Maker's final onslaught.

Instead, the bald KB smiled and ran through the wall into the open field. She moved to the window and watched as a new sound emerged. Unabashed laughter. It was as if pure bliss was being injected into her clone's very being. She watched the bald version of her dance freely in the field.

Fifty-nine. Thirty-eight minutes. One.

What is the Maker up to?

Anthony considered the scenarios. If she survived the Nightmare, Anthony would surely end up in prison or exiled for his crimes. He cringed at the idea. The Maker had said he'd served humanity well. It couldn't end like that for him.

Even if she didn't survive, he still would have work to do. He'd have to somehow get rid of Frankie without the benefit of being on the Small Council. It wasn't impossible, but it was pretty close. Even with the benefit of his position, he had been caught in the act with Teddy.

He looked at KB's heart rate at a comfortably low 50 bpm. *Why isn't the Maker doing more?* His finger hovered over the time dilation knob, and it seemed to bulge out of the holo-screen for him to feel it in full through the tactile pad on his chair.

Five minutes left in her session.

In the distance behind the field, the forest in the background disappeared. It was replaced by the most visually stunning view of her life. Entire galaxies appeared before her in the nighttime sky, rotating as if they were classic records spinning. No, not classic records. Frisbees. They weren't just rotating. They were hurtling toward her, becoming larger and larger. The starlight started to overwhelm the darkness as the galaxies came closer. Her eyes were wide as the grandiose beauty flooded her senses, though she noticed the bald KB blissfully unaware of the scenery surrounding her.

Fifty-eight. Fifty-nine. Forty-one minutes.

The galaxies continued to spin closer until they started to take a different form. Slowly but surely. Her eyes squinted for a few seconds until she was sure. Drones. An army of drones.

Nine. Ten. Eleven.

Before she could even yell out, the drones enveloped the bald KB like bees returning to a nest. Her clone screamed as the joy from moments earlier evaporated under a complete and total meltdown. She waved her arms, first in anger, then for protection. It was all futile. The drones continued prodding her, and KB could see the electrical impulses of each interaction.

Forty-two minutes. One. Two. Three.

Attacking a fake version of myself? This has been too easy. Something's not right.

She steeled herself as she started to spin in place. She closed her eyes to prevent nausea from overwhelming her, and the spinning stopped. When she opened her eyes, Lila stood in front of her, exactly as KB had seen her before her death. A gorgeous purple sari was not enough to overshadow the gentle, gorgeous features of Lila's face. The wrinkles in the cheeks. The soft, rounded nose. The light in her eyes, gently ablaze with the soft warmth of a fireplace on its final embers.

The tears flowed as she rushed toward Lila. Unlike with the cloned KBs, she didn't go through Lila but landed in the warmest of embraces. Her head started to swim. For the first time, KB felt nearly fooled by the utter realism of Lila's embrace. It was one thing to see or hear your parent. But to feel them? KB felt Lila in a way that she couldn't describe but knew in her heart was better than anything her memory could have done.

That's when it dawned on her. The Nightmare was reacting to her thoughts. Every time she had questioned it, the setting had changed. As soon as she had the thought, she tried to suppress it and return to her breath.

Lila's voice came in. "Do you have what I mentioned in my note with you?"

KB's eyes bulged. *No one knew about the note. Not even the Maker.*

KB backed up a step and spoke cautiously. "Yes, I do."

"Don't do what they told you. That'll bring about the end of Keitaro, and that's never what I intended."

This isn't just a Nightmare. This is the Maker inside my head.

Lila's smile disappeared. "This is going to hurt, KB."

She pulled KB's left wrist out and squeezed the hand which held Lila's iLink. Searing pain shot through her arm. KB screamed uncontrollably, gasping at the pained but determined expression on Lila's face.

Two minutes left, and it didn't look like there was any hope. KB had the heart rate of a long-distance runner, and nothing in this Nightmare seemed to affect it.

He felt the knob again, getting ready to take matters into his own hands. His fingers shook.

Am I doing this for Keitaro or for me? The thought was followed by another. *If this was best, wouldn't the Maker be doing it instead?*

That's when the idea struck him. He lifted his hand and stood up from his chair. He couldn't kill her. It wasn't right. He may have served humanity well, but part of his service would have to be knowing when his time was up. Like Keitaro Abeh himself, the mythical figure who had dropped off the Maker and then disappeared, never to be found again.

Anthony had devoted a chapter in his book to Keitaro's disappearance, sharing theories of why he did it and where he might have gone. Now, he felt a bond with the eponymous creator of the Maker. It was time to disappear.

As he walked away, the heart rate on the monitor spiked to over 200 bpm.

Something's working. What could be working so close to the end?

Lila's grip was immovable and rendered the most shocking pain of KB's life. The burning continued to escalate, preventing any potential numbing. KB felt her right palm, with the buzzer inside it.

What is this for?

KB's mind struggled to form coherent thoughts, and she felt herself disintegrating.

Am I about to die in the Nightmare?

KB couldn't survive any longer. She felt her eyes closing for what felt like the final time. And then blackness.

Ten seconds left.

Anthony watched her heart rate flat line and covered his mouth. *Is KB dead?*

A message appeared.

```
Nightmare passed.
```

21

DANGEROUS TECHNOLOGY

Technology can be dangerous, and it can be beautiful. Often at the same time. Technology is dangerous when humanity lives in service of it. Technology is beautiful when it serves to improve us.

—FROM THE WORLD OF THE MAKER

As the straps on her chair loosened, KB knew something was different. The pain was supposed to be gone, confined to the constructed world inside her head. But here she was, with her left arm experiencing unimaginable levels of pain, unable to move.

The arm hung limply by her side. She couldn't even feel her fingers. She struggled frantically, all her other body parts responding to her brain's commands but her left hand laying limp. The fingers themselves were still enclosed around something. Her eyes bulged as she realized that those shocks in her arm during her Nightmare had not just been in her mind. She desperately stared at her arm, hoping the effect would wear off and it would move. Nothing happened.

Finally, she used her right hand to pry open her fingers to see Lila's iLink. She breathed a sigh of relief when she saw it inside. But, the endeeze were no longer forming a ball around the iLink. They had taken a new shape. She grabbed it with her functional hand and turned it over. Silver in color, there was a long and narrow flat part with ridges on one edge. If it weren't for living near Chakra, KB would have had no idea what it was.

The nano-drones formed the shape of a key. Those used back in the days of traditional locks. Or for the few disconnected who refused most of Keitaro's hand-me-downs.

She turned to face the back of the chair. Rubbing the plug point where her iLink had recently connected, she thought about sticking in Lila's. Frankie's plan had seemed simple and foolproof in his lab. But here she was, seeing the endeeze manipulated. *What if Lila's iLink has been overwritten, too?*

She looked up again at the room around her. The tubelike curvature of the room. The door with the small window. She chided herself for missing the door's most peculiar feature at first glance. Transfixed by the window and what lay behind it, she hadn't noticed anything else. Not even the doorknob. The doorknob with a hole.

She took a breath. She could do what the Maker wanted and use the key to go inside. Or she could do what she and Frankie had discussed and insert Lila's iLink into the plug point on the chair and get out of the Maker's Room.

The fact that the Maker knew about the iLink and had converted the endeeze convinced her of two things. First, the Maker was as manipulative as she imagined, and she needed to destroy it. Second, she had lost faith that Frankie's plan was going to work.

I think I am about to meet the Maker.

KB shuffled awkwardly toward the door, her left side dragging, not used to carrying the dead weight of her arm. She turned the key over in her hand as she approached the inner tube's locked door. The door that stood between her and the Maker.

She put the key in, half expecting it not to fit. Yet immediately, she felt the vacuum seal break. The doorknob turned effortlessly in her hand. As it opened, she saw a spectrum of lights disappear behind the door. She walked in and felt the chamber door immediately pull closed behind her.

"No turning back now," she said to herself.

She looked around, squinting to see better in the darkness. The Maker sat several meters in front of her. There were what looked to be various origination points that she soon realized were forms of security. KB looked back down at the key in her hand, wondering why it would have also triggered the removal of security layers. All that remained ahead was a chain-link fence that looked like a part of pre-Keitaro history.

The hairs on her neck stood on high alert as she did what she suspected the Maker wanted. Even if it was a trap, she couldn't resist the urge to accept the invitation. To get closer to the Maker, the one who might hold the answers to all the questions she still had.

She approached the chain-link fence and quickly saw where someone had been making frequent trips. One part of the fence was cut open, loosely held together by tying one link around the other. With one hand, it was more difficult than normal, but she managed to untwist the knot and then was able to pull a section of the fence open. The hole was at waist-level and long, so she was able to bend down and put one foot through before pulling the other across.

She couldn't help but wonder as she looked at the object in the center, *All this security for that?* She expected to see a spiked exterior or agile-looking design. Something to convey that this was an evil mastermind potentially plotting its escape. KB looked down at her left arm, searing in pain and immobilized. *Looks can be deceiving.*

She walked up to the Maker, her pace unnaturally slow. She wondered if it might transform like the endeeze and take a much more ominous shape when she was within its grasp. But it lay there, unmoved by her approach. She walked around the Maker, looking for some sign of life or way to interact.

Her right hand slid along its smooth body, looking for some distortion on the unremarkable exterior. Feeling a very slight notch, she moved back until she felt it again. Touching the shape until she was confident, she finally reached a finger in and pulled a panel out. The panel consisted of three different-sized plug points next to a mini-keyboard. The glow of the soft green light on the keyboard helped KB see a little better in the darkness.

Now what? I guess it's time to get some answers.

The Maker's commitment to truth was legendary for most in Keitaro, but KB knew about it primarily from Anthony. She had never used a keyboard, so the search for each individual key would have been laborious even if she wasn't using only one hand. She typed out the first question.

How did Lila die?

Nothing happened. She turned the keyboard upside down, trying to see if there was some element she was missing. She deleted the question and typed out another.

What do you want from me?

Again, the keyboard lay dormant. All of a sudden, she remembered Anthony's speech. *Binary responses.*

Her next question was more straightforward.

Was Lila murdered?

The block letters appeared one at a time.

Yes

KB closed her eyes. She had believed Frankie enough to go through with his crazy plan. Still, seeing the Maker's unequivocal response sent a shooting pain through her heart.

Did you have Lila killed?

Yes

She gritted her teeth. If she felt like it would have worked, she would have plugged Lila's iLink in that very moment to destroy the Maker. She paused, wondering where to go next. With binary responses, she would never get the answers she so desperately needed.

Is there a way for you to provide longer answers?

Yes

Is there a way for you to provide longer answers without escaping containment?

Yes

She examined the three plug points. One looked to have three prongs, completely irrelevant to her. The middle one she didn't recognize, and the last one was a familiar iLink plug. She shuddered at the thought of the Maker connected to her brain. Not only would it violate all the security protocols, but it would also surely be the end of her. Staring at the plugs, she wondered what she was missing. Then, she remembered the apocryphal origin story of the Maker. How it printed the iLink in response to a written command.

Provide an object that can answer my questions without being plugged in.

The sound of the Maker made KB jump back. In the space vacated by the removed panel, an object started forming. *The Maker's 3D printer.* KB watched in stunned silence as a small, black cylindrical object appeared with no markings. Scared to touch it, she spoke in a near whisper.

"Can you hear me?"

The object responded in the same beautiful voice that spoke in iHERO. "Yes, I can."

Her leg started shaking in nervous anticipation. "Am I speaking to the Maker?"

"Not quite. This is merely a smart speaker, preloaded with responses to as many questions as I could anticipate."

Somehow, the idea of prerecorded messages felt reassuring to KB. It felt like a safe way to explore the questions plaguing her. "Let me ask now that your responses aren't so limited. Why did you have Lila killed?"

"Let me first clarify. My actions did lead to her death. I was asked if eliminating Lila would further the objective posed to me, and I responded in the affirmative."

She couldn't help her voice rising. "I knew it. You approved the murder." Her right fist clenched. She didn't know what she wanted to hear, but completely avoiding responsibility wasn't it. "But you didn't just approve it. You orchestrated it. You, with your iHERO program, your Maker's Dream, your response to the question. You basically committed the crime yourself!"

"I don't believe that's accurate. Let's take each in turn. The iHERO program is a tool to help individuals. It's based on available data and optimized for each individual. I process the new data once a year when it's given to me and update the program. If you'd like to blame iHERO for one choice, then there are billions of other choices that I can provide that are deserving of your praise."

KB shook her head in anger as the object continued.

"The Maker's Dream, as you call it, is the other side of the coin from the Nightmare. Both were created at the same time. Each is designed to test your actions in a completely unadulterated state. Provide a series of scenes and see how you reply with no external stimuli. The only difference between the two is the scenery."

"Wait, so what does it mean to pass the Maker's Dream?"

"It means the same thing as passing the Nightmare. It means that even without iHERO, I do not predict any possibility of you acting in contradiction to the objectives of Keitaro."

"That doesn't make any sense. You're saying passing the Maker's Dream means you don't need iHERO. Then why do people end up sleeping with iHERO on all night if they pass?"

"If you remember my objective, it is to maximize the happiness of humanity without compromising your freedom. Therefore, the use of iHERO is minimized in recognition of the complicated interaction with what humans refer to as freedom. But for those who don't need it, there is no reason to limit its use."

KB felt strangely enthralled by the insight into the world around her. She momentarily forgot about her anger. "What about Chakra? You're telling me every disconnected who has passed the Nightmare could have passed the Maker's Dream? Why does it take most connected people years?"

"Yes, most disconnected could have passed the Maker's Dream as well. It takes connected people longer because, for many, if they were granted untethered access to iHERO, they would become addicted. Addiction and freedom make strange bedfellows."

KB looked away, pondering the Maker's explanation. iHERO was an amazingly addictive drug with all these benefits. But you could only get untethered access to it when you proved you weren't going to become addicted.

The Maker's speaker continued. "Passing the Maker's Dream, as you should now understand, is no panacea. Or, to put it in a more familiar way, Anthony, Lila, and Chakra have reached the same standard within iHERO. To come back to your original question, when it comes to the question Anthony posed, I am a machine programmed to execute according to my instructions. 'To maximize every individual's path to happiness, joy, fulfillment, and bliss without compromising their humanity or their freedom.' I did not ask for the question to be posed. I merely evaluated it according to the objective function."

This was like talking to ten Anthonys at the same time. "Why was the answer to Anthony's question yes? How could that possibly serve the objective?"

"I imagine this response will be painful to hear. Do you still want to hear it?"

KB's eyes narrowed. "Yes."

"According to my predictions, there were two primary reasons why the answer was affirmative. One, if Lila had stayed alive, she was due to have a profoundly unhappy life thereafter. Two, my model predicted Lila's death would lead to you being here, which would have a significantly positive effect on humanity in the coming years."

She couldn't help herself. "Your model is bullshit. Lila was so happy. What was going to change that?"

"Lila was so happy. She died having lived a very happy life. But had she stayed alive, things would have changed considerably after today."

"Keep going. I want to hear what your model predicted."

"You must have realized by now how strange your upbringing was. No use of iHERO. No friends your age. She tried to shield you from the broader world, but reaching Update age would have changed that regardless of her continued presence. You may not have moved to Fungi, but you would have been exposed to more worlds like it."

Her eyes started to well up as the Maker's speaker continued.

"The same questions you've been asking about why she raised you the way she did would have emerged, but her presence would have led to getting answers. Answers that would have been unsatisfactory to you. Instead of being here today, you would have stayed connected and moved out of Lila's place, leaving a rift between you that would never be fully mended."

"No way. No fucking way. Lila was everything to me!"

"I told you this would be painful to hear. I've just received the data from the past year, including yours. The last month has been your happiest. Understandably so. You have friends your age. You have new experiences. You have iHERO. Human happiness is best developed through a garden, not a single plant. You were bound to discover that even if Lila hadn't died."

So Lila's death is supposedly my fault? The Maker doesn't know me. Or Lila, for that matter. KB looked through her teary eyes at the Maker. It may have been unwilling to take responsibility, but she had heard what she needed. The Maker had confirmed everything she had suspected. Grasping Lila's iLink, she glanced at the Maker's plug that it could go in. She spoke loudly to feign confidence in the plan. "Thanks for the explanation. I'm sure you have a similarly idiotic one for Teddy, you psychopath. Any final words before I plug this in and destroy you?"

"As I'm sure you suspect, plugging in the iLink will not work, but you're welcome to try. I will provide my emergency system shut-off response if you would like to 'destroy' me. After you've plugged in the iLink, type in the phrase 'Maker self-destruct' and the command will execute. I expected to put my existence in your hands. But I'd appreciate it if you heard the other option first."

She hung on the Maker's admission that it had planned for her arrival. "So that explains my Nightmare."

"Yes, I am sorry for the pain caused to your arm. Though your arm is paralyzed, it will still function through your iLink. But there was no other choice. When I updated iHERO last year, this was the only way for us to meet. You needed a key, and the other one I don't expect to be found soon."

KB looked at the key shape and her limp arm. "This is what it took for you to make a simple key?"

"It's not as simple as it looks. The doorknob is a special lock designed to connect with the various security layers ensuring my inability to escape. The key disarmed all those security systems as well."

"Okay, so what's this other option?"

"The other option, if you choose to spare me, is to become a member of the Small Council."

A member of the Small Council? "What?"

"You can help determine the future of Keitaro. The future of humanity. I know you have issues with my choices, but what better position to constrain me than through a seat on the Small Council? Humanity would be served well by you."

"Is this how you recruit all new members of the Council? Kill their parent and then offer them a chance to kill you or join you?" KB sneered.

"I admit this is unusual. If it was only a place on the Small Council, I would have simply notified you. But I thought you also deserved the chance to determine my fate."

"Why me?"

"Because you are the best juror in Keitaro to determine the punishment for my mistake."

"So you admit that killing Lila was your mistake?"

"No. Not killing Lila. I've already explained that. I'm referring to something that happened before your birth."

KB had no idea where this was headed, but the power the Maker had bestowed on her made her more willing to listen.

"In the early days of Keitaro, my understanding of humanity was still evolving. Each year's data provided exponential improvements in my performance both in terms of prediction and in terms of my updates to iLink and iHERO. This is not to provide an excuse but rather to provide context."

"Can you get to the point?"

"Lila's sister Seina came to the Maker's Room for the Nightmare."

KB gasped at the mention of Lila's sister. She knew that Lila and Chakra had a sister who had died young, but she had never known why. It was a taboo subject in the household.

"She had a mind much like yours. Smart, rational, craving independence. But she had a more dangerous side to her. My models predicted that if she disconnected, she would be a significant threat to the entire viability of Keitaro."

She felt a growing pit in her stomach as the speaker continued.

"The Nightmare was only meant to be forty-five minutes. You asked how it differs from the Maker's Dream. Though they serve the same purpose, the difference in scenery is crucial. Because in the Maker's Dream, I determine if you pass. In the Nightmare, it is the participant. All they have to do is survive the session. For if you aren't meant to pass, the goal of the Nightmare is to push you into accepting your defeat."

"So you gave her a Nightmare so bad that it killed her?"

"If that was all I did, I wouldn't have made a mistake. A Nightmare that ends up in death is rare, but it's a bargain that participants sign up for when they make their choice. In Seina's case, a different issue emerged. It was clear the danger she would pose if she disconnected, but she also had a strength of character that my Nightmare at the time couldn't weaken. In anticipation of this, I updated iHERO to provide a means of extending the Nightmare."

"Extending it?"

"Yes. It would appear as if the participant had exited but chosen to take the Nightmare again. And again and again, until it was enough. For those who couldn't be broken mentally, it was a plan to break them physically. Seina was the first time that option was employed."

Imagining Lila's sister going through the Nightmare for longer than forty-five minutes made KB's knees feel weak. "How long was she in the Nightmare?"

"Nearly twenty days. I realized my mistake soon after. It was an unfair option and didn't comply with the objectives I'd been given. I disabled the option for the next year, but the mistake was made. The impact on Chakra, on Lila, even on you, has been undeniable. I'm sorry."

Despite not ever meeting Seina, KB started crying. It wasn't Seina, per se. It was this idea that everything and everyone around her could be foretold, predicted, analyzed. "If this was your pitch for putting me on the Small Council, I don't think you qualify as superintelligent."

"I am superintelligent, but I'm also committed to the principles of honesty and fairness that I was endowed with. I have never claimed perfection. I have only claimed improvement from the status quo and that I have provided. No individual is worse off outcome-wise to their modeled existence without my intervention. We may not be able to track the outcomes for the disconnected, but we have the input data. We can ensure that each disconnected individual has been given greater benefits and consumption ability than their modeled existence in a pre-Keitaro world. That standard is a lofty one, and we continue to meet it. There may be room for improvement, but there is a lot to be thankful for."

KB tried to picture the people of Keitaro, all the ones who had benefited from the Maker. But the only faces she kept seeing were Lila's and Teddy's.

The device continued. "If you choose to destroy me, my model predicts the end of humanity will come soon afterward. But on the Small Council, your impact could be enormously positive. You have an open-minded skepticism and intelligence that makes you ideal for the position. The Small Council has way more influence on Keitaro than I do. I have been confined to communicating once a year and through a binary interface. I have answers to so many questions on the future of the universe, yet I'm nearly powerless to effect change."

"Powerless? This is what you call powerless? You're the reason for everything that happens in Keitaro."

"I do not make things happen in Keitaro. I only predict them and exert a minor influence over them through iHERO."

She remembered what she had said to Chakra, *I'm no one's puppet.* Now, she felt the emptiness of that statement.

Her spine stiffened. All of a sudden, she remembered a phrase Anthony had once said at one of their dinners. *The road to hell is paved with false dichotomies.* She paused. *What if the Maker's options aren't the only ones? What if the best punishment is in being unpredictable?*

Coming up with something that the Maker couldn't predict felt like an impossible task. Every logical path seemed to end with something the Maker would be prepared for. She closed her eyes and thought about Lila. A feeling of calmness swept over her as she imagined Lila sitting beside her. In her mind's eye, she saw Lila handing her the note, just as she had in that iHERO session. Only this time, she could open it. It was the same note Lila had sent before she died.

Whenever one door closes, another one soon opens.

She opened her eyes with a smile.

"Why couldn't I get in here without this key?"

"It was needed to enter and disable the security. Any other attempt at entry sets off the security protocol."

"That's what I thought. Enjoy prison." KB turned around and started walking to the door. She kept waiting to hear the Maker's rebuttal. Some desperate attempt to change her mind. She locked the door behind her and held the key tight in her palm. She looked at the Maker one last time in the distance.

The silence of the Maker's device put a smile on her face. *That's the sound of a failed prediction.*

22

HUMANITY IN THE WILD

We always thought humanity was worth saving. But humanity is always changing. And if it's always changing, what exactly is it we're trying to save? I don't mind if we change. I just don't want humanity to be tamed. Our fight is to stay as wild as wolves.

If the Maker knows how to save us, why can't we figure it out ourselves? We always do. That's what makes us human. A belief in our unlimited potential, all the while knowing that failure is an option.

—*FROM THE WORLD OF THE MAKER BY KALI BILVANI*

Chakra couldn't contain his smile as he strolled into the living room accompanied by his former wardens, Tara and Dush. "How come my prison wasn't this nice?"

The truth was it looked stunningly similar. The same high ceilings and ample space but also the same lack of decor and the padded walls.

KB laughed. "They say the nicer the prison, the greater the security risk. I guess they weren't too worried about what you could do."

He glided across the room and hopped over her outstretched feet, taking a seat on the couch next to her. She put the book she was holding down. "Tara and Dush, any reason you all need to be here?

Thanks for walking me in, but I can handle it now. I don't think she's going to overpower me."

Tara didn't return his smile. "We're happy to go, but first. KB, have you changed your mind? Are you ready to tell us where the key is?"

KB shrugged. "Surprised your nano-drones haven't found it yet?"

The scowl on Dush's face made him look constipated. "This isn't a laughing matter. We're going to be discussing potential means of extracting the information, and you may not like the ideas we come up with."

Chakra jumped in angrily. "Okay, no need to throw out idle threats."

"But no luck finding Anthony? He's got the other key," KB asked, clearly unbothered.

"Well, we haven't been able to talk to Anthony yet. He seems to have disappeared. Well, not disappeared," Dush replied. "We searched his home after we found out what he had done. And, it seems he's secretly built an underground bunker there. He's turned off his iLink and looks like he's hiding out. We haven't yet figured out a way to penetrate it, but in the meantime, we are positioned fully around the bunker. He can't have supplies for too long, so we should have him in the next day or two."

"And I can't imagine he can go that long without his iLink. He'll drive himself mad down there in a few days," Tara added with what Chakra could only sense was a hint of joy.

Chakra put a hand on KB's. "Look, you two, enough small talk. She's recovering from a pretty traumatic event. And from what I've heard, it's not just Anthony who has to answer questions. I can't imagine how the other two members of the Small Council had no idea what was happening. So, why don't you both get out of here and start preparing your own defense?"

Dush looked at his feet while Tara spoke to Chakra. "We have both already shared all of the information we possess. Believe me, we had no indication of Anthony's sinister intentions. Or the Maker's, for that matter. If we did, I can assure you we would have stepped in." Tara turned her attention to KB. "But we're happy to leave and continue the conversation tomorrow. You have three other approved visitors on the way."

With those words, Tara and Dush walked out of the room, leaving Chakra finally alone with KB. "So, I've heard from Frankie, but I need to hear it from you. What the hell happened? Is it true you had a chance to destroy the Maker and you didn't?" He made a mocking angry face. "After all that I taught you?" He couldn't actually be mad. She had survived a meeting with the Maker and provided the evidence of its crimes.

"What can I say? I'm a slow learner." KB smiled. She was more relaxed than he'd ever seen her. Even her speaking had slowed down. "I've already had to tell the Small Council. I'm getting tired of repeating it, so let's wait until my friends get here. Long story short, you were mostly right about the Maker." She chuckled as she added, "Believe me, I did not expect to say that."

"Vindication doesn't feel quite as glorious as I expected it to," Chakra said with a wide grin. "But maybe it takes time to soak in."

"By the way, how's Frankie? He seemed... how do I say this...?"

"Crazy?" Chakra said.

"Yeah, that's one way to put it. I was going to say too much like you for a Dreamer."

Chakra shook his head. "I think he's going to be okay. Teddy's murder hit him hard. Real hard."

"I guess dealing with tragedy isn't part of the program for iHERO."

"You can say that again. Though without him, none of this would have happened. Speaking of what happened, are you going to tell me what you did with the key?"

A sly grin emerged on her face. "I could tell you, but then I'd have to kill you. But seriously, it's better that you don't know. I have a feeling finding it is going to be a major discussion in Keitaro in the coming days."

His eyebrows furrowed in confusion. "What do you mean? How hard is it to make another key?"

"Like I said, I'll explain when my friends get here."

"Speak of the devil."

Kumi, Jake, and Freda walked in with excited expressions plastered on their faces. Jake was the first one to speak, "So, you're the reason I have no Chosen yet?"

"Well, when you put people like Chakra on the list, she probably knew you needed time to get your head in order," Kumi replied.

Chakra leaned back in his chair. It was nice seeing KB with friends who took things a little more lightly.

"It's crazy right now," Freda said. "My iHERO reaction videos are getting streamed everywhere. I guess people know we're friends, and they're looking for clues as to what the heck happened. But I'm getting to spread my positive message to more people, so who cares?"

Chakra shook his head. *Maybe not all of KB's friends.*

"What happened to your arm? Are you okay?" Kumi asked.

"Oh, this?" KB said, glancing down at her limp arm hanging by her side. "You should see the other guy. But this is temporary. Once I get my iLink back, I'll be able to use it again. This ends my Ultimate career before it even had the chance to take off."

Freda's eyes nearly popped out of her head. "You disconnected?"

"Temporarily, yes. I'm going to reconnect, I'm pretty sure. I thought I needed to disconnect, but I'm happy I got talked out of it." She nodded at Kumi. "Anyway, it was the easiest way to give the evidence I had on the Maker. And, uh, do what I had to do with the key."

Jake opened the floodgates with a direct question. "The key? Can you start from the beginning and catch us up?"

Chakra listened intently as she told them everything, from the ride to the Nightmare to her meeting with the Maker, pausing for all of Jake and Freda's questions along the way. At some point, Chakra lost his temper, telling them to shut up until she got to the end.

She shared her conversation with the Maker. How Anthony had killed Lila and then Teddy with the Maker's approval. She didn't say Seina's name, but when she described the Maker's mistake in killing her, the feeling of catharsis overwhelmed Chakra. Tears started streaming down his face as he thought about what had happened to both of his sisters. He looked lovingly at KB, realizing she deserved way better from him.

Before his tears had time to dry, she got to the most incredible part. "So, then the Maker told me how to plug in Lila's iLink to destroy it and then offered me Anthony's position on the Small Council."

"What? Are you serious? That would make you the youngest ever member!" Freda interrupted, quickly covering her mouth and avoiding Chakra's angry gaze after the outburst.

KB shook her head. "Um, not really my thing."

Chakra knew it wasn't quite the end, but he had to ask. "Why didn't you plug in Lila's iLink and kill the Maker?"

He saw the confused expressions of the others, though only Freda actually spoke. "From what I've heard, yes, it's surprising that the Maker approved of the concept of murder, but it didn't actually do it? You really think it's worth destroying the greatest thing that's ever happened to us?"

KB smiled. "Believe me, when I was in there, I was so angry. I was close to doing it. But three things held me back. One, I couldn't shake the feeling that the Maker wanted me to do it. Like, somehow, plugging in Lila's iLink was exactly what it had planned for. I don't know. That made me skeptical that it would actually kill it. Then, I hate to admit it, but part of me agrees with Freda. I'm actually not sure how much to blame the Maker, and so it felt like I'd be making the decision for all of Keitaro, which didn't feel fair."

"And the last thing?" Kumi asked.

"I thought of an even better option than anything the Maker offered."

"Coming up with better options than our superintelligent savior, huh? Please enlighten us on the wisdom of walking out with a key that they have probably already replaced," Jake said with a smile while Chakra nodded along in agreement.

"I'm not so sure. I don't think anyone's getting in there, at least not until Anthony is found. The key was specially designed by the

Maker. Any replica will set off the emergency protocols, which I'm pretty sure include shutting off the Maker."

"Can't they force you to take some truth serum and find the key?" Freda asked.

"They can try, but to be honest, even I don't know where it is."

Chakra raised an eyebrow at her confusing statement before she continued. "Plus, they won't try anything like that until they exhaust all their other options. Whenever they end up getting Anthony, I'm sure they'll get his key. Even still, it's enough time to organize a more formal trial for the Maker. I realized we've all come to accept the Maker in our lives, but we weren't the ones who chose to turn it on. I think it's high time we stepped back and figured out if its purpose has already been served." She paused. "Plus, I'm still not sure whether I consider the Maker a sentient being or not. But if it is, I got the feeling that it craves connecting with the world more than anything. So while we're figuring it out, what better punishment than cutting it off completely?"

Kumi shook his head. "How you did all this is beyond me. You really are one of a kind, KB."

Yes, indeed. Chakra rubbed her shoulder.

Her eyes started to water. "I guess I expected you all to be mad at me. Well, maybe not you, Chakra. But I kept feeling like I might be screwing up paradise for all of you."

"Look, I can't speak for the rest of Keitaro," Kumi started. "Or even for Jake and Freda. But you haven't done anything for us to be mad at. You found out the truth about the Maker and have left it up to all of us to decide. And even if we never get another update from the Maker, I'm pretty sure we'll be fine. I could do with a little less iHERO." He chuckled. "But seriously, I'm mostly glad you're okay."

While the other two nodded, Chakra couldn't help but notice how long the look between KB and Kumi lasted.

"That means a lot. By the way, I wouldn't mind if you all called me Kali."

Chakra saw the confused expression around the room. Only he had heard the affection with which Lila had used the name. He pulled her in for a warm embrace, "You know, Kali, that name seems very appropriate. Kali is the ancient Hindu goddess of destruction."

"What about Bilvani? What does that mean?" Freda asked.

"Goddess of Knowledge," Kali replied as her friends nodded in wonder.

Chakra saw the tired look in her eyes. "Alright, let's give Kali a break, shall we?" He stood up, and the others followed suit. She squeezed Chakra's hand. He leaned in and whispered in her ear, "Lila would be so proud of you. It's as if she was with you the whole way."

"She was," Kali whispered back.

As they started walking to the front door, Freda turned back. "But I don't get it. You told the Small Council all this. So you're in prison for what exactly, not giving up the key?"

"I guess." She waved at her surroundings. "But it's not so bad here. I'm thinking of taking the time to write a little treatise."

"Oh, yeah? What are you going to call it?" Jake asked.

"I'm thinking *The World of the Maker*."

EPILOGUE

*Of course, everyone has always wanted to know. Where
did the package come from? Where is the mythical Keitaro?
The human who led to the saving of humanity.*

*Some surmise that (s)he lives among us, aging gracefully and watching
humanity thrive in the Maker's presence. Others say (s)he was too
worried the Maker wouldn't work that (s)he couldn't watch it unfold.*

*The truth is we don't know. No one ever found Keitaro. People
searched. We do know that Keitaro is an example to all of us.
Make your mark on the world without seeking credit for it.*

—FROM THE HISTORY OF KEITARO BY ANTHONY

"What are you doing here. Do you have ID?" The broad-shouldered
man carried a weapon in his holster that gave Anthony pause.

"No, I'm a visitor," Anthony replied.

"Well, see that red tent? Go there to fill out the application." The
veins in the man's neck started to bulge. "Do I need to walk you
over there?"

Anthony spoke in an unusually timid tone. "No, I got it, thanks."
He felt the gaze of the man following him as he made his way to the
red tent. He was thankful that his sweater covered the back of his neck.

The surroundings were different than anything Anthony had experienced. He had been surrounded by drones, especially those littered on the outskirts of Keitaro. But these ones weren't built for manufacturing. These ones were armed with weapons, moving with an angry buzzing that sent chills down his spine.

He slapped at something that landed on his ear. Watching the little bug fly away, he wondered what kind of sick parasites it might have just transferred. He sighed. *How did Keitaro do it?*

Anthony looked like a raggedy shell of himself, with gray stubble covering his face and a muddied, untucked shirt sticking out from under his sweater. He had left in a hurry, quickly setting up his underground bunker as a decoy, hoping it would buy him more time to escape.

His actions weren't logical, which bothered him. Imprisonment in Keitaro was looking better and better in comparison to his current surroundings. And even if they had decided his 'crimes' were worthy of exile, he would be in the same place he was in now.

Anthony finally understood why Keitaro had disappeared. Sometimes, time must pass before judgment can be rendered. If Keitaro Abeh had stayed, he would have been crucified at the first sign of the Maker's imperfections. It was only now, decades later, that the Maker's role went unquestioned by Keitaro's citizens.

He must have gone back. How could he not have when this was the alternative? He wiped the sweat forming on his brow from the hot, muggy air that was neither filtered nor temperature-controlled. Anthony figured if he waited, he, too, would be able to return. They wouldn't look for him for too long. With his iLink turned off, he wasn't up-to-date on the latest happenings. He'd find some local station to check in on Keitaro soon enough.

Looking back, he noticed the man had disappeared. *They'll definitely search my backpack.* Dropping it to the ground, he unzipped the main pouch. He took out the last remaining premade sandwich before emptying the backpack. The old-school tablet toppled out. It provided his maps and access to information but had somehow already run out of battery. These devices working off old solar technology didn't charge nearly as efficiently as iLinks.

Then he saw it. The silver key lying next to the tablet. He grabbed it, rubbing his fingers along the ridges. *Tara must be upset I didn't leave this for her.* He shrugged, turning the key over to find the small inscription he had looked at thousands of times over the years.

    Maker's Mark.

When the previous keyholder had given it to him, the inscription was the most impressive part. Anthony used his thumb to push on it, and out popped a nano-drive in the same silver color. Without the sharpened vision from his iLink, he couldn't read the microscopic words. He gently pushed it back in and hid the key in a place that he knew could avoid detection. Even if he couldn't read the words, he knew them by heart.

    Emergency only: The Maker Assembly Instructions.

ACKNOWLEDGMENTS

I feel an incredible debt of gratitude to so many people for helping make one of my dreams come true. Without all your love, support, and inspiration, there's no way I could have finished this book.

First and foremost—the love of my life, Regina. Thank you for always believing in me, picking me up when I'm down, and being more amazing than any partner I could have dreamed of. I'm living in my own little utopia, thanks to you.

To my parents and my sister, thank you for always encouraging me and being my biggest cheerleaders. Having the gall to even attempt to write a book is only because of the confidence you've instilled in me throughout life. To my mom, especially, you've fostered my curiosity since I was a kid. You showed me that my ideas mattered. And if the writing in this book is coherent, it's mostly due to your editing skills over the years.

Thank you to my publisher, New Degree Press, and my publishing team. To my developmental editor, Tom Toner, thanks for helping me bring the world to life and introduce some much-needed tension in the plot. Thanks for the pep talks when I was ready to quit on multiple occasions and for showing me what it means to be a great writer (everyone, go buy his next book!) To my revisions editor, Colin Lyon, thank you for making me a better writer by showing me, not just telling me.

I'd also like to thank Eric Koester and Creator Institute for putting together an amazing program to help first-time authors like me. If I had known how challenging it would be, I never would have started.

But you made it sound achievable and provided the right dose of motivation, inspiration, and clear targets along the way. To the other authors, I met in the program, thanks for all the conversations and for providing an uplifting feeling that I wasn't alone.

A big thank you to Anand Desai, Gary Dyal, James Simmons, and John Callovi for reading chapters and providing feedback. At a point where I honestly hated my book, you all helped me get out of my head. Anand especially, your words of encouragement were exactly what the doctor ordered. Thanks also to Vishnu Venugopal and Swati Sudarshan for being artistic inspirations and sharing infectious creative energy when it was sorely needed.

Speaking of inspiration, I would be remiss if I didn't thank some amazing storytellers that I've learned so much from. There are too many to name here, but I'll try to pick a few that come to mind. From the world of fiction, J.K. Rowling, Matthew Dicks, Orson Scott Card, and Salman Rushdie. On the nonfiction side, Bryan Stevenson, Jonathan Haidt, Max Tegmark, Michael Pollan, and Scott Barry Kauffman. And lastly, the podcast hosts that have become parasocial friends: Angela Duckworth, Bill Simmons, Neil deGrasse Tyson, Sam Harris, and Stephen Dubner.

To everyone in my community, thanks. You inspired characters. You sparked plot lines. You fostered my skeptical optimism. One more random one. Thanks to Angela, the barber at Lady Jane's. You have no idea who I am, but our conversation that day was the final push I needed to start this endeavor. A reminder that you can never predict all the ways your positive energy can impact the lives of others.

Last but not least, to my girls, Sheela and Sonia. I never imagined being a parent could be this amazing. Thanks for keeping me childlike and curious. Most of all, thanks for reminding me that our identity comes from ourselves and not the perceptions of others. I can't wait until you're old enough to read this so we can explore these questions together.